The Reading Circle

ASHTON LEE

KENSINGTON BOOKS
www.kensingtonbooks.com

KENSINGTON BOOKS are published by

Kensington Publishing Corp.
119 West 40th Street
New York, NY 10018

ISBN-13: 978-0-7582-7342-0
ISBN-10: 0-7582-7342-8
First Kensington Trade Paperback Printing: April 2014

eISBN-13: 978-1-61773-244-7
eISBN-10: 1-61773-244-3
First Kensington Electronic Edition: April 2014

10 9 8 7 6 5 4 3 2 1

Printed in the United States of America

3|14

Books by Ashton Lee

THE CHERRY COLA BOOK CLUB

THE READING CIRCLE

Published by Kensington Publishing Corporation

For Will

Acknowledgments

Writing this series would never have been possible without the expert guidance of my Jane Rotrosen agents, Christina Hogrebe and Meg Ruley. They both know the New York literary market and how to make it work for the writers they sign. When they matched me with Kensington Books, I knew I had found a home for my work.

The list of professionals who support me at Kensington is substantial, but let me start with Executive Editor, John Scognamiglio, who saw the potential in my Cherry Cola Book Club series. I've also interacted with Adeola Saul, Paula Reedy, Karen Auerbach, Doug Mendini, and Alexandra Nicolajsen in publicity, production, and marketing and have always received their utmost attention and advice.

Once again, I must thank my Aunt Gail Healy in Natchez, Mississippi, for rounding up more tried-and-true Southern dishes for the recipe section at the back of the novel. The feedback on the recipes in the first novel has been prodigious, and some of my readers and librarian friends have prepared many of the dishes for my talks and signings around the country.

Finally, I want to thank all of my librarian friends, family members, and readers who have connected with me on my Ashton Lee Fan Page, at facebook.com/ashtonlee.net. That's where you'll find the latest photos, reviews, and book tour information for all the novels in the Cherry Cola Book Club series.

A Club for the Boys

"Oh, the swarms of mosquitoes we'll be swatting this summer. Better stock up now on the repellent!" were among the sentiments everyone in the little town of Cherico, Mississippi, was proclaiming toward the end of January. That was often followed by, "They'll be breeding by the thousands in the shallows of Lake Cherico with nothing to kill them off!"

It was, in fact, the warmest winter anyone could recall, and that included the couple of ninety-somethings who were still alive and kicking. There had been only two or three nights below freezing since Thanksgiving so far—with the temperatures rocketing up into the fifties or sixties only a few hours after sunrise. It was still sweater weather, but heavy overcoats were kept on their hangers in the closet. *Unseasonable* was the word all the meteorologists kept repeating over radio station WHYY, The Vibrant Voice of Greater Cherico, as well as on the television stations in Tupelo and Memphis. The extreme northeast corner of Mississippi generally felt the wrath of those Alberta Clippers roaring down from the Arctic, but it was as if some super force field had held them at bay this year, limiting their range to the upper Midwest.

Against such a relatively mild backdrop, The Cherry Cola Book Club was about to hold its first meeting of the year in its accustomed place—The Cherico Library at 12 Shadow Alley. Accordingly, Maura Beth Mayhew, the feisty, visionary young director, had been hard at work coordinating and delegating everything from the potluck menu to voting on the club's next read. Her prowess at both was hard-won, having survived a five-month ultimatum from Councilman Durden Sparks and his two dim-bulb underlings—"Chunky" Badham and "Gopher Joe" Martin—that she must show them why the underutilized facility not be shut down for good. To their way of thinking, the library was a luxury the City Council of Cherico could no longer afford.

But Maura Beth had held her fiery red head up high and come through with flying colors. She had not only created The Cherry Cola Book Club to get more patrons into the building for book reviews and those delicious potluck dinners, but she had gone proactive in circulating a successful petition to keep the town's converted, corrugated iron warehouse of a library open for everyone from students doing term papers to the unemployed seeking job leads and assistance with their résumés. She was bound and determined not to let stingy and corrupt local politicians banish such a valuable community resource.

What Maura Beth had not foreseen, however, was how deeply involved she would become in the lives of some of the book-club members. Single and still looking, she had come to think of married couples—like Realtor Justin Brachle and his wife, Becca, popularly known as Becca Broccoli because of her recipe show on the radio; Douglas and Connie McShay, respectively a retired trial lawyer and ICU nurse originally from Nashville; and spinster Miss Voncille Nettles and her widower beau Locke Linwood—as the core of an alternative family.

To be sure, she had met the McShays' nephew Jeremy, and she was hopeful that this earnest and robust young English teacher from Nashville would turn out to be "the one." But their burgeoning relationship continued to be long-distance and was going to require planning and patience to get to the next level. In fact, Jeremy had phoned to say that he had some crucial business to discuss with the headmaster of New Gallatin Academy and would have to put participation in The Cherry Cola Book Club on hold for the time being.

"You sound so mysterious," she had told him that afternoon. "If something's wrong, I'd like to know about it and try to help."

"I'm afraid this is all on me," he had replied. "But I hope to be down next weekend with some very good news as a result of all my machinations."

Meanwhile, the January 29th meeting of the book club was minutes away from starting up at exactly seven o'clock. As she had done for last year's get-togethers, Maura Beth and her trusty assistant, the sweet and eternally diplomatic Renette Posey, had arranged all of the library's folding chairs in a semicircle in front of the circulation desk. Yes, the setting continued to have a crowded and make-do quality about it, but it had served its purpose. After last November's successful showdown with Councilman Sparks during Cherico's budget hearings, the club had every reason to hope that their numbers would continue to grow and keep the library viable in the eyes of the City Council. Yet no one could forget that City Hall had given the library only a one-year reprieve. Beyond that, nothing was guaranteed. Finally, it was time for Maura Beth to take her position behind the podium, where she slowly surveyed the crowd. Besides her alternative family, she was pleased to see that her best friend, Periwinkle Lattimore, had come on her day off. As the owner, chef, and even chief bottle washer of

Cherico's most popular restaurant, The Twinkle, she would definitely add an uninhibited, down-home touch to the proceedings. Then there was Mr. Parker Place, The Twinkle's accomplished pastry chef, freshly hired in the aftermath of the closing and demolition of the old-line Memphis Grand Shelby Hotel. Even Maura's hairstylist, tall, blond Terra Munrow of edgy Cherico Tresses, had kept her promise to become a library user and reader of romance novels once again. And certainly not to be overlooked, the dressed-to-the-teeth Crumpton sisters—Mamie and Marydell—the town's wealthiest spinsters and inveterate users of the library's genealogical resources were also in attendance.

"I'm excited to see so many familiar faces here tonight," Maura Beth began, trying her best to make eye contact with as many people as possible. Momentarily, she found the process a bit dizzying and decided to stay put on the gaze of her expert treasurer, Connie McShay. "I see some of you who helped the library over the hump last November at the budget adoption, and your continued participation is crucial if we are to keep the City Council at bay. Unfortunately, we know that Councilman Sparks is still intent on constructing that industrial park north of town. He'd like nothing better than to use the library's funds to get that project off and running."

It was Miss Voncille who spoke up first. "But don't you think we've earned some breathing room here, Maura Beth? All those voter signatures on that petition made Durden back off pretty quickly, I think. In case anyone hasn't noticed, he's not here tonight, breathing down our necks the way he did at every meeting we held last year. That has to be a good sign."

In fact, it was a carefully worded threat by Miss Voncille that changed the councilman's tune. The avid researcher found that a fund had been established long ago to support the library—money that seemed to have walked away on its own.

In Cherico, Mississippi, there was nothing like misappropriated funds to spoil an election. From that point on, it was clear that Cherico's head honcho wanted no part of shining a flashlight in that forgotten dark corner.

"We can't take anything for granted, however," Maura Beth answered, wagging her index finger. "Councilman Sparks may not be here tonight, but we know he has his eye on us. We must continue to build the buzz about the library. I think we'd all agree that there was too much dust gathering on the shelves for far too long. And don't think the powers-that-be didn't notice it. It even got back to me last year that Councilman Sparks once jokingly referred to us as the Rip Van Winkle Memorial Library. But we know better now—The Cherry Cola Book Club has aroused it from its slumber."

The diverse crowd delighted in the metaphor, and there was a great deal of head nodding around the semicircle.

"Meanwhile, we have some brief but important business to discuss tonight before we all dig into these tasty dishes many of you have so graciously prepared for us." Maura Beth looked down at her catering notes and couldn't help smiling. "Mushroom and asparagus casserole, curried chicken and rice, and our usual tomato aspic and sherry custard, for starters." She took a deep breath, as if the variety of dishes filling the buffet table had just been placed beneath her nose to whet her appetite. "But for those of you who were not present at The Twinkle last year when we celebrated our budget reprieve, it was informally decided that Eudora Welty's *The Robber Bridegroom* would be the next novel we would read. It was our intention to concentrate on Southern classics written by women to start out with, and this would be a continuation of that policy. Now, do we have any feedback on that, or are we ready to reconfirm that decision?"

Unexpectedly, the sturdy Justin Brachle—nicknamed "Stout

Fella" by his wife, Becca, for his portly demeanor—attempted to raise his hand, but Becca grabbed it quickly and pulled it down in midgesture.

"Don't!" she cried out before releasing his muscular arm and gritting her teeth in the aftermath. "Leave it the way it is."

Justin—ever the quarterback—broke through Becca's interference, thrusting his fist in the air once again. "Stout Fella and Doug McShay sitting right here are gonna have our say."

"It's no use, Becca," Connie McShay said from her vantage point a few chairs away, while patting her helmet of big hair. Then she addressed Maura Beth. "I'm afraid our husbands are determined. We would have warned you, but we just found out what they were up to on the way over here ourselves. They had their boys' night out yesterday evening. Douglas rolled in at an ungodly hour just full of himself and feeling no pain, so I suspected something was up."

Both men stood up as a double team a few feet apart, ignoring Connie's comments, and Douglas nodded toward his friend. "You go ahead and take it just like we discussed."

Justin drew up his big frame, looking straight ahead and moving his lips silently for a few seconds, obviously trying to remember something he'd been rehearsing. "Well, Maura Beth, Doug and I were having a few last night out at The Marina Bar and Grill, as my wife said, and we decided that reading *Gone with the Wind* and *To Kill a Mockingbird* like y'all did last year was just fine and dandy with us. It was your club to start with. But if we fellas are gonna be a part of all this like you and our wives want us to be, Doug and I feel that the club should read something by a man writer once in a while. And, yeah, we know we don't read as much as you ladies do, but we don't see anything wrong with putting in this request. I mean, men and women just see things differently."

Periwinkle Lattimore, whose ex-husband Harlan owned The Marina Bar and Grill, joined the fray as she stilled her customary wad of Juicy Fruit. "You bet men and women don't see things the same way. Did that crazy Harlan put y'all up to this? The only thing he's ever read in his entire life is the owner's manual of his pickup truck, besides our divorce papers, that is. Tell the truth, now, is this Harlan's idea of a joke? It's got his brand a' foolishness written all over it."

"Nope, he didn't do anything but supply us with the drinks," Douglas insisted. Then he practically did a spit take. "And he kept 'em coming, too. He's a top-notch bartender!"

"And a top-notch womanizer, just in case the rest of you didn't know," Periwinkle muttered under her breath, folding her arms for emphasis and then sniffing the air for good measure.

Completely caught off guard by the verbal bullets flying around her, Maura Beth quickly exchanged glances with Connie and Becca, who were shrugging in resigned wifely fashion. But with the unerring instincts she had acquired as an even-tempered public servant, she did not miss a beat. If she could deal with and overcome Councilman Sparks and his threats of library dissolution, she could handle this little flare-up. "I think The Cherry Cola Book Club should always be open to literary suggestions, no matter the source. We don't want to be running roughshod over anyone's opinions. There should definitely be give-and-take in a book club. So, tell us—did you have a specific writer and book in mind, Justin?"

He nodded energetically in that overgrown football player way of his. "We'd like to read *Forrest Gump* by Winston Groom. That's what we decided. What really gave us the idea was that Harlan was serving boiled shrimp on the house last night out at the lake. Man, he had a huge bowl of 'em on ice out on the counter, and does he make a great cocktail sauce! It'll flat clear your sinuses, lemme say! So, anyway, we started talking about shrimp in general, and that's how we got around to *Forrest Gump* and The Bubba Gump Shrimp Company. 'I saw that movie,' Doug here says to me between bites, and I said I'd seen it, too. And then we wondered why we couldn't read the book instead of that Eudora Welty stuff, no offense, you understand."

"Yes, I'm sure you meant no offense, Justin. But I don't usually think of Miss Welty's work as *stuff*. I think she's earned a less generic description and status by now," Maura Beth said as politely as possible.

Miss Voncille got to her feet immediately, abruptly letting go of Locke Linwood's hand. "That's true, Maura Beth, but *Forrest Gump* may not be such a bad suggestion when you think about it.

"I read the book when it was first published, and then I went to see the movie," Miss Voncille continued. "The two aren't exactly the same, you know. I think it might be a change of pace for us and shed some light on a part of our history that some people want to sweep under the rug. I know the war was unpopular and still controversial to this day, but some of us have an emotional attachment to it." It was not difficult for Maura Beth to guess why Miss Voncille might be so support-ive of the men. It had only been a few months since she had revealed to the club that she had never married because her fi-ancé, Frank Gibbons, was still MIA in Vietnam. She paused briefly, resting the palm of her hand over her chest as if she were listening to the National Anthem. "We all need closure in life."

Maura Beth maintained her poise, realizing that there was now genuine conflict swirling around the room. She must do everything in her power, however, to keep the discussion calm and civil. "Well, let's delve into this a bit further, and then we'll take a vote. If our club becomes the institution we hope it will, we'll have plenty of time to read just about everything worth-while."

Everyone standing resumed their seats as Justin spoke up again. "You see, Doug and I also like the fact that the Forrest Gump character played his football for the Bear. It doesn't get any better than that, and I'm not exactly a 'Bama fan, even though my wife, Becca, is. I played my ball at Millsaps, which is boiled green peanuts compared to the big, bad SEC. Anyhow, everybody says college ball is damn near a religion here in the South, so we thought we could talk about that, too. I remember you and Becca and all the other ladies saying we should think outside the box anyway."

"Yes, I actually am a 'Bama fan, but I thought we were supposed to have literature in mind here, not football," Becca said, fighting off a pout. Then she turned to focus on her husband. "That scholarship of yours is way back in your rearview mirror. You're nearly forty years old, and you just recovered from a heart attack and an angioplasty, need I remind you. So no more wishful thinking about backyard games with the fellas—not even flag or touch. Besides, when it comes to football, what we should really be discussing is the plight of us poor football widows. From September kickoff to the end of the bowl season, it's like we're chopped liver. I admit I do keep up with 'Bama, but you guys let us out of the closet long enough to fix your meals and snacks, and maybe work up the energy to kiss us at halftime—if your team is covering the point spread, that is. But that's about it!"

"Amen!" Connie put in, a football widow herself.

Then Locke Linwood managed a sly little grin while putting in a word. "For the record, I love shrimp with cocktail sauce, if that means anything. To the horseradish, men!"

"Glad you said that, Mr. Linwood," Justin added, smiling big. "Doug and I thought that reading *Forrest Gump* might also be an opportunity for the wives to contribute their best seafood and shrimp recipes to the potluck."

Miss Voncille leaned over in Becca's direction. "You've done shrimp recipes on *The Becca Broccoli Show*, haven't you?"

"Yes, it was the Cherico version of the 'shrimp on the barbie' thing. But for the record, folks, I'm getting the impression we're suddenly all about the shrimp here, and the prose can just run away and hide for all we care. Should we change our name to The Cherico Shrimp Club, or better yet, The Cherico Cooking Club? For wives only, I might add."

Then Maura Beth realized how off topic they'd wandered. "However, we were discussing whether to read *The Robber Bridegroom* or *Forrest Gump*. Do I have any more cogent thoughts on Welty's work? There's certainly a wealth of literary criticism out there to access."

"We've read just about everything Eudora Welty has ever written!" Mamie Crumpton proclaimed, heaving her ample bosom framed by her silver-sequined bodice. "Haven't we, sister?"

Mousy Marydell offered up her customary, barely audible, "Yes."

"Of course, I've always loved that story of hers about the lady who lives at the post office," Mamie continued. "I have to admit that I don't know anything about this *Gump* novel by C. S. Forester, but I do adore shrimp." She paused briefly to run her tongue across her lips. "These potluck dinners have been scrumptious, but I don't know what kind of culinary theme we could build around Eudora Welty. Southern food, I suppose, but everything we've eaten here at the library has been Southern. Comes with the territory, of course."

"If I may correct a slight misconception you have, Miz Crumpton," Maura Beth explained, careful to sound as diplomatic as possible with such an influential library patron. "C. S. Forester did not write *Forrest Gump*. Winston Groom did. He's an Alabama writer—and quite an accomplished one at that."

Mamie waved her off in typical patrician manner. "Pish,

tosh! I vote for something new. Sister does, too. I think Voncille and the men make good, serviceable points. We should
support them and save Miss Welty for another time. I'm sure
we'd all agree that her place on the shelves is assured for all
eternity." Mamie paused and began laughing heartily all by
herself, her ample dress appearing to vibrate and take on a life
of its own.

Maura Beth frowned and waited for the woman and her
mounds of fabric to cease and desist. "Did I miss something?"

"I was just thinking," came the reply, "that no one is going
to steal *The Robber Bridegroom* from us."

There was a forced ripple of laughter, if only because most
people found Mamie Crumpton, her money and social position, to be intimidating, and few had ever dared to cross her
without a significant price to pay.

At that point Maura Beth could see that *Forrest Gump* was
going to win the day. Both Becca and Connie again shrugged
their shoulders, also knowing full well that when Mamie
Crumpton made up her mind, that pretty much settled the
issue in question. When the vote was finally taken, in fact, *The
Robber Bridegroom* came in a distant second, at which point
Maura Beth—always voting last—joined the majority so as not
to appear inflexible or holding on to a lost cause.

"Well, it looks like we'll be reading *Forrest Gump* for our
March meeting. And bringing lots of shrimp and seafood
dishes as a consequence," Maura Beth announced. She could
feel herself forcing the muscles of her face into an artificial
configuration of approval. Why, it just wouldn't do for her to
become as despotic and heavy-handed as the Cherico councilmen were! "Becca, you'll coordinate who brings what as
usual, won't you?"

Becca nodded complacently at first, then suddenly seemed
more sanguine. "Hey, why be a salmon swimming upstream

about this? As long as we're also going to be discussing foot-ball—and football widows, I trust—why don't we include some of our favorite tailgating dishes along with the shrimp? I stumbled upon a classic or two during my time at 'Bama."

All of the men present broke out in generous nods and smiles, and Justin spoke up for all of them when he patted his stomach and said, "Sounds like a mighty good deal to me!"

Nonetheless, Maura Beth struggled to fight back the un-easy feeling dogging her. In a breathtaking turn of events, *The Robber Bridegroom* had been apprehended and put away for a while, and furthermore, the all-encompassing emphasis on food was leaving a bad taste in her mouth. "I just want to re-mind everyone again that we are first and foremost a book club. I'm pleased that everyone enjoys the potluck so much. Sharing delicious food and companionship is a big part of what we're all about here. But we're also here primarily to re-view literary works. I hope we'll all read *Forrest Gump* in that spirit and remember how much we value those outside-the-box angles when we get together. That's what has given The Cherry Cola Book Club such a unique calling card so far. Looks like we now have a book club for the boys, so to speak. Of course, our ultimate goal should be to become a book club for all of Cherico."

After the meeting had adjourned, some of the members stuck around to thank Maura Beth. "I never thought I'd find the time in my busy schedule at The Twinkle to read books," said Periwinkle. "Or listen to 'em in my case, since I check out the audios to keep me occupied to and from work. Why, sometimes I think I'm in an episode of *Star Trek* the way I start out from The Twinkle after I close up and shove one of those CDs into the dashboard. Then, bam! There I am transported to my front door with no conception of any time having passed at all."

"And I have to say that I've rediscovered reading," Mr. Place said. "When I'm not turning out my desserts, that is. And I believe I'd have my mama reading, too, if she didn't have so much trouble with her eyes. By the way, she sends along her regrets that she was feeling a little bit under the weather and couldn't be here with y'all this evening."

"I'm sure we all hope she's feeling better soon. Meanwhile, you must evaluate our cookbook selection sometime, Mr. Place," Maura Beth suggested. "I have the sneaking suspicion that our collection needs weeding desperately in that area. Oh, and don't forget that we have large-print books for readers like your mother. I'm sure she can find a genre she likes."

"I'll remind her."

Renette Posey entered the exchange with her girlish excitement. "Oh, we definitely need to weed, Miz Mayhew. Just the other day I found a dusty old cookbook published way back in 1943 with a chapter on how to grow vegetables in your Victory Garden. I didn't know what on earth they were talking about until I got home and Googled it on my computer. Imagine growing everything under the sun in a terracotta pot to spite the Nazis!"

Maura Beth was decidedly embarrassed by the revelation, briefly looking off to the side. More than once she had postponed weeding certain areas of the collection for the simple reason that the library lacked adequate replacement funds. "I must apologize for having held on to such an outdated subject like that."

Renette was right, and Maura Beth knew it. They still had far to go to bring The Cherico Library up to modern, state-of-the-art standards. Forget just keeping it open; they needed more money to hire staff, improve the collection, get some computer terminals, and that was just for starters. Expanding the book club was an integral part of the equation. Determined to make that happen, Maura Beth thanked her loyal members and sent them on their way with a pep talk. "In the six weeks until we get together to review *Forrest Gump*, don't forget to remind your friends and relatives to check us out the way they did at our *To Kill a Mockingbird* meeting in November. Let's continue making The Cherry Cola Book Club and this little library the toast of the town."

2

The Infrequent Reader

Fifteen minutes or so after The Cherry Cola Book Club had officially finished with its buffet and small talk, Maura Beth found herself alone in the library, tending to such routine tasks as flicking off light switches everywhere before she went home to her little purple-decorated efficiency on Clover Street. Renette had helped her put the leftovers away in the library fridge and wanted to stay until the last key had been turned in the last lock, but Maura Beth had sent her off, sounding like a concerned mother lecturing her daughter on the great truths of life. "Go get your beauty sleep, sweetie," she had told her. "Build up your *pretty* reserves while you're still young. The bloom is off the rose soon enough."

No wonder, then, that Maura Beth jumped noticeably, even swearing that she felt her heart skip a beat or two, when a timid little voice out of nowhere called out, "Miz Mayhew?"

Maura Beth quickly turned from her vantage point outside her office door and peered toward the dimly lit entrance. "Who's there?" she said in a tone that managed to sound both frightened and incredulous. "Is that you, Renette? Did you forget something?"

The shadowy figure moved forward slowly into the illumination surrounding the circulation desk, and Maura Beth saw who it was, much to her great relief.

"Oh, it's you, Miz Duddney! What a surprise!"

Indeed, it was. Maura Beth had not set eyes on the dull, monosyllabic spinster since her dismissal as Councilman Sparks's secretary late last year. Everyone in the inner circle of the book club was convinced that Nora Duddney's firing after decades of service was an attempt to bring Maura Beth "into the fold." But the ploy had not worked. Maura Beth had seen through it, turned down the extra money as Nora's successor, and fought even harder to remain at the helm of her beloved Cherico Library. Yet Maura Beth had wondered more than once what had become of the poor woman. She seemed to have dropped off the face of the earth—until tonight.

"I've come to join your book club," Nora explained, now face-to-face with Maura Beth. "But I needed to tell you a couple of things—privately."

Maura Beth fumbled for the right key on her big ring and unlocked her office, flicking on the light switch as they both entered. "Please, have a seat, and we'll have a nice talk." Once they were settled in across from each other, she resumed. "You missed an interesting meeting here, you know. But I'm thrilled you're joining. You'll love our little group that's growing every day. There are so many wonderful novels out there to explore, and we decided tonight that our next read will be *Forrest Gump* by Winston Groom."

Nora said nothing at first, playing with a few strands of mousy brown hair that had defied her best efforts at grooming and fallen haphazardly across her forehead. For a second or two, she looked as if she might be getting ready to pull them out by their roots. What she desperately needed, Maura Beth conjectured while watching the nervous display, was a visit to Cherico Tresses for a few highlights, or at the very least a bona-fide hairstyle. Not to mention a clothes makeover and a

touch of makeup. Nothing drastic, mind you. Just a little something to bring her out of her pale, late middle-aged stupor.

"That's one of the things I needed to tell you. I'm not a
reader," Nora said finally. "Never have been. It's not that I dis-
like reading, it's just that . . . well, I have this trouble. I see
words and letters all reversed—I've been that way all my life,
like I'm from another planet. That's why people always saw
me taking my time at the typewriter—and then the computer
when we finally switched over at City Hall. I actually understood what I was supposed to be doing—it just took me a
while to get it done."

"You're dyslexic?" Maura Beth said, indulging a sharp intake of air to put an exclamation point on her epiphany. "All
this time you've had dyslexia?"

"Yes, I have. A severe case, I'm afraid. And I didn't find out
about it until many years into my adult life. While I was growing up, everyone just thought I was—well, you know . . . slow.
And that included my parents. Back then, the diagnosis wasn't
so easy to come by. They never knew what the real problem
was. Just that the doctors said I needed looking after." But she
said nothing further.

"Now I can see why you wanted a little privacy."

Again there was decided hesitation, and Nora looked distinctly uncomfortable. "Yes."

"Try to relax, Nora. I'm pretty good at listening."

Nora swept the wild strands out of her face with the palm
of her hand. "I, uh, was beyond shocked that Councilman
Sparks fired me. That job was the one thing I thought I could
count on, come hell or high water. It was my ticket to stability
in my life. But . . . I was just swept aside."

Now it was Maura Beth's turn to feel awkward, knowing
the truth about the entire secretarial situation, but she had no
intention of revealing it. It was obvious that Nora had a low
threshold for hurt feelings. "Yes, I think it was very unfair to

you after all those years of service to the town. Did Councilman Sparks even know you were dyslexic?"

"I'm not sure. I know I never told him. I was afraid he
might hold it against me."

The sadness in Nora's already drab face was too much for
Maura Beth to bear. "Shame on him if he did and still let
you go!"

"I appreciate you taking my side." Then out of nowhere,
her face brightened. "But maybe the joke's on him. It's gotten
back to me that the lady who replaced me, Mrs. Lottie
Howard, is driving him crazy. Something about abbreviating
his messages all the time and trying his patience in general. I
never tried to cut corners and somehow managed to meet his
deadlines."

The image of Nora as a dim-witted, washed-out nonentity
quickly began to dissolve as Maura Beth took in every
thoughtful sentence headed her way from across the desk.
Suddenly, there was a real person behind the blank façade
Nora had always presented to the world. And there was now a
legitimate reason for the one-word utterances and grunts that
had always characterized her behavior. Obviously, the woman
had always been in the midst of supreme cognitive concentra-
tion.

"I've gotten over the shock, though," Nora continued.
"Now I'm just angry, and I think it will help me to be with
people." There was more hesitation. "Of course, I've been
wondering if I should maybe look for another job somewhere
because—"

Maura Beth interrupted and leaned in, genuinely puzzled.
"Is this a matter of finances? If it is, I truly sympathize, but I'm
afraid I have no budget to hire you here. I'd be embarrassed to
tell you what I make, much less my front desk clerks."

Nora suddenly exuded confidence as she replied, her face
more animated than it had ever been on the job at City Hall.

"No, I'm not hurting for money. I've saved up quite a bit over the years. I was actually paid handsomely, believe it or not. But I earned every penny, if I do say so myself."

Maura Beth continued to be in awe of the new Nora, all dewy petals opening up in the light of truth. Here was someone most of Cherico had thought of as no more significant than the wallpaper in Councilman Sparks's office, and she was now standing up for herself every bit as impressively as Maura Beth had stood up for the little library on Shadow Alley.

"If you know any of this already, stop me," Nora continued. "My father, Layton Duddney, and Councilman Sparks's father, Wendell, were both on the Council way back when certain matrons of Cherico decided to contribute some of their hard-earned inherited money to start up a library—"

Maura Beth couldn't suppress the high-pitched giggle that floated up out of her like a hiccup. Would wonders never cease? Nora Duddney even had a subtle sense of humor, taking that potshot at wealthy Chericoans the way she had just done.

"What?!" Nora exclaimed. "Did I say something funny?"

Maura Beth quickly put her librarian face back on, chiding herself mentally. "Oh, no, please continue. I'm just enjoying talking to you like this. Why, we've practically become girlfriends!"

"What a nice thing to say to me! Anyway," she continued, "I do know that Daddy lobbied Wendell Sparks for my job. Daddy took me aside one time and told me that as long as a member of the Sparks Family was sitting on the Council, I was supposed to have my job as City Hall secretary. The sun and the moon might not rise and set, but I would in that outer office without exception."

"Very interesting," Maura Beth said. She remembered that Councilman Sparks had once revealed to her that he had owed Nora Duddney's father a favor or two.

"What you may not know is that Daddy has outlived Mr.

Wendell by a good many years and is still with us." Nora suddenly frowned, lowering her brows and making slits of her dark brown eyes. "Well, in a way he's still with us. He's actually been out at Cherico Nursing Manor near the lake for many years now. It's only been more recently that he's been unable to recognize me, or anyone else for that matter. But something tells me it was no coincidence that Councilman Sparks let me go shortly after Daddy was officially moved into the assisted living wing. Daddy may be pushing one hundred, but what good does it do him when he doesn't even know who or where he is? It's a sad situation all around."

"That must be very difficult for you," Maura Beth said, trying to sound as soothing as she could. But it suddenly all made sense to her. With Layton Duddney essentially out of the way, Councilman Sparks no longer needed to respect the arrangements of the past, however shady they might be. And it had left him free to pursue his offer to Maura Beth of having the great privilege of "working under him" at City Hall and other designated spots.

"Now as to the book club," Nora said, fully comfortable with Maura Beth as a confidante, "it would take me forever to get through *Forrest Gump* or any of the other books you decided to review. I'll need some sort of help if I'm going to participate with the others."

"I tell you what. I could buy an audio copy of *Forrest Gump* to accommodate you. Mr. Place's mother, Ardenia, could make good use of it, too, with her failing eyesight and all. Besides, we have more than a few people who've never entered into the discussions so far, and I don't ask them why. I suspect the good food and companionship are enough for them, and they're content to let others do the talking."

Nora rested her fist under her chin and contemplated for a while. "If you could get that audio, I'd be up to speed just like everybody else. I'm very good at listening to things. You'd be surprised what you can find out that way—especially if people don't even think you're listening or treat you like you're not even in the room."

Maura Beth reached across the desk and shook her hand. "Well, I'll do my best to get that audio of *Forrest Gump*. Meanwhile, allow me to welcome you aboard!"

"I feel better already." Nora smiled briefly while scanning Maura Beth's cluttered office, but she couldn't help wincing once she had finished. "You really do have a small budget, don't you? I'd get claustrophobic working in here day after day."

"Tell me about it."

Then Nora brightened again. "I just want you to realize that you're the only person I can think of in recent memory who has managed to outfox Councilman Sparks, even if it's just in the form of a one-year reprieve for your library. I know what I'm talking about, what with all the years I've been around, Miz Mayhew. Sometimes I think I'm as old as Cherico itself."

"You're exaggerating about yourself, but you flatter me," Maura Beth said, her smile a bit on the guarded side. "I wish I'd been able to win an outright victory for the library with no strings attached."

But Nora closed her eyes and shook her head emphatically, the wild strands falling into her face once again. "I know what I know. And the bottom line is, you cannot count on Councilman Sparks to do the right thing when the time comes—unless you force his hand."

Maura Beth continued to marvel at the words coming from Nora's mouth. It was almost as if she had been saving up this impressive display of verbosity and insights over the decades for just such a seminal occasion. Above anything else, Maura Beth was an admirer of those with a gift for words— written or spoken. She therefore was compelled to listen to everything Nora had to say without questioning a syllable.

"If this one-year reprieve Councilman Sparks has given you looks like the end of the road, you and I need to talk further," Nora concluded. "I know you never thought you'd be hearing these words come out of my mouth, but here they are anyway—let me help you."

Maura Beth sat back, feeling more optimistic about her Cherico Library mission and The Cherry Cola Book Club than she ever had before. Nora Duddney, she observed, was breathing new life into that treasured old chestnut trotted out by librarians throughout history: *Never judge a book by its cover.*

3

Hieroglyphics and Empty Pajamas

It was Evie Sparks, of all people, who had come up with the solution to her husband's secretarial dilemma with Mrs. Lottie Howard. In fact, January was nearly over when she had revealed her brainstorm over breakfast just before he had set out for work as chief executive at City Hall.

"I had this idea about Lottie because I know what a pain it is for you to go through another hiring procedure," she had begun, sitting across the table and munching on a piece of buttered cinnamon toast. "Of course, you'd be perfectly justified in letting her go, no matter what."

"You know damned good and well that's one of the New Year's resolutions I'm bound and determined to keep—waving bye-bye to that maddening woman," Councilman Sparks had said. "I just need to get all my ducks in a row first."

Then he returned to his plate of scrambled egg substitute and turkey sausage, alternated daily with a bowl of vanilla yogurt and blueberries. Durden Sparks, the consummate politician, knew that maintaining his job went hand in hand with maintaining his physique. He knew he had won election after election because of a combination of good looks and clever manipulation. Women still sighed over his deep-set, dark eyes and a mesmerizing display of white teeth, even as the gray hair continued to spread ever so slowly from his temples to the sides of his head. If it were possible for a man to become tenfold more attractive to the opposite sex in his middle years, Councilman Charles Durden Sparks was living proof and then some.

"I remember all your resolutions, Durden. There's that one, of course, and then the one about getting Maura Beth Mayhew and the library out of your hair for good. No one knows better than I do that you won't rest until you see ground broken next year on the industrial park."

He had drawn himself up proudly and underlined with his outstretched hand an imaginary sign suspended in midair. "I will continue to maintain that The Charles Durden Sparks Industrial Park has a wonderful ring to it."

But he could tell from her casual tone of voice that she was not taking his priorities as seriously as he would have liked. "If you're going to say I should have already fired Lottie and that I should take Nora back, the answer is no. That connection with Layton Duddney is over and done with. Another lifetime. Finis."

She swallowed a bite of her toast and took a sip of her coffee. "That wasn't what I was going to say at all." She cocked her head to the side, reminding him exactly of their spoiled poodle, Bonjour Cheri, who was lying at her "mommy's" feet at that very moment. Both dog and wife had that same precious little face with the cutesy, short clipped hairdo framing it precisely. "I was thinking that you ought to give Lottie a taste of her own medicine."

"How so?"

She put down her toast and sat up straight in her chair with her hands limply posed in front, looking remarkably like she was about to beg him for a treat. "I mean that you should start abbreviating the hell out of things the way she does all the time. Leave notes on her desk about important things for her to do, but instead use those big letters in all caps. Then conveniently skedaddle somewhere with Chunky and Gopher Joe, and let her try to figure out what you meant until you get back and enlighten her. Turnabout is fair play."

He enjoyed a good laugh and then nodded her way. "Now, why didn't I think of that? You're absolutely right. Two can play at hieroglyphics."

"From what you've told me, she actually seems to enjoy tripping you up. Just let her find out what that's like."

Days later, Mrs. Lottie Howard *had* found out, and he only had to do it to her once to drive home his point. She had padded into his office and earnestly apologized to him in the aftermath. "Okay, you win. I get the message. Or, rather, I didn't get it." She glanced briefly at the note he had left her, which she had cupped in the palm of her hand. "Couldn't even come close to figuring out what you meant by D-T-Y-L-B-A-U—I-B-B-A-N."

He gave her one of those triumphant "I stumped you!" looks she had delighted in giving him over the past few months. "Don't take your lunch break as usual—I'll be back at noon!"

She had taken the time to match the letters with his translation and actually chuckled there at the end. "Good one, Mr. Sparks!" Then, even though he had not asked her to, she began explaining. "I actually thought I was being efficient. Or maybe I've just become addicted to texting shortcuts. You don't know this about me—actually nobody does—but I spend a lot of time on Facebook chats at home, especially late at night. As the young people say, 'It's awesome!' "

He had leaned in, deliberately withholding his trademark smile from her. "Perhaps you should work harder at getting a life, Lottie. At any rate, your obsession almost cost you your job, I hope you realize."

And that had been the end of it. Mrs. Lottie Howard, as it turned out, was a keeper after all.

The drive out to the Cherico Nursing Manor was much longer than Councilman Sparks had remembered. So many twists and turns in the old two-lane road full of dangerous pot-holes—one that badly needed a new coat of asphalt, and one they had budgeted for back in November at the controversial hearings that had forced City Hall to continue supporting the library.

That was what Maura Beth Mayhew, pretty and enticing as she was, would never understand in that compartmentalized librarian's brain of hers. The roads, the utility poles and underground cables, the sidewalks, the sewers, the stop signs and traffic lights—indeed, the entire infrastructure had to come first in the budget. The citizens needed those things in place to conduct their ordinary lives in a successful manner without thinking about it. As for books—well, they could buy them somewhere if they were so darned addicted to them. When times were tough and money was tight, why must a struggling town like Cherico keep the library afloat at all costs? Heh, *costs* being the operative word.

Councilman Sparks had darkened the front foyer of Cherico Nursing Manor only once before, and that was to visit Layton Duddney just after he'd first been admitted a few years back. But now he needed to confirm things for himself. His "mole at the Manor," as he thought of her, had assured him that Nora Duddney had already come and gone that late January morning. He would not be running into her in what would be a beyond awkward confrontation.

"She only stayed about ten minutes, sir," Nurse Trella Goodell had told him over the phone just before he had set out. "No one ever stays much longer. I mean, what would be the point? He just sits there, propped up in bed, staring at the

TV if I turn it on for him. Or staring at the wall and all his pictures if I don't. I don't mean to be disrespectful, Mr. Durden,
but he's just a pair of empty pajamas, and that's the God's honest truth."

But Councilman Sparks wanted to see for himself as yet
another year in office moved along, as he moved toward estab-
lishing his legacy for the town of Cherico. Not that he had
doubted Nora when she had admitted her father was truly no
longer there.

"Daddy's gone south for the winter," she had explained to
him a few months earlier, tearing up all the while. "And it
looks like winter is gonna last all year now."

Finally, Councilman Sparks found himself in the parking
lot of Cherico's only nursing facility. It had all the charm of a
one-story pedestrian motel on the outside, even though he
knew the staff inside was more than qualified to look after its
many aged patients. There was a part of him that hoped he
would never live long enough to have to be "committed" to a
facility like that; but it was in sharp conflict with the other part
that was convinced he was going to live forever and go down
in The Guinness Book of World Records as a result.

Enough of these idle musings. It was time to get this task
over and done with. So he headed in with a snap to his step
and was soon signing his name in the ledger that displayed
Nora Duddney's spidery signature several lines and hours
above his. The officious receptionist, a frowning man with severely thinning dark hair whose gold nameplate on the
counter identified him as Victor Prather, picked up the phone
and notified the assisted living wing of the visitor waiting in
the foyer.

"She'll be right out to get you," Victor told him after the
brief conversation had ended.

"Nurse Trella Goodell, I assume."

For a few awkward seconds Victor looked put-upon, as if

the woman's identity should be kept secret, but he finally exhaled in what sounded remarkably like a tone of resignation. "Yes, she's the main one on duty over there today."

At first Councilman Sparks wanted to lean over the faux marble counter and make a smart remark. "You like your job a lot, do you?" came to mind. But he thought better of it.

After only a minute or so, Trella Goodell emerged from one of the corridors and shook the councilman's hand warmly. Here was an older woman who exuded empathy while obviously not having missed many meals. The roundness of her fleshy face, combined with its prominent laugh lines, surely gave her patients an additional sense of comfort as she tended to their needs. As a result, "jolly old girl" were the words that had most often been used to describe her.

"You've come at a good time," Trella continued, after they had exchanged the usual pleasantries. "He's just up from another of his dozens of naps. Of course, he spends most of his time asleep, as you probably know."

"So you've told me."

"Lookie here, Mr. Duddney!" Trella announced quite loudly, as she ushered Councilman Sparks into the man's cozy bedroom a few minutes and twists and turns of corridors later. There were lots of framed pictures tacked to the white walls for decoration, but this small assisted universe of his lacked much personality otherwise. "You have another visitor. Two in one day. First your daughter comes, and now Mr. Sparks is here to see you!"

This pale, withered specimen whose visible flesh seemed to blend perfectly into the pale beige pajamas he was wearing appeared frozen in place, propped up against the pillows of his bed. There was an unexpected dignity to it, however, as if he were patiently posing for an artist doing his portrait. Momentarily, Layton Duddney barely moved his bald head, which still sprouted a handful of wispy white strands and peered at the couple standing in the door frame.

"Time . . . t'eat . . . yet?" he managed, moving his mouth in what seemed to be slow motion.

"You just ate an hour ago," Trella told him, her professional smile still in place. "I brought you your tray."

"Didda . . . eat it?"

"You ate your string beans," she told him. "A bite of the chicken breast. It was grilled today."

He began to perk up, and there was a sudden flash of recognition in his eyes. "Dessert?"

"Yes, you had dessert. Rice pudding. You liked it. You always like it when we have rice pudding."

He began peering intently at Councilman Sparks, slowly looking him up and down. "Who's he? . . . I don't need changin'!"

Trella's tone became even more patronizing. "No, Mr. Duddney. This is not the orderly. This is Councilman Durden Sparks. From City Hall. From Cherico. From in town."

There was only the one word from Layton Duddney: "Why?"

Trella moved closer to the bed, momentarily leaving Councilman Sparks in the background. "Because he likes you."

But there was no response.

"May I speak to him?" Councilman Sparks asked, moving to her side.

"Go right ahead. Just don't expect anything."

Councilman Sparks took his time. This was harder than he thought it was going to be. He couldn't help but remember when Layton Duddney had been a much younger and far more vigorous man who had conducted the business of Cherico for many years alongside his own father. The two had been an unbeatable pair of politicians, weathering every storm that had ever come their way. They had always managed to sweep suspicion and controversy under the Persian rugs of their City Hall offices. And they had also done their fair share of good things for the community.

"If you play your political cards right, Durden," Layton had once told him, "you can lead a charmed life." And that, along with other incentives, pep talks, and revelations from his own father, had settled him on a career as a Cherico city councilman.

"Layton," Councilman Sparks said, feeling something catch in his throat as he spoke. "I'm Durden. When I was a teenager, you used to call me Durdie. I remember distinctly the summer Mom made you stop, though. She said it made me sound like I needed a bath."

Layton remained in silent posing mode.

"I told ya," Trella said, her smile absent for once.

Councilman Sparks decided to try again. "Layton?"

Suddenly, there seemed to be a spark of recognition again, and Layton gave the councilman an intense, almost angry stare. "I said . . . I don't need changin'!"

Trella was shaking her head. "It's no use, Mr. Sparks. I think he gets worse every day, like I've been telling you over the phone. But at least now you can say you've seen it for yourself."

That was all Councilman Sparks could take. He quickly thanked Trella for her time and assistance, and then headed out of Cherico Nursing Manor as fast as he could negotiate the succession of corridors. He had always told himself that the end justified the means. He had always had the best interests of the people of Cherico at heart. He had to believe that.

Long before Layton Duddney had lost it, he had taken Councilman Sparks aside and talked turkey with him. "This little town will die on the vine unless you're strong and aggressive. You think the people and the companies and the businesses with money out there know where the hell we are anymore? Your daddy and I figured out a long time ago that the main chance had passed our little Cherico by. We had the lake and the Tennessee River going for us, but we just pretended that they weren't even there. So we did what we could to keep Cherico on the map, and that's what you gotta do, son. And after both of us are gone, you gotta keep at it. That'll be your legacy, son. That'll be your legacy."

When Councilman Sparks started the engine of his SUV out in the parking lot, he had to steady himself with a couple of deep, cleansing breaths that caused his seat belt to tighten and press against his stomach. Then he glanced into the rearview mirror and was shocked to see the single tear coursing down his right cheek.

Out loud, he said, "Now where the hell did that come from?"

4

A Bump in the Road

As they had done every now and then over the six years of
their friendship, Maura Beth and Periwinkle were closing
down The Twinkle. Of course, all the votive candles on the
two-seaters were still flickering, the silver and gold star mobiles
were dangling above them, and the quiet stylings of a Diana
Krall CD were working their magic in the softly lit background. But the last customer—a paunchy carpet salesman
passing through Cherico by the name of Bubby Bentworth—
had headed back to his motel, having enjoyed his entrée of
Periwinkle's grilled rosemary chicken with roasted new potatoes and a slice of Mr. Parker Place's silken grasshopper pie.
The front door had been locked and the OPEN sign flipped,
and now it was time for some genuine girlfriend talk on an
otherwise uneventful Saturday night over a last glass of white
wine.

"You go first," Periwinkle said, seating herself at Maura
Beth's dinner table as she served their nightcaps. "I know
you've been kinda worried about Jeremy and all. So you say
he's coming down to see you tomorrow with some sorta
news?"

Maura Beth took a sip of her wine and nodded approvingly. "Haven't heard anything to the contrary. He's supposed to show up around two o'clock. I have no idea what he's been up to, though. He said telling me in advance might jinx it."

"Don't you hate it when men act so mysterious?"

Maura Beth managed a reluctant little nod, briefly drawn to the flame of the votive candle sitting halfway between them. "I wish I could say I'd had enough experience to agree with you. Of course, right before Al Broussard ditched me at LSU at the tender age of twenty-two, he did start acting strangely distant. Then he dropped that bomb of his that if I wasn't willing to join the Catholic Church, he wasn't going to marry me. But so far in our relationship, Jeremy's been pretty straightforward. And romantic enough to keep me interested. He's a really good kisser, for starters. Soft lips, lets you come up for air now and then, lets you guide him to the spots you want him to go to, but also respects your limits."

Periwinkle quickly wrinkled her nose twice while working her gum. "All that's a good sign. But try to keep your eyes wide open if you can. I was way beyond naïve when I married Harlan Lattimore. Of course, I've wised up since then." Then she leaned in the way she always did when something resembling a lecture or testimonial was forthcoming. "He'd just gotten the construction loan to build The Marina Bar and Grill out on the lake, and I was just as gung ho as he was. He even drove me out to the muddy spot where the restaurant was going up, but the moon was shining on the water, and it really dressed things up like a lot of fancy scenery in a stage play. I just thought this was gonna be a business made in heaven. I told him I'd be more than happy to be his secretary and keep the books and all. They say couples who work together have a better chance of staying together. That's what they say. But I shoudda seen trouble brewing because, honey, the devil was in the blueprints."

"You mean fine print, don't you?"

Periwinkle shook her head emphatically and pounded her fist playfully on the table. "No, I meant just what I said. When he laid out the blueprints for the restaurant, I shouldn't have been so darn trusting. There was this extra room in the back next to the pantry, and I said, 'What's that for?' And he explained that he thought it'd be a good idea to have a little place to take a nap if either of us got really tired. Or even to spend the night in an emergency or if some other situation ever arose. Can you believe I fell for that?"

Maura Beth tried to suppress a smile but couldn't. She'd heard the story of Periwinkle's divorce too many times. But this little detail about the additional square footage was a brand-new twist. "Sorry. So that's how he went about his business on the side."

"Lemme tell you how innocent I was. I even went out and decorated that little den of iniquity for him. Is that beyond lame or what? There I was, fooling around with swatches and fabric bolts until I was nearly cross-eyed, worrying about what the curtains would look like and if the color scheme was gonna be cheerful enough for him, when all he cared about was the mattress. Oh, it was a sweet setup for that nasty rattlesnake a' mine. My work was done by six every day, but as I eventually found out, some cutie'd come wandering in by herself later, sit herself down on one of his bar stools, and way too many times she'd end up evaluating my decorating skills on her back during one of Harlan's quickies!"

They both were actually laughing now and did not speak for a while. Maura Beth returned to the candle flame until she thought it was time to break the awkward silence. "No wonder you haven't told me about that part. I've always admired the way you've handled yourself since the divorce, though. I think I would've been crushed by what you went through."

Periwinkle tapped her index finger on the table a few times, as if she were a teacher trying to get the attention of a daydreaming student. "That's where the settlement helped. As I've told you before, Harlan wanted to pay me off and cut me loose for practically nothing. But I hired me a great lawyer—Curtis Trickett, matter of fact. I'd recommend him if you ever need legal help. I told Curtis I'd helped Harlan build up that business and kept it square with the IRS and all our creditors, and I wanted my share because I intended to open my own restaurant. And here we are sitting in my very respectable success story."

Just when Maura Beth thought Periwinkle had wrapped things up neatly, however, there was more inside scoop. "Harlan's been on my mind lately because apparently I've been on his."

"Really? After all this time?"

Periwinkle was staring at the mobile above them, looking as if she were talking to one of her trademark stars. "Oh, I have no idea what to make of it. I get this phone call last night from him saying that he'd like to treat me to a romantic little dinner tomorrow. Just the two of us. And I said, 'Are you out of your mind?' To which he says, 'No, just to remember the good times.'" She brought her gaze down to the table again. "He's up to something. I don't usually hear squat from him, not even on my birthday. Of course, I don't bother to remember his, either."

Then she leaned in for one of her "girlfriend gossip" moments. "In fact, I'll tell you something interesting, girl. The only man in my life these days is Parker—I mean professionally, of course. He's such a dream to work with, and his desserts have really brought a different group of customers into the restaurant. We never used to get the 'sweet tooth' crowd, and more black families have started to come in because of him. He says he's been spreading the word to all his friends at church, and they even mention him when they order. Sometimes they even ask if he can come out and talk to them. It's all good."

"I'm so glad the hire has worked out for you. I had a good feeling about Mr. Place from the start," Maura Beth said.

Periwinkle brightened even further. "Oh, more than you know. Sometimes Parker goes out of his way to do thoughtful things for me. Why, one time he even brought me some flowers—he's the Southern gentleman Harlan never was. And there's something else I've come to realize. At first I kinda thought of him as belonging to another generation. But he's just a few years past fifty, and I've finally admitted to forty, girl. I've gradually begun to think of us more as contemporaries."

Maura Beth finally drained the last of her wine and lightly smacked her lips in a gesture of finality. "That all sounds delightful. My workplace environment is just plain drab and depressing with no man in sight. At any rate, I'll give you the lowdown on Jeremy as soon as I know what it is, and you do the same with Harlan. Oh, wait—did you agree to that dinner?"

"I did. Don't know why." She began moving her eyes about, apparently projecting an amusing vision. "Maybe he needs to have his little playroom redecorated. But lemme tell you, girl. I am good and through being his clueless Martha Stewart."

Maura Beth had never seen Jeremy looking so depressed before. She knew something was seriously wrong when he walked into her Clover Street apartment just past two the next day with his shoulders slumped and his eyes downcast. It also came to her that she had never seen him dressed in anything but his New Gallatin Academy navy blue blazer and red tie. Today he had decided that a pair of jeans and a faded yellow shirt with the top button missing would do the trick, and she didn't mind at all. He was still just as handsome and appealing out of his schoolteacher drag. They briefly hugged and kissed but had barely seated themselves on the sofa when he launched into an explanation of the project that had been occupying so much of his time lately.

"I thought I had this 'Living the Classics in the Real World' field trip in the bag, Maura Beth. I don't think I've ever been so disappointed in my life, not even last year for your *To Kill a Mockingbird* meeting. Man, sometimes I wish I didn't care about my students the way I do," he began. There was no mistaking the anger in his voice as he began flexing his right hand several times, fist to open fingers. He couldn't seem to stop, as if he were doing some sort of isometric exercise. Finally, Maura Beth reached over and put her hand over his.

"Calm down and tell me—but take a deep breath first."

He complied, but his tone was still agitated and his breathing still labored. "I researched everything. Ways to cut corners on the motel and meals for my students, checking out availability of reservations on certain dates, lining up parents as chaperones, and all of it well in advance this time. As I mentioned, I've been working on another literary field trip—this time to take a school bus down to Oxford to see Rowan Oak and have the guys learn all about Faulkner. Why shouldn't my students be exposed to the literary world within reasonable traveling distance? I thought I got turned down last November for your *Mockingbird* review because everything was too rushed and last minute, which it was."

Maura Beth reached up and gently rubbed his shoulder, feeling the tightness of his muscles beneath the shirt. "So you're saying the headmaster turned you down again?"

"I really thought Mr. Yelverton would approve me this time. I spent most of last weekend drawing up a proposal, and then I had dinner with him and his wife for the verdict. But it looks like it was all for nothing." Jeremy's features darkened, and he made another fist, which this time landed emphatically on his thigh. "What really burns me is that Yelverton never blinks an eyelash when it comes to approving bus trips for the football team. Long live the Fighting Frontiersmen! Hey, he'll send them all over Middle Tennessee from August to November to represent the athletic priorities of New Gallatin Academy. But let an English teacher try to expose his students to a little literary history and culture, and suddenly it's a case of 'Old Mother Hubbard went to the cupboard.' He says my students can read Faulkner in the classroom like they've always done, plus go online if they want to see pictures of Rowan Oak, and that everybody knows the sports program brings all the alums together, particularly football." Jeremy drew back sharply, practically spitting out the next word: "Football! It's undeniably a religion here in the South. And don't let anybody even think about standing in the way of the Immaculate Church of the Holy Pigskin!"

To say that Maura Beth was beginning to feel decidedly uncomfortable would have been an understatement. She found this version of Jeremy to be both peevish and unattractive. Did she dare bring up the results of last week's book club meeting in the face of his outburst? Unfortunately, Jeremy forced the issue.

"Well, I guess I needed to get that off my chest," he added, taking another deep breath afterward. "I trust your Cherry Cola Book Club went off like clockwork. At least I know there's still a vestige of sanity in the world. Reading Eudora Welty again will do both of us good. We've at least got that going for us."

Maura Beth suspected there was no way of easing him into what had happened, no matter how she fashioned it. So she got it over with right away, speaking faster than she normally would have. "The truth is, we won't be reading *The Robber Bridegroom* after all. Your Uncle Douglas and Justin Brachle proposed that we read *Forrest Gump* instead. We took another vote, and *Forrest Gump* won quite handily."

Jeremy's eyes glistened as he leaned in a little too closely. "What? You replaced a classic like *The Robber Bridegroom*? Somewhere I think Eudora Welty must be turning over in her grave!"

"Over the selection of a small-town book club? Oh, I suspect she's more secure than that up in her literary heaven," Maura Beth answered, bringing her hands together prayerfully in an attempt to lower his adrenaline level. "Besides, we can always read her next time out." She attempted a conciliatory smile, but he didn't even notice, turning away while he conjured up more angry words.

"My Uncle Doug as an expert on literature?" Jeremy's sarcastic laugh was making Maura Beth even more uncomfortable, and he showed no sign of letting up on his pique. "You know as well as I do that Uncle Doug is totally addicted to Lake Cherico and his fishing lures. You've seen his collection mounted out there at his lake house. He ought to open up a museum and charge admission. I know it drives my aunt Connie crazy."

"Oh, not anymore," Maura Beth protested. "Didn't you know that your uncle will be teaching her how to fish come springtime? They're going to become a team out there on the water."

Jeremy's face was becoming more and more a mask of disgust. "Good luck with that. And as for Mr. Brachle, my uncle's partner in literary crime—um, what did I hear them calling him?"

"Stout Fella is the nickname you're looking for."

"Yeah, well, I don't think he's any great shakes at Shakespeare or any other literary figure. And now everybody has to toss out Eudora Welty and read *Forrest Gump* because those two want to? What's really going on here?"

Maura Beth resented the fact that his rhetoric was intimidating her. "But everybody voted on it, Jeremy. I had to go along with the majority. Miss Voncille liked the Vietnam part of the story, and even the Crumpton sisters thought it was a good idea. And, yes," she admitted sheepishly, "they will all be discussing the football angle in the plot and eating tailgating dishes for the potluck. You might as well know that right now. I went along with it because I'm just not cut out to be a dictator."

He shot up from the sofa and began pacing around the room like an expectant father in a hospital waiting room. "Well, that's just great, isn't it?! Here you fought hard against the mentality of the good ole boys like Councilman Sparks on the City Council all last year to keep the library open, and now it looks like some more good ole boys are taking over your book club. One step forward, two steps back."

He kept at the pacing, and for a while Maura Beth said nothing, following him with her eyes. "I don't see it that way at all. You're overreacting," she said finally, trying her best to salvage what was rapidly becoming an ugly confrontation.

"No, I'm not!" he snapped back. "You really expect me to come down to your next meeting and talk about how great football is, when all my efforts to get a fair shake from New Gallatin Academy have basically been dashed by the love affair the South has with that silly game? Actually, it's more like an addiction, if you want to know the truth! Who do you think got all the girls when I was in high school: The jocks, or the guys like me who wrote for the school literary magazine?!"

Maura Beth's discomfort had now morphed into shock. She could not believe Jeremy was acting this way and feared that anything further she said to him would be pounced upon mercilessly. Yet, her independent spirit was not about to be silenced. "So is that what this is all about? We're going all the way back to high school? The last thing in the world I'd like to do is dwell on that painful period of my life. I was teased at first because of my red hair and freckles. Of course, I learned how to toughen up. Maybe you shouldn't act like this is the end of the world. If you stay the course regarding your goals, you'll eventually win out."

He continued his lecture while pacing, though he did lower his voice somewhat. "Okay, so maybe I was oversimplifying things. But I thought we saw eye to eye on this issue. You've let me down. I realize I'm in a terrible mood because of Yelverton's decision, but I guess I'd already begun to think of The Cherry Cola Book Club as a voice in the wilderness."

"You do love your metaphors, don't you? At any rate, that's a lot of pressure to put on one little librarian in a little town like Cherico. *The New York Times Book Review* hasn't asked for my opinion even once," Maura Beth said in an attempt at peacemaking. But one look at Jeremy's face told her there was no truce.

"Hey, if I don't try to change things up at New Gallatin Academy, and you don't hang tough here in Cherico, we might as well revert to cave drawings to communicate!" Jeremy continued, finally coming to a sudden halt and planting his feet firmly in the middle of the room. It was as if he'd found his mark for a scene they were shooting for a movie. Only then did he resume his monologue. "Shouldn't we have loftier goals than who scores the most touchdowns on Saturdays and Sundays? How low should our common denominator actually be allowed to go?"

Maura Beth sensed the posturing, the playing to the crowd of one, and remained unmoved. Furthermore, she intended to show him she was no slouch in the speechifying department herself. "Can't we make room for both? Though I will admit I feel like I have to fight the good fight practically every day of my life. But part of my mission as a librarian is to be inclusive of all ideas and interests in the collection that we make available to the public. We're not supposed to choose sides, but we're asked to frequently, believe me. Some people want us to remove any books on witchcraft, while others want to know why we don't have more information on gay issues. The truth is, we're the first line of defense against censorship whenever it rears its ugly head. Meanwhile, I just don't want to be known as the Dictator of The Cherry Cola Book Club."

"I have a terrific headache," Jeremy told her, massaging the tips of his fingers into his forehead. "Do you have something I could take?"

After Maura Beth had excused herself and retrieved a couple of aspirin and a glass of water for him to wash them down, Jeremy again took a seat on the sofa where he sank back and considered. Then he dropped the bomb. "I don't want to participate in the *Forrest Gump* review. I'd probably end up saying things to people that I'd regret, even to my uncle Doug. Not that I have anything against Winston Groom, you understand. More power to any writer who makes a name for himself. It's just that this last-minute reversal thing is getting to me. I'll gladly come down for *The Robber Bridegroom* whenever you schedule it, but not this."

Maura Beth resumed her seat beside him, taking his hand and smiling gently. "I'd still like for you to be here, Jeremy. You don't have to say anything. Just be here for me, and for the good of the club and what it means to the library. We've already had a couple of spirited debates—I see nothing wrong with continuing that. You above all should respect the value of the free exchange of ideas."

He looked down at his lap where his hands had gone limp and then shook his head. "I just can't do it, Maura Beth. The way I feel right now, I'm wondering if I even want to return to New Gallatin Academy next year. I think I'm butting my head bloody against the bleachers of the football stadium. Maybe I should have been born in a simpler time."

"How far back do you want to go? Before indoor plumbing? You really are in a negative mood, aren't you?" Maura

Beth said. Then it occurred to her that she should be drawing a line in the sand, so she did. "Maybe we shouldn't see each other until you get things figured out. I don't particularly like the side of you I've seen today, and you seem to think I don't measure up to your lofty literary standards and that I'm suddenly a huge disappointment to you."

There was a long silence filled with tension, and neither of them seemed willing to break through it. Finally, Jeremy rose from the sofa and headed toward the door. "Seems like we've both said too much this afternoon. I was going to invite you out to Aunt Connie and Uncle Doug's for dinner tonight, but I guess maybe that's not such a good idea now. They'll be disappointed that you're not coming, but I'll make up something to tell them."

"We seem to have hit a *Gump* in the road," Maura Beth said, trying for levity at the last minute.

Jeremy produced a weak little smile and gave her a peck on the cheek. "Sorry. It's been a really bad weekend for me. You're right. I need to figure things out and get back to you."

"I understand all of that, Jeremy, but please, for the sake of our friendship, don't take too long."

She watched him marching to his car with those long, angry strides and wondered if this might be the beginning of the end for a promising relationship that was only a few months old. Over even before it had begun?

It was the sort of evening given over to romantic walks and whispering sweet nothings in the ear, not to mention a good deal warmer than it should have been for February in the extreme corner of Northeast Mississippi.

"This is practically that same moon that was shining when we first drove out here to see where our little eatery was going up in the mud," Harlan Lattimore was saying to his ex-wife after he had cooked and served up their dinner. With the restaurant closed and no one around to disturb them, they were standing on the deck of The Marina Bar and Grill whose pilings jutted out daringly over the slack waters of Lake Cherico. For her part, Periwinkle was having none of his selective remembrances of things past, including his repeated attempts to slip his arm around her waist.

"That was oh so many moons ago, Harlan John Lattimore. And I no longer have those girlish stars in my eyes." She moved away from him slightly and then took a swig from her bottle of beer. "Otherwise, not much has changed out here. You can still turn out a mean medium-rare steak and loaded baked potato, which I thank you for. And you still got this same old faded gray deck with the picnic tables for the ones that like the fresh air, and the same old neon jukebox with all the country line dancing tunes indoors by the bar. Even though line dancing is so over, it's not even funny. And I imagine that back room I unwittingly decorated for your extracurricular activities is still up and running."

He seemed to take her sarcasm in stride and even cracked a smile. "Now, you'd be wrong about that, Peri. I got rid of it and expanded the pantry over two years ago. If you'd like the grand tour, I'd be happy to oblige. But it's just a collection of canned goods and spices with a few cardboard boxes thrown in for good measure. I gave the bed and the mattress the old heave-ho and drove 'em on down to the Cherico Salvation Army."

"And they took something that worn-out?"

"You can make jokes all you want, but I really am a changed man," he insisted. "I wanted to tell you that tonight here under the moonlight. Ordered it up special just for you."

Periwinkle looked him over with a skeptical expression. He hadn't changed much since their divorce, at least not physically. He still sported a lean and tall physique with rugged features accentuated by a neatly trimmed mustache, a full head of curly hair with a few grays here and there, and he had yet to give up on his blue jeans and cowboy shirt costumes. Somewhere along the way, he had died and gone to Line Dancing Heaven. But she had her doubts as to whether he had truly renounced his philandering ways, back room or no back room. No matter what, she was not about to be sweet-talked into anything she felt was not in her best interests. She was forty now, over two decades removed from the guileless country teenager who had once fallen for his macho Marlboro Man charms.

"So what's caused this so-called change in you?"

"I was hoping you'd ask," he said, giving her a roguish wink. "The old me wouldn't even admit to what I'm gonna tell you, but here goes nothing. A few years back this sweet young thing in a skirt leaving nothing to the imagination wiggles her way across the floor and takes a bar stool right smack dab in front of me. I could tell she was definitely gonna make a move and—"

"Seems to have happened to you all the time, as I found out in no uncertain terms," she interrupted.

He briefly closed his eyes and shook his head. "Okay, okay. But this little item was different. 'What's your name?' I asked her. And she said it was Tammie, spelled with an I-E—"

"I'm sure that set her apart from the others."

"Please stop interrupting me, Peri. You may not believe it, but I have a real good point to make here." He waited a few seconds to see if she was going to comply, continuing only after she shrugged her shoulders and nodded with a look of resignation. "Anyhow, she happened to stroll in on my birthday, and a couple of the regulars mentioned that fact while we were all talking our typical bar talk. So Tammie says, 'Hey, how old are you anyway, barkeep?' And I like a fool tell her the truth. 'Forty-nine,' I say. And that's when I get the surprise of my life. Tammie looks me straight in the eye and says I need to go see the doctor right away. Of course, I have no idea what she's talking about, so I ask her to explain. And she goes, 'Anyone that old is bound to have something wrong with 'em.' "

Periwinkle started up with her heartiest laugh and took her time letting it die off. "Man, did you get your comeuppance!"

"I guess I did. And you know what? I really did go to the doctor for that checkup I hadn't had in a long time. After all the blood work and the X-rays came back, I was thankful there was nothing wrong with me. But it did start me thinking about the future. I mean, how long was I really gonna settle for these one-night stands? This generation gap that was all lipstick and legs right in front of me was only gonna get wider as time went on." He frowned for a moment at what he'd just said. "Wait . . . that didn't come out right."

"It's nothing I haven't heard before. I'm a big girl."

He moved in, bringing the smell of beer on his warm breath and the English Leather he had dabbed on his neck closer to her. "Fact is, I was crazy to fool around on you, Peri. I didn't know how good I had it. Look at you, just as slim and beautiful as you were when we first started dating. I even like your new blond hair."

She was still in no mood for such tactics, however, and again backed away from him ever so slightly. "Yeah, well, it's getting time for another one of my root jobs over at Cherico Tresses. But that's neither here nor there. Harlan, what on earth do you really want? Can't you come clean?"

"Of course I can. I really want to be with you again," he answered, lifting his right eyebrow seductively. "I thought I made that clear."

"And you expect me to believe that?"

He took his time, taking a swallow of beer first. "Well, I can see why you would have your doubts. But I noticed you haven't found anyone, either—at least not that I know of. You're not hiding a boyfriend in your attic, are you?"

"No, besides, I'd have him chained in the basement so he couldn't play around on me like you did."

They both laughed; then he said, "I had that coming, I guess. But I was thinking maybe we could try again. What's the harm in that?"

She put her beer down on the deck railing and it nearly fell off as it made contact with a protruding rusty nail head. Then she gave him an intense stare after rescuing the bottle quickly with an impressive acrobatic move. "Break my heart once, shame on you. Break it twice, shame on me." She turned toward the lake and marveled at the way the dark water had dissolved the moon into thin, uneven shards of light dancing on the surface. "I let that pretty sight out there lead me out to sea once before," she continued, pointing to the horizon. "I'm not about to up and do it again."

Surprisingly, he appeared amused at her remarks. "I see I have my work cut out for me. But that's okay. You won't mind being courted again, will you?"

She returned his laughter, only louder. "No, not as long as you don't mind being rejected."

"We'll see about that, Peri," he told her, finishing off his beer in one great chug and rather unromantically stifling a belch. "We'll just see."

For Maura Beth, Monday morning was not a day to rejoice. Unlike some people with a predictable work routine, she had never had any trouble getting her week started in her cramped little library office. She considered herself nothing if not a woman on a mission. But this Monday was different, and it showed on her face and even in the way she was moving about in a kind of slow motion. She just couldn't get it out of her head that Jeremy had exploded yesterday over something as relatively inconsequential as a book club read. That was nothing in the larger scheme of things. What kind of relationship could she expect with him over the long haul when things really got tough? The incident did not inspire confidence that he might actually be the man she had ordered up on page 25 of her LSU journal almost a decade ago. At the moment he did not resemble marriage material.

A few seconds later, Renette Posey popped her head in. "Nothing much going on out there at the circulation desk, so I thought I'd catch up with you a bit."

Maura Beth managed a smile, but it faded quickly. "Nothing much going on in here, either, I'm afraid."

Renette took a seat across from her superior, smiling genuinely. "Miz Mayhew, I've worked for you long enough now to know when something's wrong. You dragged yourself in here this morning, and I was wondering if I might help somehow. You know I'll keep anything you tell me in strictest confidence."

Maura Beth made another weak attempt at holding up the corners of her mouth but couldn't stop her lips from trembling. "That's sweet of you, Renette."

"Weren't you and Mr. McShay supposed to get together over the weekend? Did he not show up or something? Being stood up is the worst."

Maura Beth decided she needed to confide in someone, since she hadn't had the chance to run anything past Periwinkle yet; and even though Renette was ten years younger and just out of high school, she knew she could trust her Monday, Wednesday, and Friday front desk clerk with the slightly edited details of her private life. "Oh, Jeremy showed up, all right," she began. "It would have been better if he hadn't, though." Then she recounted their surprisingly antagonistic exchange, complete with her own exaggerated hand gestures—right, left, up, and down—and finished with a long, calming intake and release of air.

"I wouldn't have seen that coming," Renette said, her pretty young face creased with frown lines. "Mr. McShay was so professional when he brought down those three students from Nashville for the *To Kill a Mockingbird* review. He was so composed and made such intelligent comments. I wish I'd had a teacher like him 'cause I know I would've gotten better grades. Anyway, I was gonna tell you that my girlfriends and I have started reading *Forrest Gump* for the March meeting. We compare notes over the phone as we go along. We all like Forrest a lot as far as we've gotten, even though he doesn't speak good English and some of the things he says are downright hilarious. But I can think of a few boys I went to high school with who didn't sound too much better, and they weren't nearly as funny. That Mr. Groom sure has captured the South so far, and that little first-grade romance with Jenny is just as cute as it can be. I had my first crush at the age, too, and I've never forgotten it."

Maura Beth held out both hands, palms up for emphasis. "Thank you! Those are the sort of comments I would have expected from Jeremy to get a review off to a good start. Instead, he just got completely bent out of shape about how football was stealing all his thunder, and I can't believe he said he wouldn't even come down. Really, now, how mature is that? I think I can remember fusses I had in junior high that were more reasonable than that."

"No wonder you're so upset."

They sat with everything for a while; then Maura Beth put the tips of her fingers together thoughtfully. "Well, he has to make the next move. I as much as told him so. I'm not saying he owes me an actual apology, but the Jeremy who showed up yesterday afternoon can take that show on the road."

Renette grinned and leaned in with a wink. "That's the best thing about working for you, Miz Mayhew. You've got loaded book carts of spunk, and I keep telling myself that when I grow up, I wanna be just like you."

5

"Duck and Cover"

Miss Voncille had come to the conclusion that more drastic measures were in order. Locke's favorite dinner of pork tenderloin with mushrooms, sweet potato hash, and homemade biscuits, which she lovingly prepared for him whenever they spent the night at her Painter Street cottage, wasn't getting the job done by a long shot. So when they had finished off their dessert of bread pudding and coffee, she hauled her grade-school scrapbook out of the bedroom closet, rummaged through it extensively, and found just the image to move the object of her affection off dead center. Or at least she hoped it would. Merely reading *Forrest Gump* together for the upcoming March meeting of The Cherry Cola Book Club wasn't getting her where she wanted to be, either.

"Remember this foolishness?" she said to him, pointing to a faded black-and-white snapshot of what looked like a deserted elementary classroom. It was surrounded by other old photos of children on the seesaw, playing dodge ball and climbing on the jungle gym, many staring at the camera with their tongues sticking out for no other reason than they were seven, eight, or nine years old. It came with the territory.

"A bunch of children playing. So what?"

Her impatience was quite evident in her tone. "No, not those. Just the one I'm pointing to."

They were seated on her long green living room sofa, flanked by a couple of her many potted palms, and still he could only manage a frown. "There's nobody in that picture."

She briefly shifted the scrapbook, bringing it up closer to his face as if she expected him to inhale the enticing aroma of some delicious entrée. "You aren't looking close enough."

He was squinting hard now, but to no avail. "It's just a bunch of desks somewhere, Voncille. I have no idea what it is you expect me to see."

She produced an exasperated sigh. "When was the last time you had your eyes checked? I'm thinking it's been too long, because you should be able to do better than that." She placed the tip of her index finger beneath one of the desks in the foreground and moved it quickly from side to side as if try- ing to rub out a stain. "Zero in on this, if you please."

Finally, he saw what she was getting at. "Oh, that's a little girl all crouched underneath that desk." He couldn't have looked more surprised. "Don't tell me that's you? What were you doing under there?"

"It most certainly is me," she told him. "And everyone else in the room besides. We were all just following orders. Now do you remember?" She could tell by the way his eyes were moving rapidly from side to side that he was searching for an answer but couldn't find one. "Oh, for heaven's sake, Locke, didn't you have these drills at your school growing up over in the Delta? It was all the rage in 1952 or 1953—somewhere around there."

The smile that broke across his face was one of relief as much as anything else. "Oh, yes, you're right. We did. I'd for- gotten all about them. Those beyond ridiculous H-bomb drills."

"Had to be the silliest things human beings have ever

thought up to do. Our teacher, Miz Sallie Cowart, called them 'duck and cover,' " Miss Voncille explained further and then started laughing. "Imagine. Ducking under our desks and covering our heads on cue was supposed to save us from any kind of nuclear blast. We had them here in Cherico once a week, so imminent was the threat of nuclear attack from the Russians, they seemed to delight in telling us. And when you went to the movies at the Starbright, they were practically in every Movietone newsreel with that narrator and his booming voice: 'Today's schoolchildren smartly prepare for nuclear war in the classroom while they take a break from learning their lessons! See how they respond bravely and quickly to their teacher's command!' Or something like that."

Locke joined her in a fit of laughter. "Hey, my school even went one step further. They decided to issue us dog tags so our bodies could be identified after the nuclear blast. Like there would be anybody around to clean up the mess and say, "Hey, over here in this corner is what's left of Locke Marshall Linwood! Oh, and look over there—that's little Roe Anne Stacey! Their parents will be so glad to know we've found them!"

She nudged him gently with her elbow. "Ashes to ashes, dust to dust!"

After the laughter had died down, Locke frowned her way. "What made you bring all that up? I haven't thought of it in years."

"The truth of the matter is, I was just thinking that you and I are survivors, mainly," she began, speaking as calmly as possible to drive home her point. "We came through these nuclear blast drills as gullible little kids and then the loss of our loved ones for real as adults. But nothing could take us out. We ought to give ourselves a pat on the back and then move on." She waited to see if he was tumbling to her ploy, but he appeared to be mostly perplexed as she closed up the scrapbook and put it to one side.

"But I think we have moved on," he said, fingering his lapel absent-mindedly. "I mean, we're smack dab in the middle of this very comfortable relationship, aren't we? Is there something you aren't happy with?"

Well, the scrapbook "duck and cover" ploy hadn't worked, either, it seemed. Enough of all this beating around the bush. Miss Voncille now realized she was just going to have to be more direct and hope for the best. Men could be so obtuse sometimes.

"Locke, I'm sure you know I have the most profound respect for your beautiful and beloved wife, Pamela," she began, taking the bull by the horns. "Why, if it hadn't been for that touching letter she left you encouraging you to get on with your life the way she did, you and I might never have become an item. It was just lovely that she gave you permission to try for love again after her death, and I'll forever be indebted to her for that."

He patted her hand and beamed. "She thought we might be perfect for each other, and she was right. Her woman's intuition, I suppose. So what's the problem? I got together with you just as she suggested, didn't I?"

Miss Voncille forged ahead. It was too late to retreat now. "It's just that your Pamela enjoyed something I don't have. She was happily married to you for many, many years. I'd like that to happen to me—or us, rather. But I haven't been asked yet. The truth is, I'd like very much to do this up proper at the altar."

He withdrew his hand from hers and sat up straight, giving her a look of disbelief. "Really? You want a church wedding with all the trimmings? I thought we could go on indefinitely the way we have been. You know, back and forth between our two houses as the spirit moves us. One night it's your sleepover, the next night it's mine. That way we never get in a rut."

She did her best to smile at his response, but what she really wanted to do was shake him by his lapels until he came to his senses. This was no laughing matter, no "spend-the-night company" issue to be resolved rationally with not even a nod to the underlying emotions about to bubble up and over.

"I would have to say no to the 'all the trimmings' part. We're too old for that. Why, we probably wouldn't even get the first present. Not even a gift certificate. People would figure we have everything we need, and they'd be right about that. But we're not too old to walk down the aisle or exchange vows in a small ceremony somewhere," she told him. "Why, it could even just be the two of us with a justice of the peace. We're both on polite speaking terms with Henry Marsden, even though he makes that awful whistling sound with his teeth whenever the letter *S* comes along."

"Sibilance," he noted immediately, quickly returning to her suggestion. "But why go to the trouble? Weddings are for people starting out in life. After that, who's really paying attention?" His tone was earnest enough, and she could have strangled him again for that.

Instead, she kept it soft and cuddly, brushing up against him. "Look at it from my point of view, Locke. I was cheated out of my first marriage to Frank by the Tet Offensive, and maybe there's this old-fashioned part of me that wants you to make me an honest woman, to use a term you don't hear very much these days."

He looked confused, as if she were suddenly speaking a foreign language. Then came several open-mouthed starts at conversation before he finally settled on the right words. "This doesn't sound like you at all, Voncille. You don't need to justify yourself to anyone. You're practically a Cherico institution."

"I couldn't care less about gossip," she said, the irritation rising in her tone as she reverted to her prickly alter ego. "Although I've been an easy target for many years. Still, I've always shrugged and walked down the street or in and out of the library for all those 'Who's Who in Cherico?' meetings with my head held high. 'There goes that crazy old retired schoolteacher whose house looks like a jungle inside,' I could almost hear them whispering the moment I passed by. But this is just about you and me, Locke. Something inside me wants to make this relationship of ours legal. I've been hinting around for weeks now, but between you actually sitting down to read *Forrest Gump* and enjoying my cooking, you don't seem to have room for anything else in that distinguished gray head of yours."

His face was a perfect blank, his eyes and mouth an inverted triangle of zeroes. "I had no idea you felt this way."

"Men!" She let her little exclamation lie there for a while. "I don't know what else to say to you at this point."

He made a strange little noise in his throat at first, but she could tell he thought he was being charming when he finally answered her. "We're creatures of habit. We like the nests our women build for us."

But Miss Voncille was in no mood for settling or being summarily dismissed. "Yes, well, I think I'd like some credit for the nest. It's been gnawing at me, and I can't change the way I feel about it. I'm just too set in my ways."

"Could I have some time to think about it?" he said, the color returning to his face. "I'd probably like to sound my children out, if you don't mind."

Miss Voncille couldn't fight off the displeasure that settled into her features. That was a new one. He had rarely brought up either his daughter or son in their everyday conversations. He had told her that both Carla and Locke Jr. were married, had two children apiece, and both lived out of state with his grandchildren—but had not volunteered much more. Locke remained the reserved, gentlemanly type who would never force pictures from his wallet upon anyone, even if they asked in the insincere manner that people sometimes do, and she had spent enough time with him now to know that there just never seemed to be any letters or postcards lying around, no long-distance phone calls to report—not even any e-mails showing up on his computer to answer.

"Why does that sound like an excuse to me, Locke?" she wanted to know, refusing to let up. But she realized she had pressed some sort of hot button when he matched her mundane frown with a startling one of his own.

"Voncille, are you trying to ruin what we've got going?"

"Good heavens, Locke, I'm not asking you to approve my riding naked the length of Perry Street on a horse," she said, her prickly temperament now full-blown. She had promised him several months earlier she would try to stop being such a diva and knuckle-rapping schoolmarm around him, and she had largely lived up to that. But he was testing her sorely, and she took a deep breath before continuing. "Why, I was even thinking it could be as simple as our exchanging vows at one of my 'Who's Who in Cherico?' meetings at the library. After all, that's where I first really got to know you and Pamela. Neither of you ever missed a meeting."

His face showed no signs of cottoning to the idea, and he took his time reacting to her proposal. "I'm well aware of that. But getting married in that crowded little library? How would that work? Whoever has a library card has an automatic invitation? I know Miz Mayhew is trying hard to promote the library and stay one step ahead of Councilman Sparks by expanding the book club, but don't you think that's going too far?"

"If you don't like that idea, we could always use a church," she continued, steeling herself further. "I'm a Presbyterian and you're an Episcopalian, but I'd be comfortable getting married

in your church if you want it that way. I've always been comfortable with you bobtail Catholics. All the pomp and ceremony without the guilt, my mother used to say."

He was wincing now. "Why do we have to rush into this?"

At that point she decided to back off. If this was round
one, she had lost it. It was time to bandage the little jabs and
cuts, and move on with new footwork for another day. It was
still a match she had no intention of losing. She was going to
hold him to his gentlemanly ways or die trying.

6

Reading in Bed

Becca sat propped up on her bright blue pillows at nine-thirty one chilly February evening, working her way through more of *Forrest Gump*. Anyone walking into the Brachle master bedroom suite might have thought that she was also posing for a Victoria's Secret catalog, what with the see-through pink negligee clinging to her petite but inviting figure. She had read up to the point where Forrest and Jenny were playing together in a college folk music group, and she was wondering once again just how far her Stout Fella had gotten with his copy. Deeper into the novel than she had, she was reasonably certain, at least judging by the way he always immediately jumped into bed after dinner, found his place with the leather bookmark she had given him, and fell to with great relish. In fact, he was doing that very thing right now on the other side of the bed. He might as well have been a mile away.

"You really are living up to your promise, Justin," she said to him, after coming to a stopping point in her reading.

"What?" he managed reflexively, his eyes still trained on the page in front of him.

"You told Maura Beth you were going to take The Cherry Cola Book Club seriously, and you have. I'm very impressed. Really, I was talking to Connie the other day about it, and she said that Douglas is digging into the novel, too. You boys are making us proud."

"Wait a sec, honey," he said, turning the page. "Let me just get through this part here."

The nonchalance in his voice annoyed her. He was dismissing her as he had so often lately. And since when had reading become more important than a satisfying roll in the hay? That was most un-Justin-like, and she was missing the intimacy besides. "You've been at it for a half hour. Aren't your eyes getting a little tired? Don't you want to call it a night even though the night is still young?"

He glanced her way briefly, and she saw that he had become annoyed himself. "Seriously, Becca—Forrest and Jenny are making crazy love all over the house. This is a really good part I've gotten to. You know, the book and the movie aren't exactly alike, either."

Those were difficult words for her to hear. Particularly since she had on her most provocative negligee, had shaved and rubbed lotion on her legs, taken extra time with the blow-dryer so she could drape her locks just so around her shoulders—and here he was enthralled with some steamy fictional action on the pages of *Forrest Gump*. It was unflattering, to say the least. Plus, he was all bundled up in his pajamas—tops and bottoms—in this case, the navy blue ones she had given him after he'd lost all that weight following the heart attack. Leading up to that traumatic event last year, he had never failed to come to bed in anything but his birthday suit—and what a big, burly birthday suit it was! But that was beginning to feel like a distant memory.

Becca decided to try a different tack. "As I said, you and Douglas certainly meant business about *Forrest Gump*. But we've got several more weeks until the club meeting at the library. No need to rush the way you are. It reminds me too much of the way you used to wolf down your food, and you know what that led to. That was the worst night of my life when you had your heart attack at The Twinkle."

"Uh, huh," he said, still glued to the novel.

"You're not even listening to me. You're treating me like I'm not even in the room." Then she jumped out of bed and stood beside the nightstand, glaring at him as if he'd just told her she looked fat or needed to brush her teeth and use some mouthwash pronto. "What's up with you?"

He came to finally, looking baffled as he turned her way. "What are you doing out of bed?"

"Oh, that does it!" she cried out. "I want to know what's going on with you, Justin Brachle. Tell me the truth—let's get this out once and for all. Are you or are you not having an affair?"

Finally, he returned her glare after inverting the book and resting it on his stomach. "What the hell are you talking about?"

She pointed to her clearly visible cleavage and arched her eyebrows dramatically. "What else am I supposed to think when you've been completely ignoring me lately? Except for that one time."

If anything, he looked even angrier as he gritted his teeth and exhaled. "I thought we weren't going to bring that up."

She climbed back into bed, fluffed her pillows, and sank back against them before she answered him, softening her tone. She knew only too well that her Stout Fella had never responded to her nagging. "I didn't mean to. I'm just confused. Lately, you haven't even tried. Are you having an affair with that Donna Gordon from our 'In the Flesh' meeting last month? I can't stand this not knowing."

She was referring to the series of cooking demonstrations that the two of them had agreed late last year to undertake in the library, much to Maura Beth Mayhew's delight. It was another feather in her cap, yet another creative way to get more people into the library. The premise was that the programs would be an opportunity for Becca Broccoli of the eponymous local radio show to meet her public "in the flesh," if you will, with Stout Fella thrown in for good measure as her smiling, eye-candy assistant. That first outing had gone over well, attracting a dozen or more people, as a recipe for white meat, chunky chicken salad with grapes and chopped walnuts was followed to mouthwatering perfection.

"Yes, ladies—grapes!" she had declared at the very beginning to pique their interest.

"White or red seedless grapes, by the way. And a handful of chopped walnuts. Oh, the textures and the savory and sweet you'll experience all in one here!"

But it had not been lost on Becca that the audience was composed entirely of women, and to Becca's experienced eye—unmarried women on the prowl at that. Especially Donna Gordon—she of the fluttering false eyelashes, age-inappropriate ponytail, and outdated pink Capri pants. Becca discovered she wasn't imagining things, either. She had excused herself to run to the ladies' room after the demonstration was over and returned to find her Stout Fella making a bicep for the gawking woman. She was actually trying to get her hand around his impressive muscle, saying things to him like, "Oooh! I bet you like to work out all the time, don't you? I bet you could ring that bell at the State Fair in Jackson!"

Becca was floored, to put it mildly. Really, how corny could people get? This silly woman talked and dressed like she lived in an alternate universe composed exclusively of '50s TV shows.

"I'm serious, Justin," Becca continued. "I know you're not sleeping with me, so who is it?"

He spoke as calmly as he could, but the spacing between words betrayed his exasperation and the effort he was making to restrain himself. "I . . . am . . . not . . . sleeping . . . with . . . anyone."

She mulled things over for a while. He had still not given her a straight answer about their sex life, and she was more frustrated than ever. "Is there something you're not telling me?" she ventured finally, hoping the question wouldn't trigger another display of barely controlled anger. "Do you think you need to see the doctor?"

He shook his head, staring straight ahead. "I'm taking all my medications. You see me doing it in front of you every morning and evening. No more disobeying doctors. I'm just fine."

"So I should just shut up and go back to *Forrest Gump*?"

He turned the book over and brought it up to his face again. "For now, that's what I think we should both do."

"This is getting way old," Maura Beth said out loud as she climbed into her brass bed, holding her LSU journal in her hand once again. Here she was, revisiting page 25. How many more times would she do it in search of her dreams? In five more months she would be twenty-nine, leaving only one year to accomplish her bucket list before she hit The Big Three-Oh. It was the milestone she had always dreaded in theoretical fashion.

No, she had not won the directorship of a town of 20,000 or more. Cherico was only 5,000 souls with no real possibility of falling into the category of growing by leaps and bounds anytime soon. So that goal no longer seemed as important to her as it once had. She had fought too hard to keep The Cherico Library open to even consider abandoning it now. It was enough that she had held on to her job and overcome some significant obstacles in doing so.

No, she had not gotten married. Jeremy McShay had seemed like a promising candidate only a couple of weeks ago, but now their relationship was in limbo. Her feisty Scarlett spirit, so hard-won during the first few months of the book club's existence, would not let her be the first to break down and call, write, text, or e-mail. He had to be the one to make the first move. That was just the way it was going to be, and if he never darkened her door again—so be it.

And, of course, no, she had not yet borne children of any kind. Not a boy, not a girl, not a redhead of either gender. She had played a game in her head during the brief period things had been going well between Jeremy and herself; when they were finding a day in their busy schedules for him to drive down from Nashville, take her out to eat, and then back to her efficiency for some quiet, tender exchanges and explorations. After he had left, she would climb into bed as she had done now and think out loud.

"Okay, I'm a redhead," she would say, sounding for all the world like she was ten years old. Then, "Jeremy has that dark brown hair." Next came, "So what are the odds I'll get someone who looks like me on top?"

Fifty percent had never sounded hopeful enough. That was basically just the flip of a coin. So she would sometimes go online during slack times at work and try to find articles about dominant and recessive genes for hair color. In the end, however, she had to resign herself to the fact that inheriting genes of any kind was just a crapshoot. You ended up stuck with whatever came your way.

Tonight in bed, Maura Beth put the journal away early and returned to her copy of *Forrest Gump*. She must be thoroughly familiar with it to lead a literate discussion on March 9th, and she had never actually read it before. Nor even seen the movie. At least she still had her library and The Cherry Cola Book Club to shepherd, no matter what. But she couldn't help envying settled couples like Becca and Justin Brachle, and even the brave and daring Miss Voncille and Locke Linwood, who were well on their way to matrimony late in life, she suspected. Why, she had even thought about inviting them to hold the ceremony in her library when the time came!

Now, why couldn't she have a seamless relationship with someone the way those good folks had with one another?

7

Forcing the Issue

This first early March outing with his wife Connie on *The Verdict* had Douglas McShay hoping for the best but steeling himself for the worst. What he really wanted to do was clear the air and call the whole thing off, but he felt compelled to at least give it the old college try. Nonetheless, why on earth had he agreed to go along with it all a few months ago in the first place?

"Take me out on the bass boat with you," she had suggested back in November at the end of a polite argument they were having about the state of their marriage. "Teach me how to fish. We'll finally be sharing our retirement." It was her idea of something that would bring them closer together; but after an initial surge of endorphins, he had become silently skeptical about it all.

Then he had summoned his courage and gone up one afternoon recently to Bass Pro in Memphis and bought her a Zebco spinning reel on sale. It had come to a little under eighty dollars and was widely acknowledged as the best reel for children and beginners. Connie certainly was the latter, and Douglas tried to remain hopeful that everything would be smooth sailing on the slack waters of Lake Cherico from that point forward.

Then came the balmy March afternoon that had coaxed them out of the lodge, taking them away from quietly reading *Forrest Gump* and sipping coffee in front of the great room fireplace. It had not started particularly well from Douglas's point of view. He had spent an inordinate amount of time assuring his wife that the combination of sun block and the big straw hat covering her bouffant hairdo would more than eliminate any possibility of a sunburn.

"I don't want to look like a lobster," she had said. "I hate that look, and it takes forever for your skin to get back to normal." She had then recited a litany of such unpleasant images as blisters, peeling skin, and vinegar baths.

But he had shrugged her off with authority. "I guarantee you won't. Now, let's get *The Verdict* under way, okay?"

That exchange had taken place on their dock. After they'd gotten settled in the boat and headed off to one of his favorite spots, Douglas had shut off the motor, taken a deep breath, and forged ahead with his wife's very first lesson. "I know you're gonna do just fine, honey. A child could operate this reel without half-trying. Don't be nervous. There are all kinds of fish just waiting for you to catch them in that cove over there. That's my favorite spot. All you have to do is push down on that little button right there," he told her, pointing to it as he let her hold the reel for the first time. He could tell she didn't like the way it felt by the way her mouth went all crooked with her lips out of alignment. "Then all you have to do is let up, and the line will lob out on its own."

Little did he realize that what seemed simple and straightforward to him was not nearly so cut-and-dried to her. "What do you mean? I thought you only lobbed in badminton and tennis."

He told himself that, above all else, he must find a way to smile. "That's a different use of the term. Just trust me. All you have to do is press down on the button."

And she did.

"Good girl!" he told her, gently patting her on the back. "Now let up."

She did that, too, but only after twisting herself around and aiming the reel at the shore, whereupon the line quickly unspooled, made a noise like a dentist's drill, and headed straight for the branches of an overhanging willow tree in the cove Douglas had praised so highly. What had he been thinking? Why hadn't he just aimed the reel that first time for her and let her watch a pro in action? Visual learning—that was the ticket. Had he subconsciously sabotaged her? Whatever the case, he was already sensing that the worst might be well on its way.

Connie was tearing up now as she tried to pull back on the line. But the willow seemed to have the strength of a grown man and would not release the lure easily, at least a dozen of its young, spring leaves fluttering down into the dark water as proof of its exertion. "How did it end up going there? Oh, I've messed up, haven't I? What do I do next?"

He felt bad about the whole thing, stepped up and took the blame like a man, all the while hoping she wouldn't think he was being too patronizing. "No, no, I wasn't paying attention. I didn't tell you not to cast toward the shore, and I should have. It's all on me. You didn't do anything wrong, honey."

But he spent the next five minutes standing up in the boat and untangling the line, grunting and muttering barely audible things under his breath all the while.

"You sound like you're mad at me," she said, watching him intently. "I think I heard a *sonuvabitch* a second or two ago."

"No, honey. I'm not mad at you. It's just that I haven't had to untangle a line since I was a boy with a cane pole using worms and crickets for bait. It's a pain in the butt, believe me." When he had finally gotten the job done, cutting away a twig or two with a pocket knife and carefully prying the hook out of the wood, he took another deep breath and wiped the sweat from his brow with the back of his hand. More willow leaves fluttered down from his shoulder as he spoke. "Let's take a break, why don't we? Get us a couple a' cold ones from the cooler, why don'tcha?"

That brought a smile to her face; then they both popped their tabs, sat back, and sipped for a while. Momentarily, Douglas was thinking that this part wasn't half bad. For him, drifting peacefully on the brown waters of Lake Cherico was what it was all about most of the time. Catching a big one counted, and mounting it when it deserved trophy status did, too, of course; but even when he came back with nothing, the time spent alone had always been worth it.

Then Douglas realized his mistake. Alone. That was the part he was giving up by letting Connie aboard *The Verdict*. By letting her talk him into it. She was distracting, even though he knew she couldn't help it and didn't even realize she was doing anything wrong. On the way over to the cove, for instance, she had rambled on about the muumuu she was wearing. It had little green fishes with bubbles coming out of their mouths all over it—against a sky blue background, no less—and she had bought it especially for her very first fishing lesson with her handsome husband. Did she look all right in it? Did he like it? It didn't make her look too fat, did it? Was it the sort of thing other wives wore when they went fishing with their husbands?

Now, what kind of questions were these to pose on a bass boat? Who the hell could see or would even care what she was wearing in the middle of the lake? And then it came to Douglas that he and Justin Brachle had nailed it when they had proposed that The Cherry Cola Book Club read *Forrest Gump* instead of *The Robber Bridegroom*. Men and women really did view things differently. They each had their own viable, separate priorities. It wasn't necessarily a good or bad thing. It just was. His lawyer's brain zeroed in on it exactly: Equality was a legal concept only.

"Ready to try again?" Douglas said, after they had drained their beers before the cans had warmed up too much in the sun bearing down. He tried his best to make it sound like it was something he really wanted to continue doing.

With a little help from her beer buzz, Connie saw through it, the straw hat on her head moving slowly from side to side in disapproving fashion. "This isn't fun for you, is it? I mean, I can tell that even what we've done together so far is not what you expected. Give me that much. We've been married too long for me not to recognize when you're trying too hard."

He mulled things over an awkward amount of time without saying anything, and even that was a tip-off for her.

"Quite frankly, I wondered if I'd have the patience for this," Connie told him. "I really don't think I do, you know. This whole thing is forced, isn't it? Here I am out here worried more about getting sunburned than anything else. I can't remember when you haven't come back to the house with a little extra color in your face, and it doesn't matter to you one iota. It just makes you look even more dashing than you already are, you devil, you."

He was squinting at her, shading his eyes with his hand while accepting her compliment with a broad grin. "Well, we really haven't given it a shot yet. You haven't even made your first successful cast."

She lifted up her chin proudly as if she were a soldier snapping to attention. "Okay, then. Let's make sure we can both say I've done that." On her own she took the reel in hand, faced away from the willows overhanging the cove, and pushed the button down, making a perfectly respectable cast.

He applauded the light *kerplunk* it made out on the still water. "I'd give you a ten out of ten! Olympic gold quality!"

"Excellent. Then that's over and done with!"

"You really don't want to continue? If you're really serious about fishing, you have to start somewhere, you know."

She handed over the reel and pointed to her big straw purse next to the blue plastic cooler full of beer and bottled water. "I came prepared in case things didn't go well. Or I chickened out, whichever came first. I brought along my copy of *Forrest Gump* to read, and that's just what I'm going to do. I'll keep you company, watching you fish while I see what mischief Forrest is up to next. How does that sound?"

Well, that was music to his ears, and he couldn't help laughing. "You know, I went along with all this to keep the peace. I haven't forgotten that you pointed out that we really weren't doing a lot of things together since moving down from Nashville. I certainly agree we shouldn't be off in our separate corners with our hobbies, though. So if this isn't the right thing to share, I promise we'll just find something else."

"Spoken like a true retired lawyer," she said, leaning over to give him a peck on his sunburned cheek. Then she reached into her purse, retrieved her copy of *Forrest Gump*, and picked up where she had left off. A huge sigh followed as she found her place. Even though she was still floating on the waters of Lake Cherico, she knew she was once again on solid ground.

It was Saturday night, the evening before The Cherry Cola Book Club would be reviewing *Forrest Gump*, and Maura Beth had just finished icing the chocolate, cherry cola sheet cake she was bringing to the event. Baking the cake in her kitchenette had given her a brief respite from her frazzled emotional state. It was driving her crazy that she had not heard a peep out of Jeremy since their fallout nearly five weeks ago. Oh, she was still holding on to her stubbornness, her absolute requirement that he be the first one to break the ice and apologize to her for his immature and outrageous display of temper in her apartment that afternoon. But she knew only too well that her rigidity was just that, containing nothing of the soft kisses and the tender touches she had enjoyed from Jeremy when things were going well between them. No consolation at all, this business of being unyielding because she knew he had been in the wrong.

"He must not care," she had told Periwinkle over the phone somewhere in the interim, struggling to repress all the indecision and doubt that was dogging her. "Or he would have made a move by now."

"I should just forget him," she had also told Renette at work one day, sounding robotic and stern, yet somehow un-convincing. "It's obviously over, and I should just move on."

Neither woman had the answer for her, and she had not been able to put him out of her mind. The whole quandary was even interfering with her preparation for the *Forrest Gump* meeting fast approaching, and she could ill afford that. Every review, every potluck dinner must leave the members clamor-ing for more. She must make every topic interesting, try to keep every discussion balanced and literate, not allowing any-one or anything to monopolize or scuttle the evening's agenda as Councilman Sparks had done last year. But she kept post-poning an outline to fine-tune her role as moderator. Worse still, she had yet to collect her own thoughts about Winston Groom's work and the unforgettable, now-iconic character of Forrest Gump—simple and brave, loyal and straightforward to a fault.

It had gotten so bad that two days ago in her little office, Maura Beth had broken down and taken a stab at forcing the issue. She had composed an e-mail to Jeremy, taking the better part of an afternoon to get everything just the way she wanted. Over and over she had deleted and rephrased, sometimes only a word here and there. At other times she found herself think-ing that several sentences needed to bite the dust. Finally, she finished.

Jeremy,

I never thought I would find myself in this position. Since I have not heard from you, I assume you are still working your way through your quarrel with New Gallatin Academy and your unsympathetic headmaster. But I clearly remember asking you not to take too long to get back to me with any decisions you made. I won't go into our quarrel over The Cherry Cola Book Club vote that set you off so. I will just say that we are going ahead as planned with Winston Groom's novel and with no regrets. It is a fine work, and I know our members are enjoying reading it.

But I want you to understand that perhaps I overreacted during our misunderstanding. I didn't mean to make things more stressful for you. Maybe I didn't make a better effort to appreciate your position on football and how it has affected your attempts to expose your students to the rewards of reading great literature. As a librarian, I certainly support you in that. At any rate, I don't think this silence between us is accomplishing anything. Frankly, I miss "us." So I wanted to say that I definitely have feelings for you and that they are far more important than winning any argument. Can't we at least start talking to each other again and go from there?

Affectionately,
Maura Beth

She had taken a deep breath and read it over a second time. Did it strike the right tone? She couldn't let anyone else read it and decide for her—not Periwinkle, not Renette, not any of the other female club members she respected as friends and confidantes. This, she knew without a doubt, was strictly on her.

In the end she had not pressed Send. She had not even saved it to her Drafts folder. She had chosen not to force the issue, deleting it in cyberspace, exiling it to a place the human mind could not go or even fathom. That much she could do without flinching. Unfortunately, she could not delete the ongoing conflict from her brain so easily.

8

Debussy and Flying Deer

Jeremy McShay glanced at his watch and saw that he had put things off until nearly three o'clock Sunday afternoon. He had gone back and forth about it the last few days but had finally made up his mind. Better late than never. If he hurried, there would be just enough time to drive down to Cherico for the *Forrest Gump* review from his cozy little bungalow rental on a dead-end street just off Nashville's busy West End. In truth, he did not have appreciably more square footage than Maura Beth did in her efficiency on Clover Street down there, but it somehow made him feel like he was actually getting somewhere in life to be living in a house and not in some generic apartment complex for singles.

He had tried that once at Walking Horse Place when he had first gotten his job at New Gallatin Academy and had found everything in the complex to be noisy and frenetic. There were even times he had been unable to concentrate on grading papers with the booming wall vibrations from his neighbor's thumping electronic equipment.

"Can't you do something about all that noise?!" he had complained to Mrs. Bit Wilson, the chain-smoking, haggard-looking apartment manager. Her diminutive office always smelled like a cross between cheap, floral room deodorizer and an ashtray overflowing with cigarette butts.

She had looked at him briefly as if he had lost his mind but agreed to send out notices reminding the tenants of the regulations regarding playing stereos and TV sets too loud, too late in the evening. He was certain, however, that she had done no such thing since his neighbors above, below, and on either side of him kept right on booming away.

Ugh! As he had so many times before in his life, he devoutly wished he had been born in another century. He would gladly forego some of the creature comforts of the millennium for some peace and quiet, and a genuine appreciation of great literature among the general population. Was that asking too much?

His stylish but practical mother, Susan McShay, who ran a successful crafts boutique in the Cool Springs Galleria south of Nashville, had warned him more than once about expecting the lowest common denominators in life to fade away anytime soon. "I cater to a small percentage of people at Beads and Crafty Needs who want to make quirky, original things with their own hands—fair enough! But I don't pretend they're the norm. Sweetheart, I know you want everyone to appreciate William Faulkner, Nathaniel Hawthorne, and Shakespeare as much as you do, but unfortunately there are far too many who prefer to buy their throwaway reading material at the supermarket checkout counter these days." That had not stopped him, however, from believing he could somehow make a difference, or from overreacting whenever he didn't get his way, unfortunately.

As for today, he wanted to get to Cherico in time to show up and apologize in private to Maura Beth, preferably at her apartment before the *Forrest Gump* hoopla got under way at the library. What had gotten into him that afternoon when he had flown off the handle the way he had? More than once, he had replayed everything in his head and ended up cringing every time. Not that he had made his peace with football and Headmaster Yelverton. He still thought the priorities of New Gallatin Academy were misplaced and that there was genuine merit in his "Living the Classics in the Real World" program he was determined to implement. But he had finally come to his senses and realized that he would just have to bear down and work for change instead of cursing the status quo and driving up his blood pressure; and that would require that he remain with the job he had and not run away from the challenges ahead of him.

He also genuinely missed Maura Beth, and he wanted her back in his life. Whenever he said her name—sometimes silently, sometimes out loud—something inside of him seemed to vibrate pleasantly. Perhaps it was not too late. Perhaps he could still turn things around. He debated whether he should give her a call and let her know he was coming. In the end he opted to surprise her, hoping that would pump up her adrenaline enough to make it easy for her to forgive him. So he bounded out of his bungalow at precisely a quarter after three, climbed into the old Volvo he had brought back to life with his tinkering, and headed west on I-40 out of Nashville to the exit that would lead him to the Natchez Trace. Maybe he would even catch a break and not get stuck behind some tourist going fifty miles an hour on the scenic, but interminably winding, two-lane parkway.

Jeremy had listened to his Debussy CD containing "Prelude to the Afternoon of a Faun" three times in succession now. It was one of his favorite classical pieces, and although it was only ten minutes in length, he never tired of its soothing, delicate passages. Sometimes he thought how miraculous it would be if he could somehow live inside those strains, inhabit those melodies in a way no one had ever thought of before. In effect, he would become the music.

But it was going to take more than Debussy at his best to get his little Volvo past the hulking white Winnebago with the blue Michigan license plate that had caused him to suck its exhaust fumes for the past twenty miles. GREAT LAKES, it read on the bottom of the plate, and Jeremy found himself wishing that this thing hogging the road in front of him was on the bottom of one of the Great Lakes right now.

He was falling further behind his ETA in Cherico by quite a bit. At this rate he would be walking into The Cherico Library with the *Forrest Gump* review well under way, and he definitely did not want to reenter Maura Beth's life coming off like someone who could not be bothered to show up on time.

He remained focused enough to know that honking his horn and flashing his high beams off and on would do him no good. That was what jackasses given over to road rage liked to do. That said, there were long stretches of the picturesque parkway that had obviously not been designed with passing in mind. It was a project that forbade commercial traffic of any kind—truckers beware!—and any emphasis on speed, therefore, made no sense. Every now and then, there were roadside exhibits prepared by the National Park Service that allowed vehicles to pull over and partake of history lessons regarding this important pioneer link between Nashville and Natchez; but unfortunately for Jeremy, none had appeared in quite some time.

"Okay, Michiganders!" he said out loud, leaning into the steering wheel. But he knew whoever had invested in that monstrosity—and it was usually retired couples traveling around to see the countryside at their leisure—had not deliberately plotted to be in front of him as they both headed south. So there was more frustration than anger in his tone of voice. If only he had left the house five minutes sooner. Maybe even a minute or two earlier. He might well be ahead of them now, giving them the slip in his rearview mirror.

With no choice but to follow, he lost himself in thought. What *did* you call people from Michigan? Were they Michiganders or Michiganites? Did it matter? He was still trapped behind them and powerless to do anything about it. Nonetheless, he decided to keep thinking of them as Michiganders.

He recycled Debussy, hoping that the music would keep him calm. Or at least calmer than he would have been otherwise. Both vehicles and their passengers were starting to lose the light, and if anything, the Michiganders slowed down even more as they negotiated the hairpin curves that wound their way through thick pine and hardwood forests just beginning to bud out from winter weather.

Jeremy checked his watch again. It was getting close to a quarter to six, and he hadn't even gotten to the Alabama line yet. The last wooden exit sign had pointed the way to the nearby town of Collinwood, Tennessee. From past trips, he calculated it would be another fifteen miles or so until he hit the border—then another fifteen minutes from there to the Mississippi line.

"C'mon, c'mon, c'mon," he was saying absent-mindedly, knowing the Michiganders could not possibly hear him. But he kept uttering the words anyway. They kept coming out of his mouth while Debussy simultaneously filled up his head and the small space inside the car. How ironic to have such an idyllic environment surrounding him while only enormous and constant frustration loomed directly outside and ahead!

He considered his cell phone. Never one to embrace new technology, he still used the flip variety that came free with the plan. Maybe he should forget about surprising Maura Beth and just tell her he was on the way but was probably going to be a little late. One of the drawbacks of his ancient phone was no hands-free dialing, so he began looking for a spot to pull over safely. Then he would make that call.

He tried Maura Beth's home number first. If he failed to find her there, then he would try the library. She had to be in one place or the other. But he had no sooner finished his task than technology's ultra-annoying graphic flashed onto his cell screen.

NO NETWORK! it said. The phone might as well have been telling him to go to hell in a handbasket.

Well, he should have known. Why would there be a network available way out here in the middle of nowhere among these stone outcroppings and unspoiled forests of rural Middle Tennessee? Who would be making the calls anyway—wild turkeys needing to catch up on their gossip, raccoons wishing each other, "Happy Birthday!" and deer telling their friends about this brand-new place to graze that they simply had to try?

Jeremy managed a smile, but he suspected he needed to get where he was going to avoid further inane speculation. So he tried Maura Beth's number again just to be certain. The same message all but slapped him in the face.

He had no choice other than to drive on, hoping eventually to enter a viable cell. The time and the light were both slipping away, so he began speeding up. With the Michiganders no longer blocking his way and his view—and what a relief that was!—he quickly reached sixty. Patrolling park rangers had been known to give tickets for going much over that, so he decided to put the car on cruise control. After a couple of tries, he got the Set button to stick right around sixty. There might still be enough time to make it to Cherico if he could continue at that speed instead of crawling along under fifty behind some recreational behemoth.

Then his little Volvo crested the top of a steep hill, and that was when he saw he was home free. "Yahoo!" he shouted, surprising himself with his choice of words. He had never used that expression in his entire life, but at the moment he was smiling as the Yahoos of *Gulliver's Travels* came to mind in brilliant literary fashion. Jonathan Swift—at least the political satirist side of him—had long been a favorite of his, often echoing his own dissatisfaction with the foibles and failings of today's society.

What suddenly had him so pumped, however, was the sight of the Michiganders and their moveable residence pulled over to the side and parked in one of the many picnic areas that had been so thoughtfully included for the convenience of tourists. It was getting a little dark for a picnic actually, but Jeremy hardly cared what whoever was inside intended to do at that particular mile marker. The important thing was that he would no longer be drafting them all the way to Mississippi.

"Free at last!" he cried out next, as the Michiganders shrank into a small patch of white in his rearview mirror.

He focused once again on the winding road ahead. He was becoming more and more aware of the beams of light streaming out from the front of his car as the dusk continued to drain the landscape of its color. When he crossed into Alabama very soon now, he would pull over to the side of the road again and try to pick up another cell. Surely he would have left no-man's-land behind by then.

No such luck was in store, however, when he tried Maura Beth's number once again a few miles and minutes later. This was still a very unpopulated area of both Tennessee and Alabama, as his cell phone informed him in no uncertain terms.

He drove on, playing Debussy yet another time. It crossed his mind that this would be a very effective version of hell for someone like himself. The same beautiful music over and over, but with no chance of communicating with anyone ever again. What unbearable torture!

Then, out of the corner of his eye, he caught a glimpse of a dark shape emerging from the nearby woods. In the second or two it took Jeremy to identify what was about to intersect with him at a moment in time, the small but graceful doe appeared to leave the ground and fly across the asphalt in a frantic effort to avoid a collision with Jeremy's Volvo. It all came off like a scene from a movie playing across the surface of the windshield, and somehow, deer and car were able to fend off the impending disaster. But while the deer scampered into the piney woods severely frightened but untouched, the car did not fare nearly as well. Jeremy's violent, last-second tug at the steering wheel sent the vehicle careening down a steep embankment and toward the oldest and sturdiest pine tree in one of the many venerable stands lining both sides of the parkway.

The strains of Debussy were still filling up his head as he saw what was coming up at the speed of light. "Maura Beth!" he cried out reflexively.

And then there was only the sound of metal bending and glass shattering as the car struck the trunk of the tree head-on.

9

Battle of the Sexes

What a cornucopia of delicious aromas and bright colors graced the buffet table of the March Cherry Cola Book Club meeting! First and foremost was the shrimp in deference to *Forrest Gump,* and it came in all varieties: garlic, barbequed with shell on; grilled; and finally, boiled with new potatoes and lemon wedges. Of course, all manner of dipping sauces, from red with ketchup to white with horseradish, were on hand as well. Then there were the football tailgating offerings: fried chicken wings and drumsticks, hot dogs, pulled pork, mustard and sweet pickle potato salad, smoky baked beans with bacon, taco makings, and all kinds of sandwiches from turkey and cheese to tuna fish, and for dessert—brownies, chocolate-chip cookies, fruit pies, and cheesecakes. To be sure, healthier fare was also available, so that Maura Beth was certain no one could possibly go hungry.

She was also pleased to see that the numbers of The Cherry Cola Book Club had held fairly steady since the *To Kill a Mockingbird* review back in November. Just about everyone who had attended then was present now for *Forrest Gump*—the Brachles, the McShays, Miss Voncille and Locke Linwood, the Crumpton sisters, Terra Munrow, and James

Hannigan of The Cherico Market, just to name a few. She was especially thrilled to find Nora Duddney present, after having tracked down an unabridged audio copy of *Forrest Gump* for her listening pleasure and participation in the review. She even found a moment to take Nora aside to chat with her about it.

"Now that was one sure way to give dyslexia the old heave-ho, right?" Maura Beth said.

"It was a godsend," came the cheerful reply. "I can't thank you enough. I'm feeling more and more connected to the world every day."

Indeed, Nora Duddney's transformation from nearly mute bystander to interesting and involved human being had progressed by leaps and bounds since the two women had met earlier in the year. Maura Beth was quick to note Nora's choice of wardrobe—she had clearly gone shopping and bought an outfit that didn't look like a drab hand-me-down from her mother's closet. It consisted of a blouse dotted with sunflowers and an earth-toned skirt. Could the heart of spring be far behind? And was that lipstick and foundation skillfully applied to the woman's face?

"Well, I just wanted to say that I think you look fantastic. I love your new look!" Maura Beth told her after she'd wrapped up the impromptu fashion assessment. "And I hope you'll feel free to give your input in our discussion this evening."

"Thanks for the compliment. I feel like I can take on anything now. I won't be afraid to express my opinion."

There were also a couple of fresh faces to learn besides. The most intriguing was a tall, attractive, forty-something woman wearing a slinky, floor-length black outfit with her long black hair parted straight down the middle. The ensemble suggested an aging hippie who had spruced herself up just a tad bit for a cocktail party. She introduced herself to Maura Beth just after the two of them had finished serving themselves in the buffet line and found a couple of chairs next to each other.

"I'm Sarah Key Darwin," she said, balancing her plate on her knees and offering her hand. "No relation to the evolutionist that I know of, of course. Please call me Sarah Key. All my friends do. This is my first meeting, and I'm very excited."

Maura Beth thanked her for showing up, shook hands while identifying herself, and then rattled off a brief history of The Cherry Cola Book Club. "Are you from Cherico? I don't believe I've seen you around town."

Sarah Key swallowed the bite of mushroom and asparagus casserole she had just speared so carefully and then energetically tapped her fork on the edge of her plate a couple of times. "Oh, this is scrumptious! And I can't wait to try the boiled shrimp! But to answer your question, I just came up from Jackson to look after my brother, Lanny, for a while. I'm sure I don't look the part tonight, but I'm actually a nurse. When I left Lanny's apartment this evening, he told me I looked just like a vampire. Or would that be a vampiress? Anyway, he's healing up after a terrible motorcycle wreck he was in. He's out of the hospital now, but I volunteered to look after him until he's back on his feet again."

"Then the prognosis is good?"

Sarah Key nodded eagerly. "It is. But you wouldn't have thought so if you'd walked into the emergency room and seen him right after it happened. He cracked a couple of ribs, and his face was a mass of abrasions and contusions and—" She briefly glanced down at her food and then looked up with an apologetic expression on her face. "Oh, we're eating, aren't we? I probably should stop right this second with the gory details."

"It's probably for the best, Sarah Key," Maura Beth said, wincing noticeably. "I'm a bit squeamish about such things.

But don't get me wrong, as I told my good friend Connie Mc-Shay—oh, she's a retired nurse by the way and she's here tonight—I appreciate all you medical professionals so much. I couldn't even begin to do what you do. But I pretty much get dizzy at the sight of blood."

Sarah Key swallowed more of her casserole and made a quick hissing sound. "It doesn't come naturally to a lot of us, believe me. It's an acquired taste." She paused, widening her eyes and repressing a grin. "Well, that really does make me sound like a female vampire, doesn't it?"

"No, but I like your sense of humor."

The two women continued to eat and chat, but Maura Beth was unable to keep a peculiar sensation from nagging at her every now and then. She couldn't seem to maintain her focus the way she usually did. There was something about the conversation with this Sarah Key Darwin that was vaguely unsettling, but she couldn't put her finger on it. She shrugged it off soon enough, however. It was probably just her usual discomfort with anything even remotely connected with medical trauma and emergencies.

"I assume you're a reader, or you wouldn't be here," Maura Beth was saying by the time they had finished. "I'm just curious, would you mind telling me how you found out about the club?"

"Oh, at The Twinkle on Commerce Street. I dropped in one evening for a quiet little dinner. Lanny was having a good day, and that sweet brother of mine told me I needed to take a break away from him. So I did. The minute I walked in the door, that very nice lady down there gave me a flyer along with the menu."

Maura Beth was beaming. And then she took the time to explain her shared history with Periwinkle Lattimore.

"She sounds like most of the people living in Cherico," Sarah Key said. "Lanny really likes it here. He works as a mechanic at Greater Cherico Ford, and he swears by how friendly everyone is. He's not a reader, though. I'm the booklover in the family. I read everything I can get my hands on, so when I found out about the book club, I didn't have to think twice about coming. Except I did ask Lanny about it, and he told me not to worry about him, and to go and have a good time."

"Well, once again we're really glad to have you with us," Maura Beth told her, glancing at the clock behind the front desk. "And it's nearly time to get the meat of our meeting under way. I hope you enjoy it."

Maura Beth moved to the podium and was just about to open the proceedings when two latecomers walked through the front door. Periwinkle, she had been expecting, even though she had also been wondering why her best friend hadn't shown up earlier for the buffet and all the socializing. The woman knew how to cook food with the best of them, but she also liked to enjoy it, particularly when other people gave her a break from the kitchen and had to prepare it themselves. No dainty, picky, "Oh, I couldn't eat another bite," girlie girl, she! The big surprise, however, was the tall, rugged man in jeans and boots trailing her with what looked like a copy of *Forrest Gump* in his hands. Now that had to be a last-minute development of some kind, since Periwinkle had not mentioned bringing anyone with her to the meeting.

"Sorry we're bringing up the rear like this," Periwinkle announced, as the two of them found a couple of seats on the back row and quietly settled in. "Harlan and I got a little sidetracked."

Maura Beth caught Periwinkle's gaze and playfully arched her eyebrows. There would be plenty of time after the review to extract the latest from her on what was going on with her "ex."

Then she put that out of her mind but soon found herself replacing it with another, more personal and painfully emotional speculation. Why couldn't it have been Jeremy who had walked through that door at the last minute, giving her hope that their relationship was not over and done with? More to the point, why hadn't she just sent that e-mail she had spent the better part of an afternoon composing and offered him an olive branch of her own?

"Welcome to The Cherry Cola Book Club, and our first review and potluck of the year," Maura Beth announced from her position behind the podium a few minutes later. "I know we've all enjoyed this delicious food that some of the members were kind enough to contribute. By the way, if you'd like to bring something for our next gathering, our very own Becca Broccoli Brachle is the person you want to talk to. Stand up so that everybody will know who you are, Becca. I'm sure she'll be happy to get together with you later and explain the 'double-broccoli thing' if you're one of the few who doesn't know who she is or what on earth I'm talking about."

There was muted laughter and a sprinkling of applause as Becca popped up briefly, nodding her head and waving.

"But now it's time to get down to club business," Maura Beth continued. "As you all know, we will be reviewing and commenting on Winston Groom's *Forrest Gump*. First, let me call your attention to the movie posters we've placed around the room." She began gesturing broadly. "On one side we have Tom Hanks as Forrest Gump sitting on that iconic bench by the bus stop, just waiting for someone to come along and listen to his stories. On the other side we have Tom Hanks accepting the Oscar he won for his outstanding portrayal." She turned and pointed to the circulation desk. "And there at the check-out counter we have a capture of that celebrated actress Sally Field as the devoted Mrs. Gump."

Connie McShay quickly raised her hand, jangling her multicolored, beaded bracelet to get everyone's attention. "And just for the record, folks, those posters didn't cost the library a cent. That was an issue last time out with certain local politicians who shall remain nameless but who are well-known to one and all." Then she glanced around the room. "And unless they're hiding in the closet, none of them is present tonight."

"Thank you, Connie," Maura Beth said, winking at her friend smartly. "So back to our review tonight. We like to say here in the club that outside-the-box angles make for a livelier and more personal discussion, and we hope we'll achieve that once again." She glanced down to consult her notes. "A couple of our esteemed members have already proposed questions, so I thought we would go ahead and tackle those first."

She pointed toward Justin Brachle and Douglas McShay, who were sitting next to each other on the front row. "These two fellas here proposed that we discuss the football aspects of the *Forrest Gump* plot since the character played the game for Bear Bryant. From that starting point, I believe they intended to apply the old adage that football is indeed a religion here in our Deep South."

"Who can deny that?" Becca said, shrugging her shoulders with a resigned expression on her face. "Our husbands are living proof. Certain wives, for that matter. Okay, I'll confess—I'm probably an example of football worship myself to a certain extent. But we women are nowhere near as bad as the men down here. They might find the time to go to church maybe once a year around Christmas if we nag them enough. On the other hand, you better believe they don't miss a college or pro game during the regular season, the bowl season, the playoffs, and, of course, they wouldn't dare miss the Super Bowl. That would be a betrayal of their gender."

Justin raised his fist. "Super Bowl rules! Right, Doug?"

"Right!" But Douglas kept his hands in his lap as Connie gave him a skeptical stare.

"Maybe I should just come up there to the podium and re-move all doubt about this," Becca said, gesturing toward Maura Beth. "I have this little tale to tell. And it's all true, I swear."

Maura Beth smiled back. "By all means. Enlighten us."

Becca took the podium and in no time was in the midst of her story. "Well, to cut to the chase, I've kept in touch with some of my Chi O sisters since I graduated from Alabama." She paused, took a deep breath, and let out a modest, "Roll, Tide!" There was a mixed reaction to her subdued cheer from the crowd, many of whom were fans of the two SEC schools in Mississippi, but Becca brushed off their lack of enthusiasm and continued.

"Sorry. I couldn't help it. As I said, it's not like I haven't taken part in this pigskin worship, too. I like to think that I've been more reasonable about it, of course. Anyway, back to the contact with my sorority sisters. You know the type of thing I'm getting at—you exchange Christmas cards with the newsletters that fall out when you open them up, birth an-nouncements with pictures and so forth. Well, as it turns out, three of the girls I've kept up with somehow all managed to marry LSU grads, and the six of them do practically every-thing together. Now, what are the odds of that, I ask you? Sounds like some sort of lame reality show, doesn't it? But in the world of football, it's what's called a mixed marriage, and it's every bit as difficult to manage as one that involves race or religion, believe me. Sometimes it can get even worse. Perfect example was the 2011 season. It was for all the marbles for the 'Bama and LSU fans. LSU beat 'Bama during the regular sea-son in Tuscaloosa, but my Tide beat the Tigers the second time when it counted down in the Superdome for the Na-tional Championship."

That raised the level of buzzing throughout the crowd, but Becca just stood there smiling and looking innocent until it tailed off. "So now I've set up the story for you. The payoff is that those three LSU husbands were so hot and bothered that their beloved Tigers had lost the game—hey, they were even blanked, 21-0—that they all withheld the other kind of hot and bothered in the boudoir that night back in their hotel rooms in the French Quarter. All my 'Bama girlfriends wanted was a little mattress magic, but the boys weren't having any and said, 'No, ma'am, not tonight!' Can you believe men would give up . . . you-know-what like that?"

Most of the men in the crowd sprang to life over the comments, almost as if someone had lit a match and given them each a hot foot. And Douglas seemed to be speaking for all of them when he said, "It's not as crazy as it sounds, but it's easier to believe the other way around. Women are pretty good at that withholding business themselves. Hey, we've all been there."

Connie balled up her fist and punched her husband on the arm. "Douglas, I can't believe you said that in front of all these people!" Then she inched closer to him and whispered out of the side of her mouth. "Everyone will get the wrong impression about us."

He was massaging his bicep, and the scowl on his face indicated she had hit him a bit harder than was necessary. "We're all grown-ups here, aren't we? It's not the first time adults have discussed the subject of withholding sex."

"And it won't be the last," Becca added, giving her Stout Fella a stern look as she headed back to her seat. But he did not respond, staring straight ahead at the podium as if he had not even heard her.

Maura Beth knew she must try to dissipate the tension in the room quickly, so she consulted her notes once again and cleared her throat with authority. "Be that as it may, we were supposed to be talking about football as a religion and the plight of football widows. And somewhere along the way, we were supposed to be relating it all to the plot of *Forrest Gump*.

Please, let's try not to forget that and return to those topics, why don't we?"

"I'll bite," Periwinkle said, getting to her feet and moving to the front to face the crowd as Maura Beth stepped aside. "There's a lot to cover on the subject of the football widow." She began moving back and forth slowly and deliberately, giving a passable imitation of a lawyer addressing a jury in a courtroom trial. "Now, let's examine some of the evidence we wives—or ex-wives in my case—know to be factual. First, everything is often indeed on hold when it comes to men getting their football fix. And I do mean everything—with no exceptions. I have a good friend over in Corinth—and I'm not about to reveal her identity—whose husband waited until halftime of the big game to get his first glimpse of their fourth child in the hospital. Just happened during this past football season, matter a' fact. He figured it was all no big deal by the time they'd had three, and he managed his time pretty doggone well as he raced the clock, his wife told me. He worked in a kiss on the forehead to her and a peck on the cheek to their latest bouncing baby boy with some sweet talk thrown in and still got back to the flat-screen TV in the waiting room before the third quarter started. Last time I heard from her, she said she was seriously thinking of nicknaming this last child Halftime."

The laughter that followed eased the tension somewhat, but it took the gathering by surprise when a voice from the back row posed the question, "May I add something to your insights there, counselor?"

Most everyone turned in their seats to see the man who had come in with Periwinkle out of his chair with a twinkle in his eye.

"Now that was very clever," Periwinkle put in. "So why don't you get on up here and finish what you started? Ladies and gentlemen, this is my ex-husband, Harlan Lattimore."

He was soon standing beside her, scanning the crowd with that rugged smile of his. "Well, the gist of it is, I'm here to say before all a' you good witnesses that I was as guilty as the next fella when it came to ignoring his wife during football season. If I'd paid more attention to my wife in general, football or no football, I believe Peri and me'd still be married. But, fellas, let's be honest here. Some of us really are fanatics about the game. I've got my share of customers who spend most of Saturday afternoon at the bar guzzling beer, peeling shrimp, and watching the games with their wives nowhere in sight. It's become the most important thing in their lives, I do believe. Now, I read this *Forrest Gump* book here because Peri was so high on your book club. Seemed like it was something we might do together."

He reached over and rubbed her arm gently a couple of times, looking her straight in the eye. "So that's what I'm doing. As I told Peri here on the way over, I'm not much of a reader, but I liked this book. I thought this Forrest Gump was a fine fella with a great sense a' humor who tried hard, whatever he undertook; and I just wanted to say to you right here tonight, Peri, that if I'd tried as hard as Forrest Gump did in his relationship with that pretty Jenny Curran, I know for dang certain we'd still be married to each other."

A few of the women in attendance let out an "Aww!" for starters; then there was light applause that briefly grew louder before finally dying out. Maura Beth, however, was astonished to see that Periwinkle was actually blushing, something she had never witnessed in the six years of their friendship.

"And furthermore to that," Harlan continued, "I think this Winston Groom fella who wrote this was smart as a fox to connect Forrest Gump with Bear Bryant the way he did. Why, you can't go wrong in the Deep South if you talk about legends like that. A whole lotta people will take a peek, even ones who aren't Alabama fans."

"Yes, I believe the idea was to have the fictional character

present for many watershed moments of the twentieth century, and it obviously worked quite well," Maura Beth said.

"That's what I liked most about the novel," Nora Duddney
put in next. "All the iconic figures during the time I was
growing up are there—JFK, Lyndon Johnson, the first astro-
nauts. Even though Forrest Gump was a fictional character,
that made him seem all the more authentic, giving him a place
in the march of history like that. There were times that I for-
got he really didn't participate in all those events. There's brilliance in that concept."

"Good insight," Maura Beth said, smiling generously at her
new friend and confidante.

"I kinda thought of Forrest Gump as Everyman, myself,"
said Justin Brachle. "You know, not the two-word version but
the one-word spelled with a capital E."

"Excellent point, Justin," Maura Beth added with a grin,
"and I think Forrest Gump would have explained it exactly
the way you just did. And I mean that in a complimentary
way, of course."

Justin beamed, puffing out his big chest. "Stout Fella
thanks you. And I agree that Forrest Gump seemed real, since
he ended up playing football for The Bear. It made me want
to be him because I was just a small potatoes quarterback at
Millsaps. Our big rival was Sewanee—the Methodists versus
the Episcopalians, ya know."

Miss Voncille's hand shot up. "This has all been very interesting, I'm sure, but haven't we talked about this football angle
enough? We get it. Some people love their football, and others
take the game too seriously. Then that leads to marital problems and yada, yada, yada. If you'll permit me to say so, there
are lots more important things to fight over than football. So I
respectfully propose that we move on to discussing the Vietnam angle of the plot that I submitted to Maura Beth. I'm sure

I'm not the only one here tonight who's interested in discussing that."

"I'm just one person," Mamie Crumpton said, thrusting out her bosom as usual. "I don't mind the football topic, but I think we've had more than enough of this sex talk. Let's return it to the bedroom where it belongs."

Ever the diplomat, Maura Beth scanned the gathering and said, "Well, what do you say, people? Show of hands to move on?"

Everyone appeared to have had their fill of the men versus women topic, as there were far more hands up than down. Periwinkle and Harlan resumed their seats. Maura Beth consulted her notes once again and then motioned to Miss Voncille. "Please come up and get this part of the discussion started, then."

Miss Voncille rose from her seat on the front row, her face solemn and her pace to the podium deliberate. There was an initial grand exhalation; then she began reading from a prepared speech, looking up now and then to make eye contact. "My years as a schoolteacher serve me well tonight. If I know nothing, it's how to organize my thoughts in a cogent manner. So I will begin by saying that our country hasn't been the same since the Vietnam War. We had some politicians—and you know who they are—who wanted to have it both ways: trying to please those who wanted to win the war, while placating those who wanted us to withdraw from it unconditionally. The media began to take sides, of course, and I'm inclined to think that that's when objective journalism began to die in this county. The press stepped away from merely reporting and started advocating. When the war was finally over and done with, some came home—but many didn't. The phrase *life and limb* comes to mind. Some gave their lives, as Bubba Blue did, dying in Forrest Gump's arms. Others gave their limbs, as

Lieutenant Dan Taylor did, Forrest Gump's commanding offi-
cer. They weren't real people, but they represented real people.
Too many to count, unfortunately."

Miss Voncille paused to take another breath for courage.
"Meanwhile, back in the real world we all live in, I found myself affected by another phrase—*missing in action*. My connection
to the war—Sergeant Frank Gibbons of Corinth, Mississippi—
never came home. As many of you know, his status remains MIA.
I never got the kind of closure that Forrest Gump did as he
neatly concluded every episode of his fascinating life journey.
That was entertaining fiction, but the MIA issue is a heartbreak-
ing one for those of us who live on. It's always in the back of our
minds, dogging us no matter how many years have passed. If only
we could close that chapter of our lives as easily as we could finish and close up a copy of *Forrest Gump*. And that's what I wanted
to say here to all of you tonight. I needed to try and once again
exorcise my demons, and I thank you for listening."

The gathering was stunned, to say the least. No one said
anything—not even Locke Linwood—and there was no applause as Miss Voncille headed toward her seat.

Maura Beth quickly moved into the breach. "That was
certainly a speech from the heart, Miss Voncille. You've
touched on so many good points. Group, shall we discuss any
of this further?"

It was Sarah Key Darwin who spoke up next. "The thing
is, the Vietnam War is not a subject that lends itself to such
easy analysis. I think the biggest problem most people have in
resolving the subject today is that so many soldiers thought
they were being patriotic in becoming a part of the military
effort. Back then, it was the definition of being an American,
and you didn't ask questions the way people do now about
everything. The simpleton aspects of Forrest Gump's character
reflect that precisely. It was what you were supposed to do
without thinking."

"What are you saying?" Miss Voncille said, her tone tinged with anger. "I'll have you know my Frank was no simpleton. He was a brave and thoughtful man. He knew what he was getting into, and I know for a fact that he found time while he was deployed over there to weigh the consequences of the war. I have his beautiful letters to prove it."

"I wasn't trying to attack your friend personally. What I meant was, we'd have been far better off if more people had questioned our presence in Vietnam from the get-go," Sarah Key returned, refusing to back down.

Miss Voncille got to her feet, even though Locke Linwood made an effort to restrain her. "I just have to ask—how old are you?" she said, pointing her finger directly at Sarah Key.

"I beg your pardon? What has that got to do with anything?"

"Never mind," Miss Voncille continued. "You're probably one of those people who views history as something to revise constantly, omitting the truth when it suits your agenda. You have no idea what some of us lived through in the last century!"

"Please, ladies," Maura Beth said, trying to calm things down. "We don't need to get personal here. This is supposed to be a polite discussion. Let's keep that in mind as we proceed."

"But she doesn't even know me!" Miss Voncille insisted, completely ignoring Maura Beth's plea for restraint. "And she certainly didn't know my Frank. Here she is forty-something years later with her political hindsight and easy answers that come with it. Implying that the men who signed up for duty in Vietnam were dolts of some kind is completely out of line!"

Maura Beth was surprised to see that Sarah Key continued to fuel the fire. "No, not dolts, but definitely manipulated. More to the point, I think, is the fact that if we don't learn from the lessons of history, we are doomed to repeat them.

Why, look at all these little wars we still get involved in at the firing of a rocket or bullet? We seem to be a very trigger-happy country."

"Please, Voncille," Locke said to Miss Voncille under his breath. "Don't get your blood pressure up. This is getting out of hand."

"I will not be silenced!" Miss Voncille proclaimed, gesturing dismissively toward Sarah Key. "Who is this person, anyway, Maura Beth?"

"No, you don't need to ask *her* who I am. I can speak for myself. Sarah Key Darwin is the name," came the curt reply, "and I was not aware that agreeing with everybody was a requirement of participating in The Cherry Cola Book Club. I certainly don't remember it being on the flyer I read at The Twinkle."

"Of course it isn't a requirement," Maura Beth put in, determined to restore order but sensing it all slipping away. "No book club worth its salt would ever discourage differences of opinion."

Miss Voncille bristled. "This is more than that, I'm afraid. As far as I'm concerned, this woman is going out of her way to be disrespectful to me and to the memory of Frank Gibbons and the many other men like him!"

Sarah Key rose to her feet, turning up her nose as she faced the podium. "Maura Beth, I'm sorry. But this is not what I had in mind when I decided to come here tonight. You are certainly a lovely person, and I've enjoyed meeting most of the rest of you. But if you'll excuse me, I have better things to do than be insulted for disagreeing with someone. The last time I looked, this was still America!"

"Oh, please don't leave!" Maura Beth cried out.

But it was to no avail as Sarah Key turned on her heels and marched out of the library in a huff.

"Good riddance!" Miss Voncille exclaimed, sitting down at last and folding her arms in disgust.

The uneasiness in the air was palpable as everyone else sat stupefied, and Maura Beth quickly glanced at the front desk clock. Perhaps it was time to pull the plug before more confrontation reared its ugly head. These meetings of The Cherry Cola Book Club had been cut short all too often by something unforeseen. Would they ever go according to plan?

"Well, I certainly hadn't anticipated anything like that," Maura Beth began, forcing herself to smile. "But maybe we've accomplished all we can here tonight." She brandished and then thumped her notes for all to see. "We certainly got around to the football angle—or angles I should say—and, of course, the controversial Vietnam angle; and a couple of other things emerged as well about Winston Groom's work. Unless anyone else has something to add, shall we adjourn?"

"If you don't mind, there was something I wanted to contribute," James Hannigan said, timidly raising his hand. "And it was about football being a religion and all. It was just that I have this friend who is a big Arkansas Razorback fan, and it used to be that the Texas Longhorns were their biggest rival back when they both played in the old Southwest Conference. My friend Johnny told me about this sign he saw once on a church marquee up in Fayetteville that read, 'FOOTBALL IS ONLY A GAME. SPIRITUAL THINGS ARE ETERNAL. NEVERTHELESS, BEAT TEXAS.' "

The pall that Miss Voncille and Sarah Key had generated quickly dissolved into easy laughter, and when it finally died down, Maura Beth said, "Thanks, Mr. Hannigan. We definitely needed that. So, on that note, shall we adjourn?"

"Fine by me," Miss Voncille said, obviously still holding on to her pique. This was followed by similar utterances from the others.

It was Connie, however, who reminded Maura Beth of something important. "Don't we need to discuss our next read? Or were we just going to resurrect *The Robber Bridegroom*? We've had Eudora Welty waiting in the wings for her cue for what seems like forever."

Maura Beth chuckled and immediately went back to her notes. "Good catch, Connie. I had another suggestion, however. Since I'm originally from Louisiana and we have quite the flamboyant reputation for politicians down in the Pelican State, I thought we might consider reading *All the King's Men* by Robert Penn Warren. It's another Pulitzer Prize winner like *To Kill a Mockingbird*. Some of you may know that the novel takes its inspiration from the reign of Louisiana Governor Huey P. Long, who was assassinated on the steps of the capitol in Baton Rouge. The same thing happens to the fictional Governor Willie Stark in this novel. Naturally, our very own Councilman Durden Sparks came to mind, particularly all the trouble we've had lately with him and his cronies. Of course, I trust all of you know I'm not encouraging any gunplay here on the steps of City Hall."

More much-needed laughter erupted. But when it finally died down, it was Connie who reacted first. "Poor Miz Eudora, a Southern legend being swept under the rug twice now."

"Well, how about this?" Maura Beth said, thinking on her feet. "We could go ahead and approve our next two reads, if you'd like. First, *All the King's Men,* then *The Robber Bridegroom.*"

There was general buzzing throughout the room, but soon enough they were taking a vote on Maura Beth's suggestion. It won unanimously, and the date for the next meeting of The Cherry Cola Book Club was set for the second Sunday in May.

"You've been keeping things from me, haven't you?" Maura Beth was saying to Periwinkle as the two of them visited in her library office after everyone else had left. For his part, Harlan had headed out to pick up a few odds and ends he needed at The Cherico Market and would return in about a half hour for his ex-wife. Meanwhile, Maura Beth's curiosity had been ratcheted up several more notches. "I thought the deal was, we were supposed to keep each other up to date about the men in our lives."

Periwinkle looked down at her lap, entwining her fingers in a display of nervous energy. "I didn't mean to shut you out. Things just moved along a lot faster than I thought they would. I mean, it was just a drink here, another little dinner there, not to mention lots and lots of phone calls, and I guess he just wore me down after a while. I was going to tell you everything sooner or later, though." There was an awkward pause, and somehow Maura Beth sensed what was coming next. "And, yes, I've gone to bed with him—after all these years. In fact, that's why we were late. Can you believe it?"

Maura Beth leaned back in her chair and scratched her head, trying her best not to sound as surprised as she was. "Wow! It seems things really have moved along fast for you. The last time we chatted about this, you were more impressed with Mr. Place than Harlan."

Periwinkle gave a sweet little shudder and her eyes went all dreamy for a second or two, reminding Maura Beth of a teenager getting ready to share her innermost secrets with her slumber-party girlfriends. "Oh, Parker is still attentive in that professional way of his, but things have changed dramatically with Harlan. I know this sounds crazy, but it was like it used to be when Harlan and I were first dating. It was like no time had passed at all. I really believe he's a changed man, I really do. Despite everything that was said here tonight about men and women not getting along for the most ridiculous reasons, I think there are times they can come together for all the right reasons. When that happens, there's nothing better in the whole world."

Maura Beth considered her reaction carefully. She had never seen Periwinkle acting this way and must not give her friend the impression that she was cynical or disapproving. "Well, what can I say? I'm very happy for you." Then she reached across the desk and patted Periwinkle's hand a couple of times—a completely unconvincing display, as it turned out.

"Something's bothering you, I can tell. I know you too well, Maura Beth."

"No." Then Maura Beth decided to tell the truth. "Yes, I just have one question, and then I'd like to give you a real, honest-to-goodness hug, no matter what."

"Shoot!"

"You two didn't do it back in that . . . you know, that god-awful room you decorated, did you? Oops, I meant the room was god-awful, not your decorating."

Periwinkle produced her usual hearty laugh and waved her off. "I knew what you meant, girl. And absolutely not—he was telling the truth. He really did convert that little sex den of his into more pantry space—all extra jars of relish and bottles of ketchup galore. I got to see for myself when he gave me the grand tour. No, we got reacquainted, so to speak, back at his new place. Which I have to admit, he's done up right nicely all by himself."

Maura Beth got to her feet, feeling tremendously reassured. "That's good enough for me. You come right around here pronto, and let's have that big hug."

"So what's the latest with you and Jeremy?" Periwinkle said, after they'd pulled away from each other a few seconds later.

Maura Beth plopped back down in her chair and sighed while Periwinkle again took her seat. "No change. Oh, I've had my moments of weakness when I picked up the phone and started to punch in his number. And just the other day, I composed this spectacularly emotional e-mail, asking him to give us a chance to start over. But I didn't have the guts to send it. I guess tonight tells me everything I need to know."

"Which is?"

Maura Beth gently massaged her eyelids with the tips of her fingers and then brought her hands together prayerfully in one smooth motion. "Which is that he knew well in advance about the review tonight and how much I wanted him here, even if he never opened his mouth. I told him how much his presence would mean to me, but it appears it meant nothing to him. So I have to conclude that it's really over between us. He's obviously not interested anymore, and it's high time I got that through this red head of mine."

Periwinkle moved to her side quickly, leaning down and kissing her forehead. "I'm so sorry, girl. Nobody knows better than I do how tricky things can be in this battle of the sexes. Sometimes you win, sometimes you lose."

10

Youthful Indiscretions

Councilman Sparks was seated behind his plush office desk, biding his time while playing tic-tac-toe against himself on his notepad. It was about a quarter to nine, and he knew his proxy would be arriving any minute with her report. This was fun, playing games with Maura Beth and her busybody friends, but he fully intended to enforce the terms of the one-year reprieve he had reluctantly granted to her precious library. Voter petitions be damned—he knew what was best for Greater Cherico and how to continue the sort of tangible legacy his father and Layton Duddney had begun. Charles Durden Sparks would leave his name on some building or project in the general vicinity for posterity, or there was no justice in the world!

After all, it was resourceful politicians, not inconsequential librarians like Maura Beth Mayhew and her predecessor, Annie Scott, who had put money into the infrastructure that today's Chericoans took for granted. True, the Sparks and Duddney families had siphoned off a percentage for themselves and their posterity here and there. But they had been careful not to leave a paper trail and had never neglected the public good.

Momentarily, the attractive woman who had attended the

meeting of The Cherry Cola Book Club at his clandestine bidding appeared, posing in come-hither fashion against the door frame. What could only be described as a wicked smile dominated her face.

"Is that what you wore, Sylvie?" Councilman Sparks said, looking her over from head to toe. "You remind me of either a witch or a vampire. Inspired by what all the kids are reading and watching on TV these days, were you?"

"Funny you should say that. I used that line about the vampire myself, as I recall," Sylvie said, sitting down across from him and leaning in to better present her cleavage for his inspection. "And for the record, I was Sarah Key Darwin for the evening. I had a really tough time keeping a straight face every time I heard your librarian friend call me that. Can you imagine? Such a name and they believed it? Don't know how I came up with it. Except I've always thought Charles Darwin was a marvelously adventurous soul, and someday I'd like to travel to Key West. Wouldn't mind retiring there, as a matter of fact. Do you think you could arrange it for me one fine day?"

He muttered something under his breath.

"Was that a 'yes' or 'no,' Durden?"

"That was a 'we'll see.' But please, your summary of the evening."

"First, I will admit your Maura Beth's a looker. I can see why you're smitten; that is, if redheads are your type."

"Never mind that. How many people were there?"

"I counted forty-five."

He was gazing at the ceiling now, finally nodding his head sharply when he had finished his mental review. "Good. That's not quite as many as they had in November for *To Kill a Mockingbird*. I knew that was a dog and pony show Miz Mayhew went all out to stage. They can't sustain that momentum. By the end of the year, I'll have all the ammunition I need to shut her down."

Sylvie Louise Morgenthal, as she had been christened by her late parents, then began recounting in earnest everything pertinent that had occurred, while Councilman Sparks listened intently, taking a few notes along the way.

"You came up from Jackson to nurse your biker brother? He was in a really bad wreck, was he?" he interrupted after she'd gotten to that part. "The things you come up with. I think I'd believe it, though. You always did have a good imagination." But he perked up considerably when she reached the argument she had managed to provoke with Miss Voncille about the Vietnam War.

"It was a walk in the park," she was saying. "You'd have thought she was addressing the United Nations the way she went on and on with her moral high ground approach and everything. Oh, she couldn't be bothered with a different viewpoint. Not that one with the prim, salt-and-pepper hair. It wasn't too hard to zero in on her soft spot."

"Good deal. Miss Voncille Nettles was just as prickly as her last name when she taught me in school way back when. I know she resented my abilities. I could debate the pants off anyone who ever went to Cherico High School, but she was always about putting a damper on me and holding me down. I bet you really got under her skin with the Vietnam thing."

Sylvie tossed back her long hair as she enjoyed a laugh. "Oh, you should have seen me. It was an Oscar-winning performance the way I spewed political rhetoric and then stormed out of there like a whirling dervish. You could have heard a pin drop in the place as they all watched me leave. I hung around outside in my car for a while, and the place emptied out not too long after I made my grand exit. All in all, I think I was effectively rude and subversive, take your pick."

"I know the feeling," he said. Then he furrowed his brow ever so slightly. "But for future reference, nurses don't generally go out dressed like that. They're serious people, and they have their reputations to consider. Florence Nightingale may be turning over in her grave even as we speak."

"Florence Nightingale may have had her own secrets. Who knows? Most people do, including you." Then she rose and turned to point her shapely, black-clad posterior at him, wiggling it with abandon. "Too bad you're so hung up on red-heads these days, Durden."

"Stop that, Sylvie." He sounded like a drill sergeant barking orders. Then he lowered his voice as she reluctantly obeyed him. "That part of our relationship is way over, but I've always appreciated what you've done for me and Chunky and Gopher Joe when we needed you."

She shrugged, her eyes looking glazed and lifeless, better suited to a mannequin. "Hey, sometimes the money works. Sometimes the woman works. Whichever gets you guys the votes you need, right?"

"Whichever."

"Tonight was different, though," she added, absent-mindedly coiling a thick strand of hair around her index finger. "I always thought I could be an actress, if I'd gotten the right breaks, you know. All those people getting so worked up over a book was a scream tonight." She made a noise with her lips that sounded re-markably like it could have come from the mouth of a winded horse. "The food was good. Nothing to drink, though. No hard stuff, I mean, and I was dying for one. There was just some sort of Shirley Temple punch with lots of cherries and slices of lime floating around in it. It made me think of a children's party."

"Yes, potluck," he said, his tone completely disinterested now. "You can get the same thing on any Wednesday night at any Methodist church in the Deep South, punch and all. And the truth of the matter is, they could hold those book reviews in the fellowship hall of any church in Cherico. They really don't need that library."

"Which reminds me. They discussed religion tonight, too.

Well, sort of. It was insane. All this resentment built up between the husbands and the wives." She had settled back down
in her chair again, behaving herself for the time being. "That's
why I never got married, Durden. Although I would, if you
would ever divorce Evie and ask me. How are things between
the two of you these days, by the way? Still no children? Still
no heir to the family fortune?"

He had had enough. "That's none of your business,
Sylvie." He checked his watch. "It's getting late now, and I've
got to get on home. I appreciate the report, and I'll call you
again if I need you for something. I trust your direct deposit
was sufficient?"

She nodded, her eyes now half-lidded. "More than generous, as usual." She rose, giving him one last seductive glance.
"It's such a shame that you and I couldn't have made it perma-
nent, you know."

His smile was at once pronounced and insincere. "Hey,
what could you expect of a horny Mississippi College law-
school student? I was looking for a good time one night at the
State Fair, and you took me for a wild ride that lasted until the
day I graduated with honors."

She clasped her hands together and mockingly cast her
eyes heavenward. "Ah, my ingenue days when I was just getting my . . . feet wet! But you have to admit, I still look pretty
good."

"That you do. Don't look your age by a mile."

"Sure you don't want a little ride on the roller coaster for
old time's sake?"

"Thanks, but no thanks." He rose from his chair, indicating
with a sweep of his hand that she should leave. "I really need
to get on home to the wife, Sylvie."

She licked and then pouted her lips. "One little kiss,
then?"

He escorted her to the outer door and granted her wish, lingering longer than he really wanted to. Then he pulled away forcefully. "Have a safe trip tomorrow back down to Jackson."

He watched her walk away, some long-buried part of him wishing things had worked out for them. She might have been an inferno in bed in the days of their youth, but even then he was savvy enough to know that her profession was a liability she would never be able to escape. After all, he had political ambitions and no intention of being dragged down with her if her past ever came to light. Things were just fine the way they were. He knew she was still hopelessly in love with him and would never do anything to harm him or his career.

Miss Voncille was an emotional wreck. Locke had driven them to his place on Perry Street after the meeting was over and was trying his best to soothe her with a glass of his best Madeira. "Here, sip on this a little, sweetheart," he told her, handing it over as she settled in on his living room sofa. "It'll help calm you."

But she downed the whole thing in one big swallow and handed the glass back immediately. "I think I'd like another one, if you don't mind."

He complied, bringing back a glass for himself this time and taking a seat beside her. "You know I support you one hundred percent, Voncille. But who cares what some strange woman thinks about the Vietnam War? She means nothing to you—to either of us. You made an eloquent speech, and I'm sure everyone else at the library agreed with you."

This time she settled for sipping her little drink. "You're probably right. But that awful, strident woman still triggered something in me I hadn't thought of for a long, long time. I think I may have painted a false picture for you of what my fling with Frank was really like. Over the years, my memories have grown rosier and rosier. I know I've put him up on a pedestal, and I realize that's been hard on you."

Locke inched closer to her, gently slipping his arm around her shoulder. "Don't worry about that. I'm a big boy."

"You're a kind, wonderful man is what you are," she said, giving him her best smile. "And that's far more important in the scheme of things. Anyway, the logistics of my relationship with Frank were a nightmare. If I hadn't still been living with my parents at the time, it all might have been a lot easier. As it was, I was always sneaking out of the house, struggling to make up excuses to Mama and Poppa that sounded halfway plausible, and always feeling guilty about everything, no matter what. I look back on all that and—" But she broke off, tearing up again as she had during the drive over from the library.

"What is it?" he asked, putting his sherry glass down beside the Oriental cat lamp on the end table and taking her hand. "You can tell me anything at this point in our relationship."

She alternated sniffling and sipping for a few seconds, then dabbing at her eyes with the Kleenex he'd given her earlier. Finally, she straightened up a bit and took a deep breath. "The word that came to me on the way over here tonight is *payback*. At the time of my involvement with Frank, I know I thought there would be no price to pay for what we were doing. Of course, I couldn't have been more wrong. Sometimes you can get away with these youthful indiscretions. But in my case, it hasn't happened that way."

"Please tell me you don't think you're being punished for your affair with Frank," he told her. "Because that would be the most wrongheaded thing you could possibly think."

"I'm not so sure. That Darwin woman was so glib about Vietnam the way she rattled off her opinions like a college professor or something. And I think most people have gone on to be glib about it nearly half a century later. Time always does that, and as a history teacher I know that only too well. Meanwhile, here I sit with my loss still feeling as fresh and painful as if it had happened yesterday. No matter how hard I try, I can't really seem to move on. Tonight was just another example of that."

He thought for a while, taking a nip or two of his sherry in the interim. "Then tell me what I can do to help."

She looked down at the piece of Kleenex she had reduced to shreds and managed a little chuckle. "First, please get me a fresh one of these. I'm about to make a mess on your beautiful sofa, and I know Pamela and her portrait on the wall over there wouldn't appreciate that one bit." She put the traumatized tissue in his hand, and he headed for the bathroom.

When he returned and resumed his seat, she had managed to compose herself considerably. "Thank you, Locke. I'm a little better now, I think. But there is something else I've never told you about me and Frank."

"Go ahead, then."

She took an inordinate amount of time to speak, but she finally got it out. "There was a brief period there—it was right after Frank had been deployed to Vietnam—that I thought I might be pregnant. You can't imagine how panicked I was for a while. What would I do if I was carrying his child and he never came back to us? All sorts of crazy schemes went through my head at the time. Would I run away somewhere, have the baby and give it up for adoption? I don't even want to tell you what else I was thinking."

"But you weren't pregnant, right?"

"No, I wasn't. I was just good and late." She was searching his face carefully for signs of disapproval but thankfully found none. "But imagine if I had been. Then I would really have been up against it, seeing as how Frank really did never come back. That would have been a youthful indiscretion for all the world to see and judge. I don't have any idea how my parents would have acted. They were pretty rigid in their opinions, and I was such a free spirit back then. Sometimes I didn't even feel related to them."

"But it didn't happen that way. Why torture yourself with the 'almosts' and the 'what-ifs' and such?"

She looked him straight in the eye and spoke with intensity. "Because being an unmarried woman under any circumstances is not the way I want to go out, no matter how many years I have left."

He looked almost amused. "I think we've gotten pretty good at reading each other's minds, Voncille. Why did I think you were going to go there again?"

She dropped the Kleenex into her lap and inched closer to him. "Then it's been on your mind, too."

"Yes, I can't lie to you. I've been seriously considering everything you brought up a while back. Ceremony in the library, ceremony in a church, maybe a justice of the peace—all of it. I just haven't made a decision yet."

She kept at it, sensing his lack of resistance. "Do you think you might anytime soon?"

He looked more amused than anything else and gave her a sweet little peck on the cheek. "I promise to give you my decision soon."

"Maybe by the next Cherry Cola Book Club meeting?"

He laughed in spite of himself. "Yes, Voncille. Maybe by then."

11

Conqu'ring Heroes

Jeremy came to.

He was lying on his back looking up at the sky on this cloudless early spring evening. There were no stars yet, and he could not remember where he was or what he was doing sprawled on the ground. There was a light breeze swirling all around him, and he felt its chill on his face and hands. Then he sat up gingerly, crying out sharply as something caught in the vicinity of his rib cage. Whether muscle or bone was the culprit, it was uncomfortable to breathe. His head was also throbbing, and when he slowly reached up and ran his hand through his hair, he came away with something sticky clinging to his fingers. When he touched the tip of his index finger to his tongue, he tasted his own blood.

Through the filmy dusk, he stared ahead and discerned the outline of what remained of his little Volvo. It had been reduced in size by half, squeezed like an accordion against the trunk of an enormous pine tree. The entire hood and front seat of the car no longer occupied any significant portion of space. They now consisted of a few inches of twisted metal and shattered glass that had fused into pine bark to create some entirely new and hideous substance. Off to the side, looking forlorn and out of place, was the door to the driver's seat—essentially intact. Clearly, it had been shorn off at the moment of collision between car and tree, and violently cast aside, but how was that possible? Why hadn't it been compressed like the rest? Why was he alive when his car was essentially dead?

Jeremy tried his hardest to focus, but the pain filling up his skull would simply not allow him to do it. For a brief second or two, he had a flash of something—impulsively unbuckling his seat belt at the last possible second, flinging the door open and tumbling out before impact. Had he actually done that, or had something beyond his ken intervened on his behalf?

Deprived of rational thought, he began to panic. Had he somehow died along with the car? Was he actually out of his body now? At first, he dismissed the idea as pure, unadulterated foolishness. But then, as if on cue to provide an answer, he could feel a light of some kind suddenly shining upon him from behind, brilliantly illuminating the forest and the wreck that had brought man-made horror to its very edges.

It was not easy for Jeremy to twist himself around enough to face the light in the distance, but with great effort he managed to do so. He was blinded by its brilliance, and the cobwebs in his brain would allow him only one credible answer: *He had indeed died, and this was what it was like during the transition.* Never a drumbeater for the tidy organized religion his parents had bequeathed him, he had nonetheless always maintained a belief in something greater than himself. Perhaps he was now about to meet up with that something greater.

Music soon followed, but it caused him to frown immediately. This was no hymn, no heavenly choir of angelic voices accompanied by golden harps. There was singing, to be sure, but it hardly sounded like it belonged in a church. He strained to catch the boisterous lyrics, and a sickening feeling spread throughout his body. Could it possibly be? His much-despised game of college football was played to rouse team spirit in the afterlife, too? Whatever the case, he was undeniably listening to the last verse of the University of Michigan fight song while sitting on the cold ground smack dab in the middle of nowhere.

> *"Hail! to the victors valiant*
> *Hail! to the conqu'ring heroes*
> *Hail! Hail! to Michigan,*
> *The champions of the West!"*

As if that were not enough, the fight song started over from the beginning; then he heard a booming voice shouting, "Hello, out there! Anyone alive out there?!"

Was that what God sounded like? Was he a Wolverine to boot? Did he sometimes specialize in search-and-rescue missions in today's complex world?

Momentarily, Jeremy was able to discern a dark, bipedal shape, and he wasn't sure if it would turn out to be angel, demon, or something—anything—in human form. But it was fast approaching him with a flashlight that augmented the stronger, wider beam streaming out from behind. A few feet more and Jeremy could clearly make out a man—an ordinary, older man in a windbreaker and dark baseball cap with the letter *M* emblazoned on it in a lighter color. He breathed a sigh of relief, realizing at that instant he was simply not ready for a supernatural encounter of any kind.

"Here!" Jeremy managed, waving just once, but it hurt too much to stretch those particular muscles, and he quickly brought his hand down. Fiery pain raced the length of his arm. "I'm alive. At least I think I am! Are you alive, too?"

The man covered the last few feet quickly and came to a halt, looking down on Jeremy at last. "Of course I'm alive. But Mother and I were worried to death when we saw somebody had gone off the road that they might not be." The man took a cell phone out of his pocket and quickly punched up a number. "Ah, good deal. Cell works down here, too!" Then, "Good news, Mother. There's a youngster alive out here. Injuries don't seem too awful bad from what I can see. Bring down a blanket and the first-aid kit right away."

Jeremy completely ignored what the man was saying as something broke through the pain in his head. "That *M* stands for Michigan, right?"

"It does for a fact. Go Blue!" There was a brief pause and then came the recognition. "Oh, and you probably heard Mother playing the fight song CD up in the Winnebago. She's got it on a loop. She gets in the mood every now and then while we're traveling around, don'tcha know? She doesn't hear as well as she used to, either, so she turns it up real loud. First thing when we get back home after this trip down to New Orleens, I'm getting her an appointment with Dr. Brady. Oh, I believe I see her heading over to us right now."

For some reason, Jeremy just had to criticize the man's pronunciation. "It's New OR-lyuns, not New Orleens."

"Is it?" the man said, cocking his head. "Mother and I have never been there. We can't wait to tour the French Quarters."

Jeremy continued in his correcting mode. "Just one Quarter down there."

"Beg pardon?"

"Never mind." Jeremy's brain told him to switch subjects. "What do you call people from Michigan?"

"Michiganders," came the reply. "It's a lulu of a name, I'll be the first one to admit."

"I thought I was right about that. So those are your headlights that had me so mesmerized and thinking of other dimensions up there on the road? That's not the white light everybody's on the lookout for there at the end? You're just that couple I got behind somewhere back in Tennessee?"

"Afraid Mother and I don't hold the secrets to the universe," the man said, breaking into subdued laughter. "Yep, those are just our high beams up there. They're quite powerful, though, and we wanted to be sure we got a good look around. We're partially blocking traffic the way we've got our big Winnebago angled up there, but who cares about that? Someone's bound to be here soon to direct traffic around us. Mother's punched up the park ranger's number, too. But never mind all that. Thank God, you survived."

Jeremy made a feeble attempt to get to his feet, but the man quickly nixed it, pushing him back down as gently as possible. "No, no, son, don't move. You're to lie back and lie still. Mother's already got an ambulance on the way. You best stay put until the paramedics arrive. They say you can do some severe damage to yourself by shifting around like that. Something may very well be broken, and you don't want to make it worse."

"I've got a sneaking suspicion I have a broken rib. I hope not more than one, though," Jeremy told him. "Can you shine your flashlight on my head and tell me what it looks like?"

The man complied and made an unpleasant face, shaking his head. "Doesn't look pretty up there right now, son. Matted hair and blood mostly, don'tcha know. It's pretty much clotted, though. I'd know how to stop you from bleeding if it hadn't, though. Does your head hurt?"

"It did a little while ago. Seems a little better now."

"You just sit tight now. Oh, here's Mother to the rescue now."

Jeremy peered up at the woman, her gray hair pulled back severely in a bun. But the crow's feet around her eyes trumpeted her kind, always-smiling nature, and Jeremy began to feel he just might get out of this mess alive after all.

"Here's a blanket to keep you warm, young man," she told him, draping it over him. "It's a Michigan Wolverine blanket. Father and I here are big fans, as I guess you know by now."

"I do," Jeremy said.

She kept on smiling down at him tenderly, and there were moments when it felt like she was his mother and he was her little boy. "I'll just clean you up a bit until the paramedics get here. Just a few wet wipes and a little alcohol to remove some of this blood just below your hairline. Really, it's not that bad. You went off the road ahead of the right people, don'tcha know. First thing Father and I did after we retired and bought our Winnebago was to take a CPR and first-aid course. You never know what might happen out here on the open road."

While she fussed over him, the man began scouring the wreck with his flashlight. "I'm afraid your little car is totaled, son. What happened? Why'd you skid off the road like that? It hasn't been raining even the least little bit."

"A deer in a helluva hurry did me in." Jeremy decided to add nothing further, suddenly feeling weaker.

"I can certainly believe that. Why, Mother and I have seen maybe a dozen by the roadside since we got on the parkway just south of Nashville. And some wild turkeys, and even what looked like a wolf, but it may have just been a wild dog. Mother hasn't stopped with the camera all the way down."

Jeremy didn't feel much like talking now, as the Michigan fight song continued to play over and over in the background. But he felt he ought to say something every once in a while. "I like that Midwestern twang you both have. Very distinctive."

The man snickered. "Well, Mother and I like to hear you people speak Southern to us down here. We get the biggest kick out of it. We especially like all those 'you alls' we've received everywhere we go—in all the restaurants, gas stations, rest stops, you name it."

"Yeah, I guess we're famous for that," he managed. Then he was frowning. "I guess we haven't introduced ourselves yet. I'm Jeremy McShay from Nashville, Tennessee."

"Pleased to meet you, Jeremy. Though I wish the circumstances were different," the woman said, continuing her clean-up duties. "And we're Darlene and Malcolm Hayes of Battle Creek, Michigan."

A terrible weakness suddenly engulfed Jeremy's entire body, and he was unable to focus in on too much more. Just that last line from the Michigan fight song—*"Hail! Hail! to Michigan / The champions of the West!"*—along with the distinctive but distant wail of a siren.

Then everything went dark.

Maura Beth felt so guilty she could hardly stand it. "Here I was, so mad at Jeremy because he didn't show at the meeting tonight, and now I find out he was doing his best to get down here to Cherico. I'm being punished for such mean-spirited thoughts, I just know," she told Connie and Douglas as she began to tear up.

The three of them were standing just outside Jeremy's hospital room on the second floor of Cherico Memorial, and the McShays had just told Maura Beth everything they'd learned from the visit with their nephew and his doctor. "Don't be ridiculous. No such thing is happening," Connie said, giving her a hug and a few pats on the back. "It's wrong to even think such thoughts."

"She's right, you know," Douglas added, nodding sympathetically. "You need to lighten up a little. This isn't the time for second-guessing yourself."

Maura Beth was sniffling now. "Well, you just ask Periwinkle what I said to her after the review tonight. I couldn't have been bothered with giving Jeremy the benefit of the doubt. Oh, no, not me!"

Connie pulled away and gave Maura Beth her sternest glare. "You are not going to help Jeremy one bit if you go in there and break down in front of him. Just be thankful he's basically walked away from this with only a mild concussion and one fractured rib. From the looks of his car, they say it could have been much, much worse."

Maura Beth looked skeptical. "Who are *they?*"

Douglas stepped in at that point. "Dr. Tillman said the state trooper, or the park ranger or the paramedics, I forget which—anyway, somebody said that the driver of that car shouldn't have survived at all. But somehow Jeremy did. That could be a sign, you know."

"There were angels on his shoulders," Connie added. "And they're probably looking after you, too. So stop beating yourself up. Stand up tall, march straight in there, and the two of you get things back on track. That's what you want, isn't it?"

Maura Beth wiped her eyes with the back of her hand and then a smile broke through. "I didn't realize how much until you called and told me what had happened tonight."

"You just hold on to that, then," Connie said. "You lift his spirits, and you'll be lifting yours at the same time."

Maura Beth gave them both her best smile, pointing to it with her index finger. "How does this look?"

"Dazzlingly white," Connie told her. "And no spinach between your teeth. Now, go on in there. You channel Scarlett and Melanie together the way only you can. And don't forget to give Jeremy that little gift from those lovely people."

"Thanks, you two."

Indeed, when Maura Beth walked into Jeremy's room, she noted with great relief that he did not look particularly compromised. There was a big bandage on his head, and he was hooked up to the usual equipment monitoring his vital signs, but it was clear that the car and not Jeremy himself had suffered most of the severe damage.

"Here I am," she called out softly, after closing the door behind her. "Maura Beth Mayhew, reporting for duty."

"Don't say anything that'll make me laugh," he said, flashing a smile her way. "I have this rib issue, you know."

She moved to his bedside where she let go of a giggle or two. "So I've been told. I hope you're not in too much discomfort."

"Only when I breathe."

Maura Beth's expression went from sunny to taken aback. "I hope you're just kidding."

"I am. Kinda."

She decided to confront everything head-on, but with a bit of humor thrown in for good measure. "I hear Christmas came early out there on the historic Natchez Trace Parkway."

He took a moment and then shrugged faintly. "You mean the deer? No, I don't think it was a reindeer trying out for Santa's sleigh. But it did fly through the air, and that's why I swerved off the road and landed in the woods." He made the smallest of gestures with his index finger. "Why don't you relax and sit down? I assume you aren't in a hurry."

"I was told not to tire you out, though," she said, pulling up a nearby chair. "You do have some healing to do."

"I promise to let you know if I feel like I'm fading."

She was gathering her thoughts now, trying to get everything just right. "I just wanted you to know . . . that I appreciate the effort you made to come to the *Forrest Gump* review. You were thinking about us, after all, and that means a lot to me. It was practically just as good as you being there."

"About that. I feel the need to apologize—" he began, but she wouldn't let him continue.

"No, I don't want this visit to be about that fallout we had. Let's just put it behind us. You eventually made the decision to attend, and except for that crazed deer, you would have been there in my library a few hours ago saying whatever it was you planned to say. Right now, just the image of that makes me very happy."

"You're very easy to please," he said. "Especially when I was very definitely in the wrong."

She wagged a finger. "No, no. None of that." The conversation lapsed for a while, but then she said, "Have you made a decision yet about your job at New Gallatin Academy?"

"I thought I had when I left my house this afternoon," he told her. "I was determined to stick it out with Yelverton at the helm." Then he started frowning, turning away from her slightly. "After this wreck, I'm not so sure. It's going to be hard for us to make this relationship work with us living so far apart, no matter how smoothly my job is going at New Gallatin." He managed a short, forced laugh, obviously restrained by his rib injury. "I mean, we can't go on meeting like this."

Maura Beth's laugh, however, was unrestrained. "You're so right, and I adore your sense of humor at a time like this."

"Gotta have one these days," he said. "But lying here in bed, I've been thinking that I have a darned good résumé. I'm no ordinary, rote teacher. Besides, New Gallatin Academy isn't the only school on the face of the planet. Rumor has it that they even have schools down here in Mississippi."

"I've heard the same thing." Maura Beth could feel the excitement rising inside of her. "Are you saying that you'd be willing to look for a job down here? Right here in little bitty Cherico? Or as the locals like to call it, Greater Cherico?"

He turned back toward her and raised an eyebrow. "I might. But it would depend on what's available. Teaching jobs are often a matter of timing, you know."

She reached over and patted his hand gently. "But you will let me know if there's anything I can do at any time to help?"

"Of course."

Then she remembered. She dug down into her purse, making all sorts of muted noises moving things around. "I have a present for you."

"Aw, you shouldn't have."

"I didn't," she said. She produced a CD, holding it up so he could see what it was all about.

"The University of Michigan Spirit Package," he said, his face lighting up immediately. "Cheers and Fight Songs." He gave Maura Beth a quick wink and then read the neatly printed message on the Post-it note attached: *"Get well soon— Darlene and Malcolm Hayes. Go Blue!"*

She nodded eagerly. "Your Aunt Connie said they stayed until you were transferred from the ER. They wanted to be sure you were okay. Then they had to be on their way. Something about not falling too far behind on their trip to New Orleans. They gave Connie this CD and told her it was something for you to remember them by, and she thought maybe I ought to be the one to give it to you."

"I wish they'd stayed a little longer," he said, the emotion clearly registering in his voice. "It's possible I owe them my life. I might have died of shock out there if they hadn't come along in their Winnebago."

He took the CD from her and brought it closer to his face. "I'll certainly never hear the Michigan Fight Song again without thinking of them. They'll always be heroes in my heart."

12

Here Today, Gone Tomorrow

Becca and her Stout Fella were having their usual breakfast of cereal, yogurt, and orange juice at the kitchen table. Without warning, Becca loudly chimed her spoon on her water glass several times, causing Justin to start noticeably and some of his Raisin Bran to go down the wrong pipe. He coughed a few times, his face turning pink. This was followed by an improvised ritual of alternating sips of water with vigorously trying to clear his throat.

"You all right?" she asked, but she hardly sounded concerned.

He was nodding and scowling at the same time. "What the hell did you do that for, Becca?"

"Sorry, I didn't mean for that to happen." She was not about to leave it at that, however. "Justin, I want to talk to you about something very important. I thought that might get your attention, since I haven't been very successful at getting straight answers out of you these days."

He took yet another sip of water and exhaled. "Yeah, well, there are other ways of getting my attention besides causing me to nearly choke to death." He went back to eating his

Raisin Bran as if nothing had happened. For a while Becca was content to sit and watch. Finally, he couldn't take the staring any longer, looked up, and said, "What? What did you want to talk to me about? I'm not a mind reader."

She decided then and there not to back off as she had so often recently. She was going to tell him the truth. Then maybe he would level with her, and they would move on to some kind of understanding. "I wanted you to know that I went off the pill several months ago. I didn't tell you because . . . I want to get pregnant. I want us to start a family. It's way past the time we said we couldn't afford it. We've been riding high for years."

He put his spoon down and wiped the corners of his mouth with his napkin. "I see."

"That's all you have to say?"

He glanced at his watch and offered more of the same evasive behavior she had come to despise. "Could we talk about this another time? Winston Barkeley's coming by the office around nine o'clock to discuss the new lake plat. This is gonna be my biggest deal yet."

"Where have I heard that before?" she told him. "The last time you rushed off to see Winston Barkeley, you ordered a cup of coffee and the 'heart attack special' at The Twinkle. Slowly but surely, you're getting right back into that pattern of letting your job run you instead of the other way around." She brought her napkin up from her lap and haphazardly tossed it on the table so that it covered part of the bowl of cereal she had been picking at here and there. "Besides, my dear husband, I know we have a problem. Certainly one of us does."

He focused on the two pills he had carefully placed beside his water glass at the beginning of breakfast. One was small, pink, and round; the other was larger, oval-shaped, and white. He was now on their schedule. "Let me take these first."

She waited for him to finish with his medications and then

cut to the chase. "I should have gotten pregnant by now, Justin. Once we started having sex again, I know for a fact I was ovulating several times."

He stared her down and briefly gritted his teeth. "Okay, okay. You have a right to know. I was gonna tell you sooner or later, but this is not gonna be easy for me. We do need to clear the air, though, and I do want our marriage to work. I hope you believe me when I say that. I still love you, Becca. I always have."

It was the first time he had said anything of substance to her about their relationship in months, but she didn't like the sound of what was coming. It flashed into her head that perhaps she would be better off not knowing whatever it was. Then he dropped the bomb.

"I'm *afraid* to make love to you. There, I said it."

Becca sat stunned, wondering if she had heard him right.

"Say something, Becca."

"I . . . I don't know where to start." In truth, she didn't even know what he meant.

He filled up his big chest and exhaled. "It doesn't matter what Dr. Ligon says about what I can and can't do, or how the medications may affect me. It doesn't matter what anybody says, for that matter. The only thing that counts is, I'm afraid. I've been that way since I came home from Nashville last year. That first time after the angioplasty and I'd lost all that weight, I thought I might have another heart attack. Think about it from my point of view. The last thing I wanted to do was . . . well, to die on top of you. And that's the God's honest truth. After that first time when I didn't follow through, I didn't even want to try again. I kept putting you off, and that made you think maybe I was having an affair. But it wasn't anything like that. I'm a one-woman man. And then . . . and then lately, I've been—please don't laugh—I've been faking it." He was shrugging his shoulders and chuckling, but it all came off as forced and uncomfortable.

Becca immediately felt as if she were going to melt into a puddle of some kind. It would probably contain equal parts empathy, love, and understanding, and she wanted nothing more than for her Stout Fella to bathe himself in it and begin the process of healing. "Oh, Justin, why didn't you talk to me about this before now? You've been shutting me out, and that's done terrible things to my head. You don't live in a vacuum, you know. What do you think I'm here for? I'm your wife—for better or worse, remember?" She moved to him quickly, standing over him, and he rose to embrace her warmly. All the tension that had been generated between them recently seemed to break like a high fever that had run its course. Now, finally, things would cool back down to normal.

He pulled back, and she could see that he was visibly shaken. She had felt the trembling while they were embracing.

"Are you disgusted with me?" he said, hanging his head. "I guess I'm disgusted with myself."

"Of course I'm not, sweetheart. I truly understand. You just had no business keeping this to yourself. But now that it's out in the open, I'm sure we can get you back to the man I married. Have you told Dr. Ligon about this?"

He shook his head, trying his best not to bring forth his tears. But Becca could see clearly that he was on the verge.

"You must make an appointment and tell him about this, you know," she said. "I can't imagine he won't have some advice for you. Other men have surely gone through this kind of thing."

He sat back down, but Becca remained standing, massaging his shoulder while he let everything out. "Just the other day, Doug and I were having drinks out at The Marina Bar and Grill. He told me about Maura Beth's boyfriend, that teacher fella from Nashville who was in that bad wreck on the Natchez Trace. Doug said he was told by somebody at the hospital that no way should that guy have walked away from it alive. Said they still don't know how he managed it. I guess it was meant to be. But on the way home I thought I was having a panic attack when I kept thinking about that wreck. I just couldn't let go of it."

Becca stopped her massaging for a moment and frowned. "Yes, I know about the accident. Connie told me over the phone, and I've talked to Maura Beth, too. She says Jeremy's doing just fine now. He'll be out of the hospital soon. But what does all that have to do with you?" Justin looked up at her with sad, puppy eyes, and it nearly took her breath away. "Why did that bother you so much?"

"Don't you see," he told her, turning away. "That fella could've been gone just like that. A snap of the finger, and he's no longer walking the earth. And then I thought about myself. I could be here today, gone tomorrow—just doing an ordinary thing like making love to you. That's how messed up I've gotten."

She leaned down and softly kissed his cheek. "It's out in the open now. And you listen to me, Justin Brachle, you're not going anywhere anytime soon. You're going to stay right here with me, and we'll raise a wonderful family together before it's all said and done."

He managed a genuine smile, and she was pleased that she had coaxed it out of him.

"You promise?" he said.

She started talking out of the side of her mouth, sounding like a character from an old black-and-white gangster movie. "You just stick with Becca Broccoli, kiddo, and you'll be in high cotton!"

"The profession is just nothing like it was when I first started teaching way back when," Miss Voncille was saying, clucking her tongue. She and Maura Beth were enjoying coffee and her famous biscuits with green pepper jelly in her bright yellow breakfast nook. "We were dedicated to our craft when I was coming along. Until I fell in love with Frank Gibbons, there was nothing else in the world I thought I would rather do than teach history. At least I can say I had that to fall back on when my personal life didn't work out the way I wanted."

Maura Beth drained the last of her coffee and gestured broadly. "All the book club members you taught swear by you."

Miss Voncille leaned in with an air of confidentiality. "As well they should. Although Durden Sparks probably doesn't. He was the most conceited boy I ever taught. He never wanted others to win or be the best at anything. Oh, no—that was his exclusive bailiwick. And he's just carried that conceit into adulthood. Of course, I'll admit it. With those looks, he should have gone to Hollywood and gotten his name in lights as a leading man. But as for me, there's nothing phonier than false modesty, so I'll take full credit for at least a smidgen of the success all my pupils have enjoyed."

"My friend Jeremy McShay feels the same way you did about teaching," Maura Beth said, artfully switching the focus of their conversation. "It's a special mission to him. We all saw that demonstrated when he brought those bright students of his down with him from Nashville for the *To Kill a Mockingbird* review. Why, the poem that Burke Williams recited for us nearly had me in tears!"

Never slow on the uptake, Miss Voncille raised an eyebrow smartly as she split open another biscuit and slathered both halves with butter and green pepper jelly. "So I gather Mr. McShay is the reason for this little get-together of ours you requested. Over the phone you said it had something to do with teaching, but I'm guessing there's a little something more involved here." Then she pointed to the biscuit she had just fixed up so expertly. "How about I take the bottom and you take the top?"

"No, thank you, really I couldn't. The two I've already had are more than enough. But you're correct about Jeremy. He and I have become an item, at least in our own minds."

"That's a very clever way of describing it," Miss Voncille said, touching a finger to her temple. "You both have to get to the same place at the same time, and that's not always the easiest thing to pull off. Locke and I are working on that right now. Well, to tell the truth, I'm doing most of the work. I'm slowly letting it dawn on him that he simply has to marry me. I've been pulling out all the stops."

Maura Beth laughed, raising her coffee cup in tribute. "Good for you. Is he almost there?"

"Almost, but I've still got to close the deal."

"Don't let him get away, now," Maura Beth added with a wink. "Meanwhile, I have something you might be able to help me with regarding Jeremy. He's thinking about giving up his teaching position in Nashville and trying to get one down here in Cherico—or at least reasonably near. Do you still stay in touch with your contacts at Cherico High?"

Miss Voncille's sigh was accompanied by a distinct sadness around her eyes. "It's getting harder and harder. Many of the friends I started out with have died, and others have retired and moved away. But I still keep in touch with a couple. Mainly, Johnnie-Dell Crews. She's a few years younger than I am, but this may be her last year." Miss Voncille began counting on her fingers but soon threw her hands up.

"Oh, I forget how long she has to go. Of course, she doesn't realize it yet, but she's not going to know what to do with herself. She'll miss telling people what to do all day. She won't be able to grade them anymore, and there's so much behavior out there today that desperately needs grading. If it were up to me,

I'd flunk most people for their appearance in public alone. The way they dress, the careless language they use. I'm honest enough to admit that I missed all the regimentation of dividing the day into neat little periods of activity. Spontaneity? I had no use for it. Fortunately, my interest in genealogy saved me. My brain just lapped up all those deeds and records and such." She gave a little gasp as she noticed Maura Beth's empty cup. "More coffee?"

Maura Beth nodded and waited for the refill before she spoke. "About Mrs. Crews. Would she be in a position to know about any openings?"

Miss Voncille's reaction was emphatic. "Indeed, she would. She knows as much about Cherico High as I do about the history of Cherico. You should hear how she goes on and on about the young teachers nowadays. But she's right, you know. These sweet-talking young things out of college aren't looking for a career like Johnnie-Dell and I were. So many of them get married after a year or two, and then there's another group who are already married who get pregnant and have to go on maternity leave. Many never come back. It was a lifelong commitment for us, but now . . . they're just here today, gone tomorrow."

"Well, I know Jeremy would stick around if he got a job there. He'd bring so much to the position, too. Maybe Mrs. Crews could let you know if something opens up."

There was a gleam in Miss Voncille's eye that was difficult to ignore. Whenever people saw it, they knew she meant business. "I'm sure she'd be delighted to help. Both of us were all for stability on the faculty, but we rarely seemed to achieve it."

"Maybe we can do something about that by rounding up a dedicated teacher for Cherico High," Maura Beth said.

Miss Voncille seemed lost in thought for a few moments but quickly perked up. "Looks like we both have deals to close.

Meanwhile, Johnnie-Dell should know something in May. That's usually when we found out who was coming back and who wasn't."

"Maybe right around the time of our *All the King's Men* review?"

Miss Voncille nodded triumphantly. "I've got Locke on the same timetable. Let's have a little toast, shall we?"

The two women hoisted their coffee cups and clinked rims. "To sisters in quest of that elusive nest!" Miss Voncille proposed. "And may our men come home to their hot mamas where they belong!"

13

Stark Realities

It had been months since Maura Beth had spoken with Councilman Sparks or seen him in person. It hardly meant he had been out of mind, however. But suddenly, with the book club's *All the King's Men* review just a couple of days away, he had summoned her to his office to discuss "something important." As had always been the case regarding these impromptu City Hall meetings, Maura Beth was nervous, fearing the worst. But she no longer felt rudderless while sailing upstream against Cherico's political tides.

"I wanted to ask you about your choice of Robert Penn Warren's novel for The Cherry Cola Book Club," he began, once she had seated herself across from him in his office. "Evie and I picked up your flyer at The Twinkle last time we ate there." He brandished the sheet of paper that had been lying on his desk and then let it slip from his fingers. They both watched it slowly flutter to the blotter below. "All this flyer prose you've concocted about discussing political intrigue and corruption and untimely death seems thinly veiled to me." He leaned in threateningly. "I am not—I repeat—*not* Governor Willie Stark. So you can cut out the wishful thinking, and if you and that Cherry Cola Book Club gang of yours are hatching fevered plans to assassinate me on the steps of City Hall, you can forget it."

"I would have to say you're reading between the lines, then," Maura Beth answered, not about to be intimidated. But she was trying for levity. "That is, of course, if you'll pardon the pun."

He smirked. "Clever. You've always had that going for you." Then he reached down to open one of his desk drawers and retrieved a copy of *All the King's Men,* tossing it carelessly on the desk with a thud. "I suppose you think you can rouse the rabble again with this? Will you storm my castle on Perry Street with torches?"

"May I see that for a moment, please?" she said, ignoring his absurd comments.

He handed it over, and she started reading barely a few pages in, enunciating her words with great precision: *"This is a work of fiction. Names, characters, places, and incidents either are the product of the author's imagination, or are used fictitiously, and any resemblance to actual persons, living or dead, businesses, companies, events, or locales is entirely coincidental."* She snapped the book shut and handed it back to him. "I think that should put an end to what sounds like an absurd case of paranoia to me."

Councilman Sparks leaned back in his chair, once again indulging his smugness. "Miz Mayhew, we're close to halfway through the year, and the best thing I can say about your little library is that you're holding your own. But not much else. All those hundreds of people you whipped up into a frenzy with your petitions last year seem to have settled back down to reality. If they were so all-fired intent on using the library, then why haven't they? I've been monitoring everything like I said I would—circulation figures, meeting room use, and the rest—and it looks very much to me like you have that same small but loyal core of library fans actually coming in. But it's nowhere near the number you got to sign your petitions in that 'let's do something trendy' maneuver you pulled off. Today's voters can be manipulated so easily. I ought to know."

Maura Beth was about to rebut him when the intensity in his face hardened further into a mask of hostility. She had never witnessed such a frightening transformation in her life, and it caused her to pull back at once.

"I want you to realize one thing," he said, the pronounced softness of his tone somehow making his words that much more threatening. "You embarrassed me at the budget hearing back in November. You forced me to do something I didn't want to do in front of a big chunk of my constituency, and I'm not going to forget that. The kid gloves are off. The last time somebody did something like that to me was during middle school right here in Cherico. Miss Voncille Nettles started refusing to choose me when I raised my hand because she knew I always had the right answers to everything. It was her silent way of calling me out, and she never let up. You found a different way to do the same thing last year, and so I want you to know that you're on notice. The library's one-year reprieve was just that. And since you also turned down my offer to keep yourself gainfully employed here in Cherico by working for me, I'd be getting my résumé together if I were you. For the last time, forewarned is forearmed, Miz Mayhew!"

Maura Beth was stunned. Talk about the fury of women scorned! The restrained anger of men was something more breathtaking to behold by far, especially when they held superior positions of power.

Since she couldn't think of a syllable to utter, he continued his quiet little rant while staring her down. "I know you think you're on some kind of elite literary mission with that feel-good club of yours, but, really, what does that have to do with the stark realities of living? Chatting smartly about books while swapping recipes doesn't put food on the table every day, and it doesn't even come close to paying the rent or the car note. This town needs jobs and new businesses coming in so that people don't have to scrape by the way some of them are having to do. Okay, so maybe that does kinda make me a populist like Willie Stark. But my mission is taking care of Cherico, and one way or another, the Charles Durden Sparks Industrial Park is going to get up and running."

For the first time ever in her dealings with Councilman Sparks, Maura Beth had no quick response. She realized she wasn't any better off than she had been a year ago, when he had first revealed to her his complete and utter disdain for the library. He was, in fact, just toying with her until he got what he wanted.

Somehow Maura Beth managed to gather herself enough to say something—anything. "Was that all you had to tell me today?" Her tone sounded casual, but she swallowed hard afterward, and that gave her away.

"I think that's it for now."

She rose and headed for the door, her heart racing. "I'll see myself out, then."

"Yes, you do just that," he said, getting in the last word.

Connie walked into the great room to find Douglas sitting on the sofa in front of the fireplace rifling through the pages of *All the King's Men*. It seemed all the more peculiar since both of them had finished the novel over a week ago.

"What on earth are you up to at that frantic pace?"

He looked up, slightly startled. "Oh, I was trying to find a passage that's been on my mind."

She sat down beside him and watched as he continued his diligent scanning, using both his eyes and index finger. "What was it? Maybe I can help."

"Something that Willie Stark said." He kept on flipping pages. "I can't find it now. I should have bookmarked it."

Momentarily, he pounced upon it with a "Gotcha!"—pressing his finger to the spot as if he had just squashed a mosquito. He settled back and smirked. "The gist of what's on this page is you gotta find a way to make the best of bad situations. That's all anyone's got."

Connie waited for more, but Douglas apparently had finished. He was looking at her now with an intensity she had observed only occasionally in their many years of marriage. "Yes," she said finally. "I remember him saying that. He was just trying to justify everything he did, all the corners he was cutting in politics. At least, that's what I got out of it. I'm sure Maura Beth will want you to bring that up in our discussion. Good for you."

He closed the book slowly and stared into the small fire he had thrown together to take the chill out of the room. "Forget the discussion, Connie. It hit home. Here's this Willie Stark character summing up his career, and it could be me saying things like that about myself."

Connie had heard similar versions of her husband's introspection for some time now. He would return to them every so often, and her strategy had always been to listen quietly and be as supportive as possible until the latest crisis had passed. "*All the King's Men* is a great novel, so I'm not surprised you found yourself relating to it. It's appealed to millions over the years. You never know when a writer's work will reach out and shake hands with you like an old friend. I don't know how many times I've found myself thinking, 'Now that's just what I've been trying to say.' "

Her efforts to lighten things up fell flat, however. "I can never do enough fishing to clear my conscience." He spoke with no emotion in his voice, and he seemed incapable of turning away from the fire and facing his wife.

"Douglas, it was just the nature of your profession. You did the best you could," she said, trying to rouse him.

He indulged a crooked little smile. "I did pretty damned well, and you know it. For example, I earned the money to build this lodge for us when I proved that Mrs. Edna Hessmer's fortune in silver and antique furniture had been irreparably damaged by the environmental discharge from the Baker City, Tennessee, paper mill exactly ten and a half miles from her house. At least that's my 'trial lawyer-ese summation' version of it. I should never have taken that case. The reality was—it was essentially frivolous."

"Why should you feel bad about that, Doug? Would we have this house if you hadn't taken the case? You presented the evidence, and it held up. As they say, case closed."

His peculiar smile expanded right alongside the skepticism and disdain in his voice. "The connection was tenuous at best. I knew it. Everybody knew it. It was the terrible smell certain people in Baker City really objected to. Of course, what paper mill doesn't stink to high heaven? But I took the case anyway. The truth was, Edna Hessmer was a rich, crotchety old widow with denture breath who didn't care about a living soul but herself, and that judgment against the paper mill ended up putting it out of business eventually. Down the road, hard-working people lost their jobs, and I walked away with the spoils. To turn what Willie Stark preached on its head, you might say I made something bad out of good."

Connie knew it was useless when Douglas veered into "career revisited" mode. His second-guessing just had to run its course. But she continued to try and pull him out of it anyway. "If we're going to play worst-case scenario here, I'll take a shot. You had to make lots of tough decisions as part of the legal profession, same as we always did at the hospital. The difference was, when you weren't up to snuff, someone might lose some money or property or something like that. When we made the wrong decision at the hospital, God forbid, somebody might die. Try to put things in perspective."

His features finally softened as he turned her way. "Most of the time I've managed to do that, or I couldn't live with myself. But lately, while I'm out there on the water just floating around without a care in the world, I keep thinking I should make something good out of bad, like Willie Stark, now that my finagling days are over And, no, fishing on the lake doesn't qualify by a mile."

"Then what would?"

He inched closer to her, and she felt the chill of his hand atop hers. It might be May with a bright, balmy day outside and everything in bloom within view of the great room windows, but inside the drafty lodge, the fireplace had been unable to get its self-doubting owner's blood moving sufficiently.

"We have more money than we'll ever need," he said finally. "This is our home now. Maybe we can help Cherico in a significant way."

Something suddenly clicked in Connie's head and she freed her hand, gesturing with it dramatically. "I think you may finally have said something that makes sense. Haven't you had enough of looking back? Think of our future right here on the lake."

He rose from the sofa and moved closer to the fireplace, vigorously rubbing his hands together. "That's just what I intend to do, even though I haven't worked out the details. But when I do, you'll be the first to know."

Connie joined him fireside and put her arm around his waist. "I can't wait to hear what you come up with. Especially if it's something we can do together."

★   ★   ★

Evie Sparks and her pampered poodle, Bonjour Cheri, greeted the alpha man in their lives at the kitchen door of their Perry Street residence. Both of them were all over him, in a manner of speaking, so much so that he often found himself addressing them as a package when he came home from work. There were even times when he petted them reflexively on their clipped heads the same way.

"And how are my two pretty girls tonight? Did we have a good day?" Councilman Sparks said, throwing his keys on the kitchen counter with a clatter.

Bonjour Cheri offered up a couple of lively barks, as if she understood exactly what he was saying, while Evie gave him her usual wifely attention. "Here's your scotch and soda," she said, handing him the drink she had just made at the wet bar. "Then we're having takeout from The Twinkle. It's warming in the oven right now. I went with Periwinkle's rosemary chicken and new potatoes tonight, and there's a slice of Mr. Parker Place's Mississippi mud pie for you if you have room. I know you keep telling me to go easy on the desserts, but I thought if either one of us had a sweet tooth, what would be the harm?"

He pursed his lips and made a cursory smooching sound as he headed toward his easy chair in what they both referred to as the "entertainment room." Its crown jewel was the latest, widest, and thinnest HDTV set on the market, affixed to the wall with stereo speakers strategically placed for theater quality sound. There was also a handsome mahogany spinet in the corner of the room that Evie only occasionally played for her own enjoyment. She would have been the first to admit, however, that she was not very good at it and had a repertoire consisting of a handful of forgettable ditties she had learned as a teenager from her piano teacher. Bonjour Cheri, in fact, became very agitated and started whimpering whenever her mommy started missing sharps and flats right and left. Needless to say, Evie never trotted out her talents when she and her husband entertained guests of any kind.

"I laid it all out for Maura Beth Mayhew this afternoon," Councilman Sparks said after a few sips of his drink. "I let her know once and for all that she and her library won't wiggle off the hook this time."

Evie was curled up on the nearby sofa, petting Bonjour Cheri, who had nestled against her and was staring up adoringly at her mommy. "And how did she react to that?"

"I think she was in a state of shock. At any rate, she ducked out with her tail between her legs. She usually has some smart-aleck response ready, but not this time around."

Evie shot him a look of consternation. "Why don't you just shut the library down and get it over with, then? Do you really have to honor that one-year reprieve? After all, you call the shots in Cherico."

He rattled his ice cubes and scowled. "I have to go through the motions because of what happened at the budget hearings in front of all those voters. But I let her know she was on my list and also what I thought of *All the King's Men* as her book club's next read. She vehemently denied any ulterior motives, of course, but I think she'd like nothing better than for the entire town of Cherico to think their local politicos are rotten to the core. I'll bet you anything they end up discussing something scandalous along those lines."

"Why would they ever think that?" Evie said, looking down at Bonjour Cheri and making precious noises to her after she had posed the question. "Look how many times you and Chunky and Gopher Joe have been reelected. No one's come close to unseating any of you."

Councilman Sparks finished off his drink and set the delicate crystal tumbler down forcefully on the nearby end table.

A little harder and it might have cracked. "Miz Mayhew has her lovely red head buried in those library books all the time. She doesn't deal in the complexities of government the way I do. She's made a crusade of her career here in Cherico, and this town's entirely the wrong place to do it. Whether she realizes it or not, she's interfering with my legacy, and I just won't tolerate it. When my time comes, I will not be buried beside my father without leaving my stamp on this town. I want future Chericoans to know I passed this way and did some good!"

Evie stopped petting the dog as the anger level rose in his voice, and she caught his gaze. "When you get this agitated, it really makes me wish things were . . . you know . . . different for us. Maybe you wouldn't get as worked up as you do if everything wasn't so bound up in your job."

He had no intention of getting into such a painful discussion yet again. "Look, I've made my peace with it. Why do you have to bring it up this way?"

"I'm not trying to hurt you deliberately, Durden. God knows, I don't like thinking about it any more than you do," she told him. "I just don't like to see you getting so upset this way. These days it doesn't seem to take much to get you to explode."

"Look, let's eat," he said, determined to change the subject. "I didn't have much of a lunch today. I'm hungry for some of that Twinkle you brought us."

At the dining room table, Councilman Sparks found himself enjoying Periwinkle's cuisine as usual. But it could not help him crowd out completely this latest reminder of the overriding disappointment of his life. He was sterile. That was the stark reality he could never avoid; that colored every decision he made or goal he set.

"We can always adopt," Evie had pointed out when they had first received the distressing news.

But the proud and accomplished Charles Durden Sparks would have none of it. Only his very own flesh and blood would be fit to inherit the political legacy his father and Layton Duddney had begun. Under no circumstances would there be an anonymous pretender to the throne.

14

Stormy Weather

It was an early Sunday afternoon in May, and Maura Beth, Renette Posey, and Emma Frost had just finished decorating the library lobby for the *All the King's Men* potluck and review that evening. As was now the custom for The Cherry Cola Book Club, three posters had been strategically placed around the room: one of Oscar winner Broderick Crawford as Willie Stark in the 1949 movie version of the novel; another of Oscar winner Mercedes McCambridge as Sadie Burke in the same film; and finally, a photo of the author, Robert Penn Warren, in later life, projecting an unmistakable air of gravitas.

"I think it's our best display yet, ladies," Maura Beth said to her front desk clerks, standing back to assess the arrangement from a distance.

"I don't know who any of those people are," Emma remarked. "But I do know those posters'll hold up nicely with all that cardboard we backed 'em up with."

"Yep, we make a good team," Maura Beth said just before giving Emma and Renette hugs and sending them home to rest up before the big event.

In truth, she had rushed things more than usual because

she wanted to be sure and reach Jeremy in time. Two calls each to his landline and cell phone had gone unanswered, but she had left messages. Considering his near disaster a couple of months earlier on the Natchez Trace, however, she was unwilling to take any chances. So she went into her office and tried once more.

When he finally picked up, she felt the relief spreading throughout her body. But it did not last long. "Where are you? Have you left Nashville yet?"

"I'm leaving in just a few minutes," he told her. "I should be there a little after four."

Then she returned to the messages she had left. "I just wanted to be sure you got those weather warnings. You need to get down here before six. That's when that awful front is supposed to come through Cherico."

"Hey, I've learned my lesson well," he said. "No more rushing around for me. And, yes, I was aware of the bad weather you're expecting down there tonight. But I expect to be safe and warm at your place in plenty of time."

"That's all I needed to hear. I love you, and you be careful now."

"I love you, too, Maurie. See you soon."

After they had hung up, she almost felt like waltzing around the library. She liked his new nickname for her. No one had ever called her anything but Maura Beth—which was fine, but there were times when it sounded a bit too formal. But they had taken things to another level during her visits to him in the hospital after the car wreck. They had talked about everything bedside the way they had when they had first met at his aunt Connie's lodge last fall.

She always entered the room with a homemade balloon bouquet, a touch that had worked beautifully for Becca and Justin when he had been hospitalized with his angioplasty up in Nashville last year. Now, it never failed to lift Jeremy's spirits, and their conversations soared from there.

"I want you to know how much your visits have meant to me," he told her the evening before his discharge. "And the messages on the balloons. You're very original, you know that?"

She tried to be nonchalant about it all but couldn't resist. "Okay, which was your favorite?"

He thought for a while and finally rewarded her with his best smile. "I'd have to say, 'All Volvos Go to Heaven.' That was bittersweet, but I really loved it. I'll really miss my little car when I get out, you know. I single-handedly rescued it from the junk pile and took it into the millennium by putting in a CD player, air-conditioning, you name it. Of course, there's my insurance that'll allow me to start all over with a vengeance."

The look she gave him was sly and saucy. "I have to admit that all the boys I had crushes on in high school were the ones who ran around in souped-up cars. Now, don't get me wrong. They weren't straight out of the cast of *Grease,* or anything like that. But there was something appealing about a guy who knew his way around under the hood of his car. And even something a little dangerous."

Jeremy took a long sip from his water glass and shrugged. "That's me. Good ole dangerous Jeremy. And don't ask me to explain my love for both literature and old cars. Except maybe that I have a fondness for classic things."

"There you go," Maura Beth said, feeling closer to him than she ever had before. "As a librarian, I'm rather eclectic myself." Then she had reached over and taken his hand as she often did during these bedside talks. Though the air-conditioned hospital room was cold, his hand was warm, and there was something else besides. She could sense the growing bond between them, the ease with which they just sat in silence smiling and knowing that the best was yet to come.

After his discharge, he had found the time to make a couple of trips down, during which he had not stayed with his Aunt Connie and Uncle Doug out at the lake. Instead, he had been introduced to the charms of her "many shades of purple" efficiency on Clover Street, and it had not taken Maura Beth long to realize that the heartbreak she had experienced at the hands of Al Broussard, Jr., during her LSU days was powerless to hurt her anymore. Jeremy McShay was definitely "the one."

That late-spring cold front roared down as predicted from Canada to terrorize the northern third of Mississippi, having no mercy on the Cherico landscape below during the early evening hours. Driving rain, swirling wind, and even a suggestion of hail sent young, yellow-green leaves flying about, many pasting themselves to doors and windows in haphazard artistic fashion. Meanwhile, umbrellas and raincoats offered scant protection from the raging elements as people scurried about trying to run their errands and conduct their daily business.

As a result, The Cherry Cola Book Club's review of *All the King's Men* was not particularly well-attended, but Jeremy's presence—without a scratch or bruise on him—gave Maura Beth all the incentive she needed to generate a lively discussion among her loyal cadre. Fortunately, she did not have to go out of her way to draw any parallels between Councilman Sparks and Governor Willie Stark to get things started. Those insights appeared front and center without prodding.

"After we both finished reading the novel, I told Connie that I thought Willie Stark and Durden Sparks were frequenting the same back rooms as part of their 'end justifies the means' ethic," Douglas McShay offered. "Seems like populism frequently ends in corruption."

Miss Voncille waved her hand at the other end of the front row. "I couldn't agree more. What happens to politicians when they get into office and stay there unchallenged year after year? My reading of *All the King's Men* suggested to me that Willie Stark had no quarrel with the liberties he took as governor because he had this cynical, almost 'original sin' view of humanity. He thought people didn't deserve any better than they got from what he doled out to them. I'd like to take issue with that view of life. I continue to believe there's something basically good about the human spirit. In my lifetime I've seen people go off to war and still try to hang on to that hopeful notion. What could be a greater test than that?"

It was the attractively dressed and coiffed Nora Duddney who answered Miss Voncille's observations. "I can't speak for soldiers, but I think the nature of politics may be the culprit here. I saw and heard more than you can ever imagine from my trusty secretarial station in Councilman Sparks's outer office. Sometimes the door to his inner office was left cracked a tad bit, and I was dismissed and forgotten as a piece of furniture while things were said and plots were thickened, so to speak."

Miss Voncille's eyes widened as if she had seen an apparition, but she managed a reply anyway. "I have to say, Miz Duddney, that your response is as eloquent as the prose we're reviewing here tonight. I'm surprised but delighted at the same time."

"Why, thank you, Miss Voncille," Nora said, nodding in her general direction.

"Everything and everyone is so tangled up emotionally in *All the King's Men*—Willie Stark, Jack Burden, Anne Stanton," Miss Voncille continued. "And, no, I don't think Robert Penn Warren was a fly on the wall during Governor Huey P. Long's administration. But I did some research, and I happen to know that he did teach at LSU before Huey Long was assassinated. Perhaps he was privy to certain rumors here and there."

Nora's face brightened. "I don't know about that, but I do know that I was a fly on the wall all the time I worked for Councilman Sparks."

"So what's the inside story on him?" Becca Broccoli Brachle asked. "Or are you not at liberty to tell us?"

"There's not much the rest of you don't already know," Nora answered without hesitation. "He comes from a political family that's been running Cherico for most of the time it's been incorporated. He believes that it's his God-given right to continue running things as he sees fit. That's the truth of the matter. Believe me, I've heard more than one person in this town refer to him as our very own banana republic dictator."

"I may have used that term myself," Maura Beth said, risking a smile. But she soon returned to her duties as review moderator from the podium. "As for the inspiration Robert Penn Warren may have taken from Huey P. Long's reign, it's well-known that the LSU football team was a pet project of The Kingfish. I received my library science degree from LSU nearly seven years ago, so I know what I'm talking about. The governor wanted to expand Tiger Stadium back in the thirties, but there was no money available at the time. But there was money dedicated to building more dormitories. So Huey Long's solution was to expand the stadium by literally squeezing dormitories between the support structures underneath. I imagine those were some noisy dorm rooms on Saturday nights in the fall. At any rate, there's your perfect illustration of the 'end justifies the means' proposition."

"One the LSU football fans could all cheer for, I imagine," Stout Fella said, while everyone appeared amused by the remark.

The very next instant, however, a deafening boom caused

the ancient, corrugated iron structure of The Cherico Library to shake from ceiling to floor. In fact, it would have been possible to count to "five-Mississippi" with gasps and shrieks for an accompaniment.

Maura Beth verbalized what everyone in the room was thinking. "That felt like it was right over our heads. I hope lightning didn't strike that worn-out roof!"

A couple of loud rumbles akin to an aftershock followed as some people cowered in their seats. "Just as long as we don't lose power!" Mamie Crumpton cried out. "Sister and I simply cannot stand being in the dark, can we?"

But for once Marydell Crumpton did not answer dutifully. Maura Beth could see that she was too terrified to utter her usual meek, "Yes."

Then, what Mamie Crumpton had greatly feared came upon them all. The library lights dimmed once, made a valiant attempt at recovery, but succumbed quickly the second time. There were more gasps and one-word exclamations as everyone was plunged into darkness, except for the illumination provided by various cell phones that emerged from pockets and purses.

Disjointed, overlapping snatches and snippets of conversation broke out everywhere. Sometimes the source was easy to identify, other times not so much.

"Sister dear, take my hand until the lights come back on."

"Do something, Maura Beth!"

"Are there any candles?"

"Was that an earthquake or a tornado?"

"Is there a fuse box we can get to?"

"Miz Mayhew, I'll see if I can get through to the power company on my cell."

"Thank you, Renette. I'll go get the flashlight from behind the desk!"

During a brief lull, there was welcome humor from a deep male voice. "Do ya think God didn't like our review?"

Miss Voncille's distinctive voice chuckled richly, joining an assortment of snickers and giggles. "Locke Marshall Linwood, did you just say that?"

"No, that was me—Harlan Lattimore!" came the reply.

Periwinkle's hearty laugh easily rose above the others. "I'm gonna have to give you a ten for that one, Harlan John!"

But the laughter soon gave way to silence in the darkness, and Maura Beth knew she had to make an executive decision sooner rather than later. "Folks, if we don't get our power back fairly soon, I think we're going to have to call it quits." If the lights had come on at that moment, everyone would have seen her shaking her head in disgust. "I don't know why we can't seem to have one of our reviews without some incident disrupting us. But while I have the chance, I want to thank each and every one of you for coming out in this terrible weather. You really are my literary troopers."

The next comment, however, was like a ray of light for Maura Beth. "Let's just hang on a little longer and see what happens, Maurie."

Maura Beth was staring through the darkness of the library lobby at Jeremy's carefully contrived, goofy face. It was hilarious to behold by any definition of the word, and she could hardly stop laughing. His eyes were crossed, and he was sticking his tongue out for additional effect. In short, he had transformed himself into the perfect clown, and she applauded him generously for his efforts.

"My turn again," she said, holding her hand out for the flashlight. "But I'm going to have to go some to outdo you now."

"Nah, I bet you can come up with something even more awesomely silly," he told her.

She took the flashlight from him and positioned it under her chin. Jeremy began laughing even before she had moved a muscle, and she feigned irritation. "But I haven't even done anything yet."

"The flashlight's done it for you, Maurie. You look sideshow freaky already."

But she wasn't about to settle for letting the flashlight do all the work. "How does this look?" She had just made an up-turned nose with her finger and snorted.

"Terrific," he said. "You're Petunia Pig with an attitude. I love it!"

Maura Beth removed the flashlight from under her chin and pointed it toward the front desk clock. "Well, enough of making third-grade faces. We've waited long enough. Let's just turn off all the switches so we won't spike the utility bill when the power does come back on. And don't you dare slip and injure that rib of yours again. We've just got you practically back to normal."

They went around together, shining the flashlight here and there, occasionally giggling like children having a grand adventure in the dark. All the others had left long ago, even though the rain and wind outside continued to batter the streets and buildings of Cherico.

"Think your place will have any juice yet?" Jeremy said as they headed toward the front door.

"I don't know. Renette could never get through to Cherico Power. Nobody could. Here, hold this," she said, handing over the flashlight while she prepared to lock up.

It was underneath the portico a few seconds later that Maura Beth thought of the perfect words for the romantic evening ahead of them. "Let's not worry about the power, though. I have plenty of scented purple candles at home to see us through the night."

He gave her a rousing kiss and then opened his big umbrella. "You wait here and I'll bring the car around. Doesn't look to me like this mess will be letting up anytime soon."

Maura Beth allowed the buzz from his kiss to settle down to her toes. What a pleasure it was to be going with a man who still believed in chivalry and treating a woman with respect in this generic day and age!

The instant Renette turned the key and walked through the front door of the library the next morning, she knew something was wrong. She couldn't put her finger on it, but she felt it. Once before in her young life, she had encountered a similar feeling. Just a month after she had moved into her first apartment last year, she had returned from a girls' night out to find that someone had broken in and stolen what few items of value she possessed: a TV set, a CD player, and, incredibly, a handful of loose change she always kept in a small crystal dish atop her bedroom dresser. She would never be able to forget the subtle feeling of being violated that seemed to hang in the air; she could almost sense the molecules of contemptuous air that someone had exhaled and left behind while robbing her blind.

She checked her watch and the front desk clock. They were in sync. Five minutes to nine and opening the library to the public. After receiving Maura Beth's call earlier, she knew she would be in charge for a little while.

"I'm running a tad bit late this morning," Maura Beth had told her. "But I should be there by nine-thirty."

As nine o'clock approached, however, Renette simply could not let go of the strange sensation that had greeted her a few minutes earlier. After checking the petty change drawer and finding it full, she decided to walk around the library, looking for signs of something else that might be amiss. At first she found nothing—to her great relief. The fiction and non-fiction stacks were neat and tidy, as were the periodical and newspaper racks. In fact, having been plunged into darkness, Maura Beth and Jeremy had not even bothered to move Broderick Crawford, Mercedes McCambridge, and Robert Penn Warren from their strategic positions around the room. Perhaps the famous trio had kept an eye on things, and she was just guilty of having an overactive imagination. Or maybe it was the fact that she hadn't slept well with the threatening sounds of the storm keeping her up.

Then she moved to the juvenile stacks toward the back of the building. What was that sound she was hearing? Something steady and annoying like a dripping faucet. She froze and gasped. There was water, water everywhere. It seemed to have poured in through several leaks in the ceiling above, inundating most of the children's collection and leaving huge puddles on the linoleum floor. Renette did not have an insurance adjuster's grasp of damage figures, but she knew The Cherico Library had suffered a serious blow. That unrelenting storm, particularly that thunder and lightning strike during last night's review, had left its calling card behind long after power had been restored.

Renette trudged back to the front desk and punched in Maura Beth's number, dreading having to be the bearer of such distressing news. More to the point: Was The Cherico Library ever going to catch a break?

Maura Beth and Renette sat across from each other in her library office trying to figure out what to do next. They had already made a makeshift sign and taped it to the front door: LIBRARY CLOSED DUE TO STORM DAMAGE, it read. Worst-case scenarios were now swirling around inside their heads, and Maura Beth, in particular, knew she had to go about this the right way with Councilman Sparks. Adding roof and floor damage to book replacement costs might not be something City Hall was willing to do at this stage of the game.

Maura Beth could just hear the pontificating councilman now: "I'm so sorry, Miz Mayhew, but the library has become an ever bigger drag on the budget than before. We just can't afford the deductibles. We're going to have to shut you down for good. This damage proves the building has outlived its usefulness."

"Makes you think Councilman Sparks and the weather are in cahoots," Renette said offhand, as if reading Maura Beth's mind.

"Here all day yesterday I was worried about the effect that storm might have on Jeremy and his travels, while I should have been thinking about this old wreck of a building taking it on the chin," Maura Beth answered.

"Speaking of Jeremy," Renette said, abruptly changing the subject, "are things still going well for you two?"

Maura Beth leaned in, lowering her voice as if afraid of being overheard. "He spent the night again, and it was nothing but wonderful. I'm not much of a kiss-and-tell person, but let me just say that Jeremy is everything I've ever wanted in a man. He truly has leaped out of page twenty-five of my LSU journal of hopes and dreams. The only thing bad about last night was he had to get up so early this morning to get back to Nashville. There I was at the front door at the crack of dawn, giving him a kiss and reminding him once again not to speed on the Natchez Trace on the way back. I couldn't help feeling a little antsy about it all. But he got me back good. He said, 'Thanks, Mom. I promise I will!' "

They both laughed, but the reality of the library damage quickly returned. "So, have you come up with a plan yet?" Renette said.

Maura Beth nodded with authority. "Yes, but I need some help to make sure I'm on the right track. And I know just the person to call."

And with that, she picked up the phone and dialed Nora Duddney's number.

15

The Second Time Around

Having removed and carefully disposed of her gum, Periwinkle walked into her lawyer's office with confidence, shook his
hand firmly, and took her seat across from him without hesitation, sitting straight up in her chair. The fact that she was on a
mission of some kind could clearly be discerned by any objective observer, and it was certainly not lost on Curtis L. Trickett, attorney-at-law.

"I could have dropped the receiver on the floor when you
told me what you wanted to talk about, Peri," he said, sitting
down and settling back at his desk.

"I bet you were thinking that if you lived to be a hundred,
you'd never understand us crazy women, huh? Or maybe you
thought I'd been struck by lightning in that terrible storm we
had last week and my brain was scrambled."

"Well, maybe I did for a second or two. But you're one of
Cherico's real success stories, so I have to begin by giving you
the benefit of the doubt." He folded his hands in his lap and
appeared to be mulling things over, while Periwinkle couldn't
help but notice that in the ten years she'd relied upon his ex-
pertise to obtain her divorce settlement from Harlan Lattimore, Curtis Trickett had seemingly not aged by a single skin

cell. He still had that healthy shock of brown hair that gave him an irresistibly collegiate, almost boyish look; then there were those delicious dimples that appeared magically whenever he smiled, which was often. He was, in fact, the definition of perpetual eye candy who just happened to have a University of Mississippi law diploma hanging on the wall behind him.

Well, it just wasn't fair. She had to go through the time-consuming fuss of having her hair dyed out at Cherico Tresses at annoyingly frequent intervals, not to mention slathering lotion on every part of her body she could reach every night just to maintain the illusion that forty hadn't recently come and gone. Men didn't know how easy they had it!

"Let me be honest with you, Peri," Curtis continued, trying to keep a smile on his face. "After all you went through with Harlan Lattimore, you say you're seriously thinking of marrying him again? I certainly didn't see this coming. I'm—well, I'm stunned."

"Don't be. He hasn't even asked me yet."

Curtis looked more perplexed than ever, as his dimples ran away and hid. "Then why are you here? Are you going to be the one to ask him?"

"No." She said it emphatically, as if he had just insulted her in some way.

He leaned back further and shrugged. "Okay, I give up. You talk and I'll just listen."

For the first time since she'd entered his office, Periwinkle relaxed enough to lean back in her chair. Then she exhaled dramatically. "I'm no trusting teenager anymore, Curtis. That's all I was when Harlan swept me off my feet years ago. He was my first, and I just thought he had the answers to everything. Over the past couple a' months, though, we've been seeing a lot of each other, and he says he's a changed man." She sat with that for a moment, realizing that what she had just told Curtis was the crux of her problem, and she needed to emphasize it.

"I want to believe all the pillow talk, and I have every reason to believe it so far. Harlan's everything he was the first time and more. I mean that in the good sense, of course. To be honest with you, I think he's gotten even more attractive over the years. But I'd like to think I'm older and wiser now. Well, there's no question about the older part."

They both chuckled softly, but Curtis didn't let her comment stand. "I think you look even better than you did ten years ago, Peri. Your success at The Twinkle is very becoming to you, and why shouldn't it be?"

She felt herself blushing and lightly touched her cheek with the tips of her fingers. "Thank you for saying so, Curtis. A woman always likes to hear compliments like that, and I do try hard at whatever I put my mind to. So that's what my visit to you is really about. You're right—I have had a lot of success with The Twinkle. I'm also smart enough to realize that our little Greater Cherico is a zero sum game when it comes to the restaurant business. Oh, our fast-food joints'll make it no matter what—I'm not talking about them, of course. But we're too small to keep everybody trying to be more upscale in the money."

Curtis arched his brows and gave her a sideways glance. "Has Harlan ever talked about how he's doing when he's with you? Do you think he has ulterior motives here?"

"No, we haven't discussed things the way you mean. But I'm reasonably sure The Twinkle has cut into The Marina Bar and Grill's business. Some of my customers have told me how they used to go out there by the lake to eat, but now they like my ambience and food better. I haven't tried to go after Harlan's business deliberately, but I'm pretty damned good at what I do. I know I've got the touch. For instance, business has been even better since I hired Mr. Parker Place as my pastry chef six months ago. We get all the 'sweet-toothers' now, as I like to call 'em. Plus, The Twinkle is right smack dab in the middle of town. A couple of my suppliers have also mentioned to me that I'm now their biggest customer here in Cherico by far. When I was Harlan's secretary and bookkeeper, he was practically the only game in town." She paused when she saw Curtis nodding his head.

"I think I see where this is headed."

She took a deep breath again. "Good. Because this time around, Curtis, I want to do the wise thing if Harlan and I do get hooked. I have too much to lose now. So if he asks me to marry him soon—which I think could happen the way things have heated up between us—I want to protect myself. I thought having you draw me up a prenuptial agreement would keep me happy in love and solvent at the same time. It'll also tell me everything I need to know about him truly being a changed man and all. Whaddaya think?"

Curtis leaned forward, cleared his throat, and rested his hands on his desk, looking every inch the most composed and successful attorney in Cherico. "I think you're very smart to think of it. And you're right—prenups sometimes thin out the pretenders in love. Or predators, as the case may be. As a practical matter, I'll need to know all the details of your restaurant business, take a look at your tax returns, personal property, and investments, of course, but I can draw up the document any way you like."

Periwinkle looked greatly relieved. "I want your deluxe agreement. That's my style, you know."

"I didn't doubt it for a second," Curtis said, his dimples returning full force.

"So you see—I'm not so hard to understand after all, am I? I want something, and I go for it. First time I saw Harlan Lattimore, I wanted him, and then I got him, along with a lot of heartache that I didn't see coming. He's been saying to me all along that if I'll just give him a second chance, I'll never regret it. Well, if he signs on the dotted line, I know I won't."

Curtis gave her a quick, sympathetic nod before adopting a somewhat fatherly tone. "Peri, have you thought about what you'll do if he refuses to go along with the agreement?"

"I'll cross that bridge when I come to it," she said, briefly averting her gaze. "But I'm a big girl—have been for a while now. I've bounced back before, and I'll do it again if I have to."

Locke Linwood was lying in his bed watching Miss Voncille sleeping beside him in the moonlight that had flooded the room. On such occasions, she became the mature angel of his dreams, and he was reminded of how completely she had transformed his life. After another session of their gentle love-making, they had cuddled for a while. It had not taken her long to drift off, but he had stayed in the afterglow moment a bit longer. Eventually, it had faded, and once again his thoughts had turned to the issue of marriage. The *All the King's Men* review and potluck had come and gone, and he had informally agreed to give Miss Voncille his decision by mid-May. He had actually been surprised that she had not pressed him before or after the library event. Then again, they had both been distracted by the loss of power that had greeted them at her house on Painter Street later that evening.

Since then, she had not brought up the subject even once, and he was beginning to feel a bit guilty. Of course, he knew why he kept postponing things. Her name was Pamela, and her portrait was hanging on the walls in the living room; her stunning, other-worldly letter was in the bookcase beside the portrait. Perhaps it all was mostly settled in his mind by now, but the same was not true of his heart.

Stealthily, Locke drew back the covers and swung his legs over the side of the bed, finding his fuzzy slippers right away. He slowly crept to his closet and threw on his robe, tying it loosely around his waist. He looked back once to see if Miss

Voncille was still asleep and observed the barely perceptible rise and fall of the sheet covering her body. All was well.

"Pleasant dreams," he whispered while blowing her a kiss.

Out in the living room, Locke stood in awe of Pamela's portrait. Here was another angel in the moonlight, one that had borne him children and provided financial security with her family fortune. He had held her hand at the altar at the beginning and again at the hospital on her deathbed at the end. How could Miss Voncille possibly compete with that?

He decided to speak to the portrait in whispers. "You look particularly beautiful tonight," he began. "Not to belabor the popular song, but moonlight really does become you."

It did not strike him as strange at all when the lovely features captured in oil came to life and whispered back. "Hello, Locke. Don't you have better things to do than stare at me in the middle of the night?"

He took her chastisement in stride. "Honestly, I didn't think you'd notice. Incidentally, how are you doing this?"

"We have our ways."

He frowned and blinked. "We?"

It had been a long time since he had enjoyed her gentle laugh, but suddenly there it was, surrounding and soothing him like a muted church organ playing communion music. "We—meaning those of us who are no longer with you physically."

Her answer made eminent good sense to him, so he proceeded. "Do you have a moment?"

Even though her arms had not been painted, he felt strongly that she was stretching them outside the frame even as she answered him. "Oh, God, yes. I've been up here for a lifetime just waiting for somebody to say something to me. And now, God bless you, here you are."

"You have to know I think about you all the time."

"I do. And I appreciate your thoughts so much. But speaking to you like this is so much better. I'm so much more than delicate pigments on canvas. There's real feeling running all through me. At least that's what I hear people saying about me all the time—'What feeling there is in that portrait!' they like to say."

Locke paused for a moment. He had to phrase this next part just right. "I wanted to ask you about Voncille. Specifically, how you felt about her being in the house . . . in our bed? She's there right now."

There was her special laugh again, and it put him at ease. "You already have the answer to that. I put it in my letter."

He took a step back, scratching his head. "Which reminds me, how did you figure things out so far ahead of time? Voncille and I continue to marvel at everything you put in there, especially everything you anticipated. There've been times when I've even thought of charging admission to let people read what you wrote."

"I see you've kept your sense of humor," she said, every brushstroke that composed her face lighting up.

"It's something everyone should keep in their pocket wherever they go, no matter what happens."

"Aptly put."

Then he wondered if he dared ask it. If anyone would know the answer, surely she would. "Do you know when I'll join you?"

For the first time during their surprising conversation, she appeared to hesitate. "Actually, I'm not at liberty to say. What I can tell you again is what I expressed in my letter. You have to go on living your life. Don't put anything on hold because of me. I'm just fine."

"You couldn't even give me a tiny hint of what comes next?" he said, sounding just like a little boy asking her to reveal what she'd given him for Christmas.

"Doesn't work that way, Locke. You have to do the living first."

He gave her a sly smile and took a deep breath. "You know, your eyes were what made me fall in love with you. I took one long look deep into them and thought you held the secrets to the universe."

Her colors almost seemed to be glowing now. "That's what I like best about this version of me, Locke. Who would have thought that a little paint and turpentine could capture a soul so well?" Then she bore into him with those eyes of hers. "Do you have everything you need from me now?"

"I think so."

"You can talk to me anytime, you know. As I said, your thoughts are nice, but any oil painting worth its burnt umber and alizarin crimson likes to have its brushstrokes tickled every now and then."

Miss Voncille's voice suddenly intervened. "Locke?"

"It's time for me to go," Pamela said. "Don't be a stranger now."

"Locke," Miss Voncille repeated, shaking his arm gently, "you're talking in your sleep."

Locke woke up and turned to see Miss Voncille sitting up in bed, smiling at him. "What?" he said, feeling completely disoriented.

"You were talking in your sleep, honey."

"Was I?"

"Umm-hmmm. Well, actually it was more like mumbling."

He sat up and looked around the moonlit room. "How about that?" Then he chuckled under his breath. "That was the damnedest dream I've ever had. I thought you were the one who was asleep, and at first I was watching you and then I got up out of bed and the craziest part was—"

He stopped in midsentence and smiled. Trying to describe

a crazy dream always made the dreamer sound even crazier. "Never mind," he continued. "I guess you had to be there." Then he inched closer to her and gave her a sweet, lingering kiss.

She pulled back in astonishment. "Locke, it was just wonderful tonight, but I don't think I'm ready for another round just yet, sweetie. We both need our rest."

He took her hand and kissed it. "Never mind all that. May I have your hand in marriage?"

She had been waiting far too long for the smile that broke across her face. Not even the most gifted portrait painter in the world could have done it justice. "I thought you'd never ask."

16

Damaged Goods

Maura Beth focused on the rhythmic whirring of the ceiling fan above her head. Barely audible, it was nonetheless just the element she needed to get her through the session. It would cocoon her ever so subtly, and they would be none the wiser that she was clinging to it for strength and courage.

Not quite a year ago, Maura Beth had endured the distressing ultimatum from Councilman Sparks and his underlings that had set her on an unending survival track for her little library. Now, here she stood again before the terrible trio in that same meeting room without a witness, taking yet another stab at keeping her head above water. This time, almost literally.

"I've had our insurance adjuster take these photos of the storm damage, gentlemen," she was saying, while passing around her handouts. "As you'll see, they clearly show the damage to the roof done by the lightning strike, and then all the water damage to the ceiling, the stacks, and the books in the children's area. Of course, I've included the floor in that corner of the building as well. I've also given you the adjuster's estimates, minus the deductibles. I'm sure you'll find everything on the up-and-up."

Maura Beth sat back down in her chair and waited for their reactions, occasionally gazing up at the ceiling fan to steady her nerves. What Chunky Badham and Gopher Joe Martin thought or said hardly mattered, of course. She knew quite well that Councilman Sparks would give her the official position of City Hall without flinching. Soon enough she would know exactly where she stood.

"Looks pretty bad, Miz Mayhew," he said, tossing his photos and documents on the table in front of him after perusing them for a few minutes. "I have to say I'm not crazy at all about these deductibles we'd have to pay to repair the roof and replace these books. Children's books at that. Sure seems like a lot of money to spend on a few pictures of farm animals, fruits and vegetables, and such. But I have to tell you, Lottie informs me that there have been exactly two calls to the City Hall offices inquiring about when the library will reopen. Two." He was holding up two fingers and gave her what could only be described as a contemptuous laugh. "At least I know you haven't been circulating petitions to have your followers participate in a phone campaign. And don't get any ideas, either. If we're suddenly inundated, I assure you we'll know what's up. You won't catch us unprepared twice."

Maura Beth took a deep breath and spoke as evenly as possible. "Some of the more avid library users have called me personally about it at home, but I haven't really kept track."

"I'm sure," he said with disdain. "We all know the world revolves around your library."

At that point, however, it was a struggle for Maura Beth to suppress her amusement. She and Nora Duddney had scripted and rehearsed every possible scenario in preparation for her appearance today, and it was uncanny how close they had actually come to predicting the responses of the head honcho.

"I'm also sure," he continued, "that you can see the folly of all this. It would be like pouring money down a rat hole, Miz Mayhew. I think it's time we all admitted this building has had it. We'd be better off having a book sale for the remaining collection and then tearing down The Cherico Library rather than throwing our good money after bad. We can always pave it over and provide some more downtown parking. I don't have to tell you that we've needed to address that for some time now."

Chunky and Gopher Joe were nodding in unison with smug expressions on their faces, doing an uncanny imitation of Tweedledum and Tweedledee.

"No one out in the Netherfield Community where I live has said squat about the library not being open," Chunky said. "They just wanna get all the tree limbs that fell down during the storm chopped up and hauled off. Why, some people even had their driveways blocked. Out my way, folks're much more inner-rested in buzz saws than books!"

Maura Beth flashed a patronizing smile his way. "And why does that not surprise me?"

"Now, Miz Mayhew, just because people don't use the library dudd'n mean they aren't good people," he snapped back. "Seems to me you've let this library bid'ness go to your head a mite. The world'll go on nicely without your library, I do b'lieve. But I know this much—folks'll use that extra parking when they come downtown and be glad for it."

Knowing quite well she was fighting a losing battle, Maura Beth deferred as best she could. "Perhaps you're right, Mr. Badham. Perhaps I should just accept the wisdom and counsel of you good people here at City Hall."

Maura Beth's sudden spurt of diplomacy may have mollified Chunky and Gopher Joe, but Councilman Sparks was having none of it. "Ah, sarcasm! The last defense of those who cannot win the argument outright. I expected more from you today, Miz Mayhew."

"So sorry to disappoint you. I just need a clarification from you, Councilman Sparks. As of this meeting, is it your intention not only to close down the library but to tear it down as well? Have we upped the ante, so to speak? Is the one-year reprieve out the window?"

He leaned in triumphantly. "It was just a matter of time before that happened, Miz Mayhew. This violent spring weather of ours just pushed up the timetable. Maybe that's a sign we both shouldn't ignore. Mother Nature just trying to tell us something, if you will."

Maura Beth remained calm and held up her end of the projected exchange as the ceiling fan continued to soothe her. "And my position, Councilman? Is that over as well?"

"It's not as if you didn't know this was coming down the line. However, your severance will be generous. We'll pay you for the last half of the year. That ought to tide you over until you can track down a position somewhere else. As you recall, I offered you a job working at City Hall as my secretary last year, but you turned it down," he reminded her, his face hardening somewhat.

She did not blink. "So you did, and so I did. But I have to say, I still have no regrets about that."

"So I gather. We all have to live with the consequences of our actions. Meanwhile, I'll want you to put your financial house in order over the next two weeks before you leave. Clear up all outstanding payments to creditors, straighten out and close the books, that sort of thing," he continued, looking past Maura Beth as if she weren't even in the room.

"That's doable," she answered, sounding not the least bit upset by his directives. "May I request an appearance with you here two weeks from now to present all those documents?"

Councilman Sparks drew back slightly, his instincts apparently alerted. "Yes, of course. But I must say you're being awfully docile about all this. I expected a fiery speech and another threat to rally the public behind you. Of course, guided tours of all the damage would most certainly convince the average Chericoan that the library has indeed had it."

"I can't disagree with that," Maura Beth said. "I'm no fool."

Councilman Sparks resumed his haughty demeanor. "I never took you for one, I can assure you. But I'm glad to see you at least understand that the library is definitely damaged goods, whatever it may or may not have been in the past, or whatever you were trying to make it."

"It pains me to say so, but you're right." She rose from her chair and nodded quickly toward the councilmen. "So I guess I'll be seeing you gentlemen in two weeks for the last time?"

Councilman Sparks flashed his best vote-getting smile. "We'll look forward to that, Miz Mayhew."

Maura Beth nodded politely as she passed Lottie Howard in the outer office and moved energetically down the hallway. Once outside on the steps of City Hall, however, she could not help herself. "Yesss!" she exclaimed, pumping her fist.

It could not have gone any more according to plan.

Harlan Lattimore had just selected "You Don't Know Me" on his trusty jukebox—the Ray Charles classic with the slow, romantic fuse that he and Periwinkle had called their favorite when they were first courting and indulging those tentative romantic explorations.

"For old time's sake?" he said, welcoming her into his arms on the floor of the otherwise-deserted Marina Bar and Grill.

She let herself be wrapped up, and he began leading her around, his eyes riveted to her every second of every move he made. "They just don't make songs like this anymore, do they, Peri?"

"Nope." She decided to keep it short and sweet, resisting

the full effect of the music and the intoxicating neon glow of the jukebox.

"Now this is what I call dancing, Peri. The youngsters today don't know what they're missing."

She nodded her head, but what they were doing wasn't dancing so much as it was rubbing up against each other in an undeniable sexual choreography. She allowed herself to go along with it to see where it would take her emotionally on this spring evening. Yes, those old feelings for Harlan had reappeared over the last couple of months. She could not deny that; and her impression, borne of instinct more than anything else, was that tonight was the night he was going to pop the question.

"I've made some big mistakes in my life," he continued as the music played, and he hummed along here and there. "But the biggest one was letting you go, Peri. I got the big head out here on the lake, thinking I was doing it all by myself. But you and I know the truth. You're really the businesswoman—you've got the knack for the figures. And you were the one who made The Marina Bar and Grill work from the get-go. Me? I still like hanging behind the bar, pouring drinks, and just being one of the guys with the customers. Shoot the Breeze Lattimore, that's me."

Periwinkle pulled back slightly and gave him a smile. "Yep, that's you." Uncannily, she felt it coming. And suddenly there it was.

"Peri, don't you think it's time we both put the past behind us? I really think we should be a team again."

"Is that a proposal?"

He didn't answer right away, taking her by the hand even before the song had ended. "Let's go out on the deck. It's really a beautiful night out there."

Indeed, it was. Balmy, with the kind of breeze that felt delicious on the skin, like caressing fingertips. The moon wasn't quite full, but it was well on its way, and the surface of the lake seemed brushed with a layer of light.

"We always seem to end up here," Periwinkle said, once they had both settled against the railing, looking up into each other's eyes.

"Is this such a bad place to be?"

She said, "No." But what she wanted to say was, "Depends."

"This time around, I think we'd be an unbeatable team," Harlan continued. "I've grown up, so you don't have to worry about that anymore."

"Oh, I believe you," she said. "You just took a lot longer than most to sow your wild oats."

The smile on his face had a trace of relief in it. "I can't excuse my behavior, Peri. I can only hope you forgive me because, yes, I want you to marry me. You had to know I was going to ask you."

She gestured toward one of the nearby picnic tables. "I think we ought to get off our feet for this."

He looked slightly puzzled but obeyed, and soon they were sitting next to each other, facing away from the lake. She had had enough of being influenced by nature's pretty pictures. That was how all the damage had been done the first time around. "Is this because you're going to turn me down?" he said, taking her hand and giving it a light squeeze. "I'd get down on bended knee, if it'd help, you know."

"No need to do that," she told him with a pleasant smile on her face. "I was going to accept your proposal, as a matter of fact. Will there be another ring, or shall I bring the one in my jewelry box out of retirement? I haven't worn it since our divorce. I thought it was enough that I kept your name. But maybe that was because I never liked my maiden name anyway."

"Kohlmeyer, right?"

She nodded and made a disgusted face. "I always thought Periwinkle Violet Kohlmeyer was a bit much. As I think I once told you, my mother is oh so fond of flowers. It runs in the family. Mom is Pansy, and then there's Aunt Rose and Aunt Iris. What's in a name, huh?"

He gave her an easy smile and eagerly displayed the handsome gold band on his ring finger that she had given him. "I've never taken mine off, Periwinkle Violet Kohlmeyer Lattimore. I guess I was trying to tell myself something all this time. I think it'd be special to exchange our rings again, don't you?"

"I do," she said.

"Hey, that sounds like you just married me again, huh?"

She laughed pleasantly enough but managed an element of restraint as well. "All of this sounds so nice, Harlan. Like a fairy tale ending for us."

He drew back slightly, stroking his mustache in distracted fashion. "Don't you think we deserve one?"

"Of course I do. But I need to talk about something that's been on my mind quite a bit lately. You said just a minute ago that you thought I was the one with a head for business—of the two of us, I mean."

The frown lines broke across his forehead as he was obviously struggling to see where she was going. "That's not debatable, Peri."

"I agree, but I have to ask how you've been managing without me all this time," she said.

"Nobody does it like you do, Peri." He was smiling proudly at his humor now, puffing out his chest.

"No, Harlan. No more one-liners," she told him, her tone as serious as his was frivolous. "How's business these days? I really need to know. We have the same suppliers, you know. They talk."

She could see that he was becoming uncomfortable, fidgeting with his mustache again. "It's okay. Maybe not as good as it used to be, but I'm getting by. What's your point?"

Periwinkle suddenly realized how difficult this was going to be for the both of them. A part of her really had enjoyed all the lovemaking and attention, and believed he was sincere about resuming their marriage in earnest, but the skeptical half still needed to be satisfied, even if it ended up costing her emotionally. "Are you marrying me again for my superior bookkeeping skills and any liquid assets I may have in the bank? I mean, are those entering into the equation just the tiniest bit?"

His reaction was dramatic, even overly so as he looked up into the heavens for a brief moment, gesturing with his hands outstretched. "Why, Peri, how could you think such a thing? I wouldn't ask you to keep my books. You'd have to volunteer. I know you've got The Twinkle to run."

"Glad you brought that up," she continued. "When we first married, I had nothing. Now I have The Twinkle and all its resources. Naturally, a good businesswoman wants to protect herself."

He went from gesturing broadly at the sky to drawing in his arms and hunkering down close to the table as if concentrating on a poker hand. "What are you getting at, Peri?"

"If this really is all about being in love the second time around, I don't think you'll mind proving it to me," she told him.

"My word isn't good enough?"

"Why don't we go inside where there's more light?" she added, rising from the table and heading through the door onto the dance floor.

He followed her lead, but she could tell by the sound of his boots stomping close behind her on the planks that he was agitated. "Peri, I'm serious here. Let's don't play games now."

"My sentiments exactly," she said, walking over to her purse, which she'd left on one of the bar stools. She turned and handed him the official-looking document she'd just retrieved.

"What's this?" He took it and scanned it quickly, and she watched the expression on his face change from curious to angry. "A prenuptial agreement? Are you serious?"

"Perfectly."

"But why?"

She leaned against the bar stool and held her chin up to strengthen her resolve. "If you truly love me as you say you do, you won't mind signing that agreement. That way, I'll know I'm not merely an investment."

"Peri," he said, his tone almost defiant, "I can't believe you would do this to me. You're treating me like a stranger. This tells me you don't trust me at all. You say you've forgiven me for my past, but obviously you haven't."

"Then you're not going to sign it?"

"Hell, no!" Impulsively and with a great deal more force than was necessary, he tore the papers in half, letting them fall to the floor in front of her feet. "I don't know what I've done to deserve this!"

Periwinkle studied his face closely, looking for signs of hurt around the eyes. Instead, all she saw were narrowed slits of anger. She needed him to show her something besides rage, some indication that he truly had become a more stable and responsible person.

"I've earned the right to feel secure about my life," she explained after she saw he was content just to stand there fuming. "I've worked too hard. Can't you understand that? If I've proved one thing since we split up, it's that I can make it on my own. And don't think for a minute that it hasn't been a struggle. But I can't go back to the way things were when I was dependent upon you for everything. If you can't accept the new me, then we shouldn't get married." She bent down and gathered up the torn pieces of paper, gesturing with them gently when she had them all in hand. "I think this answers my question. I was hoping against hope it wouldn't come to this."

For a brief unsettling moment as he made a fist of his right hand and lifted it to his face, she thought he might be getting ready to strike her. But he quickly dropped it to his side and exhaled. "I sure as hell didn't see this coming. You going to Curtis Trickett and everything!"

She glanced down at the floor, concentrating on his boots as she spoke. "I'm sorry if I've disappointed you, Harlan. But I did what I had to do."

"So you're saying you have no feelings for me at all? These past few months have meant nothing to you?" he said, softening his tone.

When she looked up again, she saw that he had reworked his face, removing the anger and replacing it with those bedroom eyes she had become reacquainted with over the past few months. "You've dredged up some of those old feelings, yes. I give you credit for that. But sometimes it's felt to me more like a campaign instead of a real romance."

"Man," he said, shaking his head. "I had no idea you'd become so cynical and suspicious."

He was good at this—she had to admit. But she refused to let him throw it all back on her. "You can describe me that way if you want. Maybe it's more that I suffered a lot a' damage last time, and I'll never be the same. Harlan, I think the bottom line here is we need to continue going our separate ways. But I thank you for thinking of me and I wish you well."

With that, she stuffed the pieces of the prenuptial agreement into her purse, gave him a quick peck on the cheek, and walked away without looking back. But he could not see that there were tears in her eyes as she headed out of the restaurant toward the parking lot. It all felt like she was doing the right thing, of course, but there was still some small part of her that kept wishing he had behaved differently and given her a different message. Being successful but lonely was a hard lot in life.

17

Legacies

Maura Beth could not help but observe that Mrs. Johnnie-Dell Crews was not one to get to the point. This tall, gaunt woman who disdained makeup and grooming obviously liked to hear herself talk and had been doing so for some time now. Of course, nothing she was saying was remotely of interest to her three visitors, who were being mightily tested as they sat politely at attention around her kitchen table sipping coffee.

Finally, it was Miss Voncille who drew the line. "Johnnie-Dell, I'm sure we all appreciate your daily trials and tribulations at Cherico High. Lest you forget, I endured them as well during my many years of teaching history in those not-so-hallowed, institutional green halls. But if you don't mind, we'd like to hear about the faculty openings."

Both Maura Beth and Jeremy managed subtle sighs of relief, even as they were holding hands under the table. They had been eagerly awaiting word from Miss Voncille's former cohort for the past couple of weeks, and now the moment had come at last, though unfolding far more slowly than they had ever imagined. Twenty minutes earlier they had received a largely confusing and forgettable grand tour of the Crews

Family cottage, courtesy of the self-absorbed lady of the house. Then again, Johnnie-Dell Crews had always been known for her many rambling, stream-of-consciousness observations.

"And this room my husband and I always called the knitting corner," she had told everyone at one point during the tour. "I forget why. You might think this shawl I have around my shoulders is my own work, but I don't knit, and neither did Porter, of course. And it isn't a corner, as you can see. It's more like a nook. Porter did keep all his books in here. Maybe we should have called it the library. But we didn't."

Her visitors had exchanged knowing glances with each other and dutifully followed her around from room to room, keeping their comments to themselves. The truth was, nothing in the house seemed coordinated or compatible with anything else. Wall colors clashed with curtains and window treatments, which did not match lampshades or throw rugs or knick-knacks perched on shelves.

"Everyone's always suspected she's color-blind," Miss Voncille did manage to whisper to Maura Beth and Jeremy, briefly taking them aside.

Finally, however, the tour mercifully ended. Now came the task of extracting that much-anticipated information about the makeup of the Cherico High faculty for the fall semester.

"Oh, about the openings," Johnnie-Dell said at last in response to Miss Voncille's prodding. "It appears we have two. But one's for shop teacher, so I don't think Mr. McShay here would be qualified for that. I think shop is barbaric, myself. One year we had a young man cut off his thumb on the jigsaw. His parents sued the school and won because the shop teacher, Mr. Barringer, had gone outside to smoke a cigarette and wasn't keeping an eye on his students. The other opening, however, may be just what you're looking for. You'd be teaching sophomore English. That's such a difficult age with all the hormones kicking in. It does make you think coed classes may be a bit of a mistake. I went to an all-girl's college myself. There are pros and cons to that, of course. Voncille has told me you teach juniors now, is that right?"

Maura Beth squeezed Jeremy's hand tightly as the good news dramatically straightened his posture. "Yes, I've taught junior English from the very beginning at New Gallatin Academy."

"More coffee?" Johnnie-Dell put in suddenly, causing everyone to blink at the non sequitur.

"Just refill us all around and get on with it," Miss Voncille said, fidgeting in her chair. "You used to do this all the time in the teacher's lounge, Johnnie-Dell. We'd run out of doughnuts by the time you'd gotten to the point of one of your stories."

Johnnie-Dell looked momentarily as if she might be taking offense at the remark but seemed to shrug it off and efficiently performed her hostess duties. "As to the opening," she eventually continued, "it came up at the last minute, you see. Apparently, Miss Dawn Hefferly is getting married, as many of these young teachers will do. She'd only been with us for a year, though. Quite the flirt walking down the halls, I noticed. It's hard to keep track of them sometimes. At any rate, Mr. Mc-Shay, you're getting this heads-up a trifle early, so please get your résumé in right away."

"I intend to," Jeremy said, smiling at Maura Beth all the while.

"You won't find a better teacher anywhere," Maura Beth said. "He has some wonderful ideas about making classical literature come to life for his students. For instance, he organizes field trips to the hometowns of some of our great Southern writers. They get to see for themselves where the writer grew up and then walk in his footsteps. Or hers, as is very often the case here in the South."

Johnnie-Dell's long face became even more exaggerated. "You know, it isn't easy to pull these kids away from their cell phones and laptops and all that paraphernalia these days.

Sometimes I think the culture has just hit rock bottom, and I wonder what we'll be leaving behind for future generations."

Jeremy caught her gaze and nodded enthusiastically. "I couldn't agree with you more, Mrs. Crews. All my life I've felt I was born in the wrong century. It seems to me we're communicating with each other more but making less and less sense. That's no sort of legacy."

Johnnie-Dell seemed impressed. "You certainly don't hear that out of the mouths of the young people these days. Oh, the bad grammar and the profanity—don't get me started!"

"Jeremy here is a delightful throwback to more chivalrous times," Maura Beth said. "I can personally vouch for that."

"Well, if that's the case, I truly hope you get the position, young man," Johnnie-Dell added. "I have only one more year until my retirement—and then I don't know what I'll do with myself, or maybe I should actually take up knitting in my knitting corner—but I would certainly enjoy having someone like you on the faculty to talk to. In fact, I'd be glad to put in a good word for you, if you'd like."

Jeremy was beaming, leaning against Maura Beth to further accentuate the bond between them. "That would just be fantastic, Mrs. Crews. We—I mean, Maura Beth and I, couldn't thank you enough!"

During the two-week period between Maura Beth's most recent appearance and the upcoming last scheduled meeting before the City Council, she forced herself to go to work every day like the dedicated professional she was. Though the library remained closed to the public, she had accounts to close and books to balance. It was a grim task for the most part, but she kept telling herself that it would all be worth it in the end. And, in fact, she continued to receive phone calls and letters from concerned citizens about the status of the library, including most everyone who had ever attended a meeting of The

Cherry Cola Book Club. All of them wanted to know what they could do to help, and Maura Beth told each of them the same thing: *Just sit tight and I'll get back to you very soon, I promise.* These testimonials and offers of assistance she intended to present to Councilman Sparks and company in a few more days, alongside the rest of the plan that she and Nora Duddney had devised a little while back. That was what kept the fire going in her belly and enabled her to get through such a trying period when her future was very much in doubt.

Then came an unsolicited visit from Connie and Douglas McShay one afternoon, after they had called ahead to make sure she was going to be there. "We have some very exciting news for you," Connie told her over the phone. "But Douglas and I want to run it past you in person."

Maura Beth felt it was her duty to give them a tour of the storm damage just after they had arrived, however. "It's one big soggy mess," she said, leading them to the distressing sight. "I'm so tired of looking at it. I keep thinking of all those soaked easy readers as so many drowned children. Isn't that an awful image to have inside my head all the time?"

"I'm sure it is. But that's why we're here," Douglas told her, patting her on the shoulder as they all turned their backs and walked away from ground zero with its warped books and stale, moldy smells. "We fully intend to help you do something about it."

It was at the meeting room table a few minutes later that Maura Beth revealed the drastic intentions of City Hall regarding the library, but she thought it best to keep to herself the forthcoming surprise attack.

Both Douglas and Connie gave each other conspiratorial smiles, and he said, "There can't be any doubt that all of us Cherry Cola people are connected in some mysterious way. We were all meant to meet and help each other out, I'm convinced of it, because our timing couldn't be more perfect."

Connie gave him a nudge and patted her hair. "Tell her the good news and stop pontificating like Nostradamus, for heaven's sake."

He put his hand up to calm her down and then leaned in to Maura Beth. "It's as simple as this. Both Connie and I have done well in life, and we have more money than we'll ever need. I was telling Connie a while back that I felt we ought to truly make ourselves a part of Cherico, since this is where we'll be spending the rest of our lives. We want to do something good for this little town, and we can't think of a better way than to help you patch up your wounded library. Now that we've found out City Hall is balking—no surprise, I might add—we'd like to donate whatever it takes to make these repairs and get the library back on its feet. Do you have an estimate, by the way?"

Maura Beth nodded and began writing on one of the squares of scratch paper she always kept at the table for staff meetings, such as they were. Then she handed it over to Douglas. "Those two figures represent the total cost of repairs and the out-of-pocket expenses City Hall will need to come up with."

Douglas scanned it eagerly and showed it to Connie, who brought her hands together with a bright smile on her face. "Piece a' cake," she said.

"Yes, we can handle that," he added. "In fact, we'd consider it an honor to contribute and leave something behind this way."

Maura Beth struggled to keep the emotion out of her voice but failed miserably. "I don't know what to say." She paused for a deep, cleansing breath. "But I do, of course. You have no idea how much this strengthens my position with the councilmen. I'm just two days away from what they think will be my final appearance before them. I can't begin to thank both of you enough."

After their departure, Maura Beth picked up the phone

and brought Nora Duddney up to speed on the latest development.

"You know, I think we just might be able to pull this off!" Nora exclaimed.

"Well, it's do or die, isn't it?" Maura Beth said. "I'm either going to spend the rest of my career here in Cherico or leave town and never look back."

"Miz Mayhew and Miz Duddney are here to see you," Lottie Howard announced to Councilman Sparks over the intercom.

There was genuine surprise in the compressed voice coming from the inner office. "Miz Duddney? Nora Duddney?" There was a significant pause. "Take me off the intercom, please."

Lottie complied, picked up the receiver, and began listening to her boss. Then she repeated his instructions to the visitors. "Councilman Sparks wants to know what business you have with him today, Miz Duddney?"

Nora patted Maura Beth on the shoulder and said, "I'm with Miz Mayhew, and she's with me. We're a package deal. That's pretty much it."

Lottie shot her a skeptical glance and repeated Nora's words through the phone. "He says he'll be with you in a minute. Wouldn't you both like to take a seat?"

"No, thanks," Maura Beth told her. "We wouldn't want to get too comfortable, you know."

Lottie's skepticism turned into an acute frown as she hung up the receiver. "Have it your way, then."

After another five minutes had passed, Councilman Sparks entered the outer office with his customary vote-getting smile affixed to his face. Maura Beth noted, however, that it disappeared in an instant as he greeted his visitors.

"Nora?" His tone was incredulous, his expression one of

astonishment. He gestured toward the inner office reflexively but could not take his eyes off of his former secretary.

Even after everyone had been seated around his desk behind closed doors, he continued to stare, and it was with tremendous satisfaction that Maura Beth saw clearly that once again Councilman Sparks had been caught off guard. The last time that had happened, everything had gone her way. She could only hope for the same results today.

"If you don't mind my saying so, Nora," he said at last, "I wouldn't have recognized you if I'd passed you on the sidewalks of Commerce Street. What have you done to your hair and your face? Have you, uh, had one of those girlie-girl makeovers or something like that?"

"Something like that," she said, as she and Maura Beth exchanged thoroughly amused glances.

Sounding somewhat tentative, Councilman Sparks continued. "Miz Mayhew, I thought this session was to be strictly between yourself and the City Council."

Maura Beth looked around the room, gesturing with a sweep of her hand. "So it was. So where are Mr. Badham and Mr. Martin? I thought they were attached to you at the left and right hips."

Councilman Sparks cleared his throat and sat up a bit in his chair. "Very funny. I have Chunky and Gopher Joe attending to other duties elsewhere. I'm taking care of this myself. That's all you need to know. Meanwhile, even though I have no idea why it's necessary for you to be here, Nora, I think the time has come for us to get down to business."

"I couldn't agree with you more," Maura Beth said. "So let's get this started, shall we?"

Councilman Sparks extended his hand with an expectant expression. "You have the documents I requested?"

Maura Beth presented the folder she had brought in with her. "As you'll see, all library business has been zeroed out."

He took his time examining the papers one by one, nodding approvingly and occasionally looking up with a dismissive smirk on his face. Then he got to the bottom of the stack, and his eyes widened dramatically. "Miz Mayhew, what the hell is this?"

"That's where I come in," Nora said. "Please allow me to explain."

Councilman Sparks glanced down at the paper again and came up glowering. "Are you two trying to pull a fast one on me?"

"Not at all," Nora continued. "My father once told me that if I ever lost my job or needed help in any way after he was gone that I was to open his safety deposit box at the bank, and that's just what I've done."

"But your father isn't gone, Nora. He's still very much with us out at the nursing home."

Nora continued to speak calmly, keeping the emotion out of her voice. "He may be out at the nursing home, Mr. Sparks, but he's not with us at all. He hasn't been for some time now, and you know that as well as I do. Of course, I also needed help after you dismissed me so casually. You have no idea how much letting me go put me in a tailspin."

Councilman Sparks brandished the sheet of paper and then crumpled it in one quick motion, while training his eyes on Maura Beth. He tried aiming the ball at a nearby trash can, but his throw was off considerably. "What have you done with the real Nora Duddney, Miz Mayhew? Who is this woman sitting in front of me speaking these complete sentences?"

Nora ignored his insult, speaking for herself. "Never mind the compliments, Councilman. I'm pretty sure you thought our fathers left no paper trail of the liberties they took with the original library funding seventy-odd years ago. Perhaps your father covered his tracks, but, as I've found out, Daddy chose not to for his own reasons. He was a very far-sighted man, as I don't have to tell you. And he obviously didn't want to take the fall all by himself if their embezzlement was ever discovered. You'll find a copy there of the exact sums they divvied up, and even back in those days, it was a generous haul, so to speak. I can imagine the interest that has accrued by now to your account alone. And then there's what amounts to a confession with Daddy's signature at the bottom. Looking back on it all now, I realize what he did was very wrong, and I'm certainly not proud of it. But as I said before, he's also not with us anymore. You, on the other hand, are, and have everything to lose if this comes to light. Of course, that never has to happen."

Councilman Sparks was fidgeting in his chair now, his expression as dark and threatening as either woman had ever witnessed. "Just what is it you smiling lady blackmailers want from me?"

"At last!" Maura Beth said, pouncing upon his words almost gleefully. "We have a very simple solution in hand for you. First, we propose that the necessary repairs be made to the library to reopen it, and that once and for all the idea of closing it down be put to bed. Those repairs won't cost the city a cent, since insurance will cover most of it, and Douglas and Connie McShay have very graciously offered to pay the deductibles for us. Of course, I will want to continue in my position."

With daggers in his eyes, Councilman Sparks said, "Is that it?"

"Not quite. The repairs won't really give Cherico the facility it needs and deserves. That would be just a stopgap measure for an antiquated building that was never intended to be a library. The square footage, the budget, the lack of personnel, no off-street parking, and no computer terminals all need immediate attention to bring the library into the millennium."

"All that costs money, Miz Mayhew. Money Cherico just doesn't have."

Both women were shaking their heads simultaneously, and

Maura Beth said, "But you and your family have it, Councilman. You've had it for quite some time, and it's money that was intended to fund the library properly. That never happened, so perhaps it's time to make amends."

"I intend to do my part. My conscience wouldn't allow me to do otherwise," Nora added. "I have power of attorney over Daddy's estate, so I also have access to his funds. I thought you and I could match very healthy contributions to get the campaign started."

"To get what campaign started, Nora?"

But it was Maura Beth who answered. "The campaign for a brand-new library somewhere in Cherico. Anywhere other than 12 Shadow Alley. We can keep it open until its replacement is ready. One that will have plenty of square footage, lots of light and space, computer terminals to access the Internet, a children's librarian, a reference librarian, a technical services librarian, oodles of parking for the patrons, and an up-to-the-minute collection. Just imagine it: You'll go from being the library ogre to the library hero. You could even think of it as your legacy."

Councilman Sparks maintained his stubborn façade. "A library is not a legacy. It's a luxury. It's a waste of money."

Maura Beth shifted into her highest gear, having waited a long time for the opportunity to turn things around for good. "That's where you're wrong. Did you know that many companies view a town's school and library facilities as a primary asset when they're seriously considering locating there? They want to be sure that their employees and their families don't get shortchanged in that department. You've made quite a deal out of creating that industrial park of yours. But you might be better off doing what you can to strengthen the quality of the schools and the public library to make that park even more attractive to prospective plants. I'm sure Cherico is a hard sell to industry these days. Why not make your task a little easier?"

"I think I may have mentioned this to you before, Miz Mayhew," Councilman Sparks said, his expression softening a bit. "But you could run for office the way you go on about things."

"Picture it," Maura Beth continued, unwilling to let up for a second while making a frame of her hands. "The Charles Durden Sparks Public Library. It'll be a whole lot more visible than any old plot of graded land north of town. Everyone will see the building with your name on it every single day of the year. Every time they go in to use it, they'll think of your generous contribution that made it possible. There'll be a plaque in the lobby honoring your vision, and future generations will regard you as an honorable public servant."

"I was thinking that my family might be remembered as well," Nora added. "Perhaps the Nora Dean Duddney Genealogy Room and the Layton Merrill Duddney Reference Department. Maura Beth tells me there are lots of possibilities in a library that's done up properly."

Councilman Sparks considered briefly, obviously weighing his choices. "The fact remains that you ladies are flirting with extortion."

"And the fact remains that you would never hear the end of it if Miss Voncille Nettles and the Crumpton sisters, just to name a few, got wind of this," Maura Beth said. "Aren't Mamie and Marydell among your chief campaign contributors? At any rate, we all know about the rumors that have been circulating for years. So much better that they remain just that."

Councilman Sparks rose immediately from his chair and assumed a stately demeanor. "I see no problem with making the repairs to the library, especially since the McShays will be covering the deductibles. As to the rest of this so-called proposition, I'll need a few days to think it over and assess my financial situation. I'll have my decision on Friday. Until then, good day."

Outside in the hallway, Maura Beth and Nora were full of

smirks and congratulatory hugs. "I think we rattled his cage," Maura Beth said. "But my heart was beating a mile a minute there at the end."

"Oh, you were magnificent, but I was trembling, too. I've never stood up for myself like that in my life. I was always shoved to the side like an embarrassment to my parents and everyone else. I can't believe I wasted so many years living down to their opinion of me."

Maura Beth gave her another warm hug. "Well, you're your own woman now, Nora Duddney."

They walked out into the bright sunlight of late May and stood on the steps of City Hall for a while, gazing at what little pedestrian traffic there was. Then Maura Beth gave a dramatic little gasp. "I must get my mind off fictional plots. *All the King's Men* and assassinations just flashed into my head. I was thinking, what if Councilman Sparks decided to have us offed because of what we know and the documents we're hiding from him?"

Nora's laugh was carefree. "He wouldn't have the nerve, I can promise you that. I worked for him too long not to know what makes him tick. He doesn't really like to take chances. His pride won't let him. He's always taken the easiest way out—or the path of least resistance. Believe me, he'll cave rather than risk his reputation or his legacy. I heard him use that word a lot over the years. In any case, I don't think either of us needs to be on the lookout for speeding cars, screeching tires, and flying bullets."

Then they walked along the sidewalk together in the direction of the library, and that was when it happened. There were two sharp reports coming from somewhere behind them, and both women instinctively hunched their shoulders. Ahead of them, just coming out of The Twinkle, a tall man in a coat and tie started visibly and ducked quickly. All three people eventually straightened up and examined themselves tentatively for possible wounds. But there were none to be found.

And then the culprit appeared in the form of a rusty rattletrap of a car moving like molasses along the street with pungent black exhaust pouring out of its tailpipe.

With her adrenaline still flowing, Maura Beth exhaled and turned to an equally relieved Nora. "Now, how does a car like that get a safety inspection sticker?!" She was tempted to yell something obnoxious to the driver—a very old man with sunken cheeks and no teeth—but thought better of it. Above all, she had her reputation as a public servant to uphold, no matter how badly a couple of backfires had frightened her to the bone.

"I guess that's what we get for talking so glibly about assassination plots," Nora added.

They both managed a chuckle, and as they passed The Twinkle, Maura Beth said, "I must remember to give Periwinkle an update on everything when she's not so busy with her customers. She's been having a very rough go of it since she split up with her ex again."

All sorts of people seemed to be dropping in on Maura Beth and her library these days. This time, Becca and Justin Brachle claimed they had been in town for a lunch of sweet tea, sandwiches, and tomato aspic at The Twinkle and just wanted to see how things were going.

"We were so devastated when we heard about all the storm damage," Becca was saying once they'd gathered around the meeting room table. "Oh, that smell out there really is awful! How do things stand? Does it look like you'll be reopening soon? If not, we'll have to hold our next Cherry Cola Book Club meeting in somebody's home. Of course, we'll be happy to volunteer in that case."

"Help is on the way," Maura Beth said. Then she explained what the McShays intended to do and hinted that there might soon be a campaign starting up for a brand-new library.

"Oh, we'd be glad to contribute to that, wouldn't we, Stout Fella? Whatever you need us to do."

Justin's expression was quizzical, but his tone was compliant. "Whatever you say, Mommy."

Maura Beth drew back with a tilt of her head, her intuition immediately kicking in. "Mommy?"

Becca leaned in, her face a joyous study. "That's really why we dropped by, Maura Beth. We're pregnant, and we wanted you to be the first to know as we make the rounds."

"Oh, I couldn't be happier for you both. Congratulations!" The two women rose from their chairs and hugged, while Justin caught the kiss that Maura Beth blew in his general direction.

"Time for me to settle down and be a father, it looks like," Justin said in that boyish manner of his. "Gotta leave something behind besides a bank account and a big house, I figure."

"When are you due?" Maura Beth said, feeling a kinship with Becca she had never experienced before.

"Well, I'm not very far along, so it might be sometime early next year—maybe late January or early February."

Maura Beth's sigh was almost girlish, her eyes half-lidded. "It must be a wonderful feeling. I can't wait to experience it myself."

"It's a new phase of our lives, right, Stout Fella?"

"Yep, the way I see it, we'll either have a boy who likes football or a girl who likes cooking."

Becca gave him a stern look and wagged a finger. "Now, don't be sexist, Justin. We could also have a girl who likes football and a boy who likes to cook. Or maybe somebody who likes both—the best of us combined."

Maura Beth reached over and gently patted Becca's hand.

"Oh, I know you'll be happy with whoever comes along. And I have some good news of my own, by the way. We just found out this morning that my Jeremy will be teaching English down here in Cherico this fall. We're both so excited, and he'll be moving down this summer from Nashville. I'm sure I'll be helping him find a place to live."

There was a playful twinkle in Becca's eye as she gave Maura Beth a nudge. "Would that be big enough for two eventually?"

Maura Beth's voice was full of confidence. "Things are headed that way, I think. He needs to get settled first. In fact, there are a number of things that have to be settled. But a new phase of my life could very well be on the way, too."

Mr. Parker Place was the next unexpected visitor, knocking on the front door about an hour after the Brachles had left.

"So what brings you here today, Mr. Place?" Maura Beth said, once they'd seated themselves in her office. "I'd give you the grand tour of all the damage, but I know you can smell it from here."

"That I can," he told her, briefly wrinkling his nose. "Well, I just took a little break from The Twinkle, and the first thing I wanted to do was thank you for introducing Mama to all those audio books. You've opened up a whole new world for her. She'd just about given up reading with her eyes going bad and all. She's been after me for a while to mind my manners. 'Baby, don't you go too long without thanking that nice young woman,' she keeps reminding me."

Maura Beth gave him her most gracious smile. "That's why we're here, Mr. Place. Just another service from your friendly local library."

He returned her smile briefly, but soon he was looking uncomfortable and hanging his head. "But I also came to tell you how concerned I am about Miz Lattimore. She just isn't herself these days. She mopes around and just doesn't have that special Periwinkle spirit she always has. We've talked about it once or twice back in the kitchen, but she won't open up to me too much. 'I need to put everything connected with The Marina Bar and Grill behind me,' she says."

Maura Beth's sigh was full of exasperation. "I know. She's said the same thing to me. I've told her that I'm here for her any time she needs me. Lord knows, she's been there for me over the years."

Mr. Place leaned in and nodded his head crisply. "I have an idea that may get her out of this depression, though. Her birthday is coming up next week, so I was thinking maybe we could all show up right after we close that night and have a little surprise party. Maybe just her closest friends in the book club. Think it's a good idea?"

"I sure do," Maura Beth said, tossing her red hair back with her prettiest grin on display. "And I can get Becca to coordinate the potluck dishes we all bring along. We can't have Periwinkle serving her own food now, can we? You'll just have to make sure she doesn't fill up too much before we get there."

"And I'll contribute the birthday cake. How does a big chocolate caramel sheet cake sound?"

"Ooey, gooey! I'll start calling everyone up right away and really get things started."

"I knew I could count on you, Miz Mayhew." Mr. Place caught her gaze politely and then pressed his lips together, making a slit of his mouth. He appeared about to say something further but caught himself at the last second.

"Did you have another idea?" Maura Beth said, sensing his hesitation.

"There was something else I wanted to talk to you about," he began. "I just don't know anyone else to turn to. Mama's pretty old school about . . ." He trailed off and bit his lip.

"About what, Mr. Place?"

He exhaled forcefully, and everything started to pour out of him. "About interracial dating, that's what. You see, I'm starting to have these feelings for Periwinkle. She has no idea. But I can't seem to help myself. Before this breakup of hers, she used to confide in me all the time about everything. I began to see how much alike we were—self-made, good at what we do, not letting other people stand in our way. Of course, I hated to see her get mixed up with her ex-husband the way she did. She was so confused at times, or at least that's what she told me. So I feel like I can help her get over what's happened to her. But I don't even know where to start. Do you have any advice for me?"

Fortunately, Maura Beth had been prepared for Mr. Place's revelations by Periwinkle herself. More than once, she had mentioned how solicitous of her he had been at The Twinkle, and now here he was confirming more than professional friendship on his part. Maura Beth had to admit that she herself had never considered dating someone of a different race, but she had gotten to know two mixed couples at LSU who seemed to be very happy together. They had gone out of their way to make their relationship work within a culture that was not always thrilled by their existence. She hadn't given the subject much thought since then, but now that it had landed in her lap again, she felt comfortable being as supportive as she possibly could of Mr. Place.

"In the six years I've known Periwinkle Lattimore," she said, "I've heard nothing out of her mouth that would lead me to believe she would not value you as a friend or even something more. She's the type of woman who believes in a fair shake for everyone."

"That's good to hear." He was eyeing her sideways. "Do I detect a 'but' in there somewhere?"

"No, not really. You might want to keep in mind that's she's still going through a rough patch because of Harlan, though. She may need a little time away from men. I think you should stay close, which you can't help but do working in the restaurant with her all day. Then, I bet you'll know when the time is right to tell her how you really feel about her. The worst thing that can happen is that she'll tell you she just wants to remain friends. On the other hand, you might end up being exactly the man she's always been looking for. I know for a fact she hasn't given up hope."

Mr. Place was slowly shifting his eyes from side to side as he considered her advice. "Makes sense to me, since I believe you know her best." Then he started shaking his head while gazing up at the ceiling. "I know I'm a great pastry chef and all that, but I guess I don't want that engraved on my tombstone. The time comes when a man wants to settle down and give up his flings and such. Yeah, it was easy for me to play the field up there in Memphis. My fancy hotel suite in the Grand Shelby Hotel was the perfect setting for it all, too. Mama's after me all the time, of course. 'When are you ever gonna find yourself a nice woman, baby? I'm almost too old to pick up a grandchild with this arthritis I got now.' Of course, who knows what she'd say or how she'd act if I did start something up with Periwinkle? As I told you before, Mama's old school and went through a lot more in her generation than I did in mine. Of course I love her, but I respect her even more because I never had to walk a mile in her shoes. Things started to get better by the time I was growing up."

"I never had to contend with any sort of prejudice in my life—unless you consider the type of disrespect I've encountered as a librarian from the local politicians a form of it," Maura Beth said. "But the important thing is to fight back and not to abandon your dreams. Will you just listen to me—I really do sound like I'm running for office, don't I?"

"Nothing wrong with that, Miz Mayhew," Mr. Place said, giving her a conspiratorial wink. "When you come down to it, I'd a helluva lot rather vote for you than Councilman Sparks and his cronies. Since I've been back, I can't help but notice he's got this town under his thumb."

18

Stolen Thunder

Whatever Maura Beth had expected from Councilman Sparks when Friday rolled around, it was certainly not something as brazen as this. Why, he had barely given her an hour's notice, but when it came to his self-serving tactics, what else was new?

"I'm holding a press conference today at high noon on the steps of City Hall," he had told her over the phone. "I'm sure you and Nora will want to be there, since what I have to say will concern you very much. I'll leave it up to you to get in touch with her because I'm very busy right now getting ready. Please don't fail to be there, Miz Mayhew."

And with that, he had hung up, leaving her to wonder what he might be plotting now. Nonetheless, she and Nora had shown up ten minutes early, standing next to WHYY's gangly young newsman, Lester Bateman, and a growing crowd of curious onlookers. In fact, Maura Beth recognized some of the faces as the downtown business owners she had called upon last year during her petition initiative on behalf of the library. From a distance, she took the time to nod and smile at such notables as Audra Neely, Vernon Dotrice, and Curtis Trickett, among others.

"Do you have any idea what he's going to say?" Maura Beth said to Lester, fixating on the size of the Adam's apple that bulged from his long, skinny neck. In fact, the man looked as if he were a complete stranger to three squares a day.

"No idea whatsoever," he told her. "I just got a phone call about an hour ago telling me I'd want to be over here to cover and record his presser. We don't hear much from City Hall, ya know. Most of the time Sparks and that crew of his act like we don't even exist. I understand it's been that way since the *Daily Cherico* went out of business a while back."

Momentarily, the Crumpton sisters, overdressed in pearls and stoles, emerged from City Hall and took their place at the top of the steps. They were soon joined by Councilman Sparks, his wife, Evie, Chunky Badham, Gopher Joe Martin, and Lottie Howard with notepad in hand.

"Ladies and gentlemen!" Councilman Sparks began, his voice brimming with confidence and ringing out loud and clear over the buzzing Commerce Street crowd below. "Before I make the important announcement we've all come together to hear, I see two important Chericoans I'd like to ask to step forward. Miz Maura Beth Mayhew and Miz Nora Duddney, won't you join us here at the top? These two ladies are an integral part of the message I'll be delivering to everyone today, as you'll all soon discover."

Maura Beth and Nora quickly exchanged worried glances but dutifully obeyed, taking their places beside the Crumpton sisters, who acknowledged them with perfunctory nods. For her part, Maura Beth found it difficult to believe that anything terrible was going to happen under such polite circumstances right out in the open in front of all those witnesses, but she nonetheless felt her heartbeat quickening and her adrenaline flowing. After all, this was the one and only Charles Durden Sparks extending what appeared to be an olive branch, and that had sometimes turned out to be bad news in the past.

"We are all gathered here today because your City Council has made a momentous decision on behalf of the citizens of Cherico. As you all know, our little town suffered terrible storm damage not too long ago when a late-spring cold front moved through as it was predicted to do. We may have been forewarned, but that did not stop Mother Nature from wreaking its havoc upon us. Unfortunately, The Cherico Library sustained the most damage in the downtown area, and it brought to the attention of your City Council the urgent need to address this problem. It also focused the attention of your elected officials on the inadequacy of our current library facilities." There was a brief pause during which Councilman Sparks lifted his chin even higher, flashed his patented smile, and took the time to survey the crowd below him much as a Roman Emperor might have done thousands of years ago.

"In the recent past The Cherico Library has been the focus of some controversy—but no more. As your duly-elected head of the City Council, I have taken it upon myself to put an end to the era of library negligence. If the storm did us any favors at all, it was to point out to us that the modest little facility on Shadow Alley must not continue to represent the needs of Cherico's readers in the millennium. Therefore, the following benefactors have stepped forward to kick off a campaign to construct a brand-new library: your Councilman Charles Durden Sparks and wife, Eve Williams Sparks; Miz Nora Duddney on behalf of the Layton Duddney Family; and the Mesdames Mamie and Marydell Crumpton on behalf of the Crumpton Family. We at City Hall are especially indebted to Miz Duddney for her extraordinary foresightedness in this matter, and to the lovely Crumpton sisters for responding quickly to our request to be a part of the initial funding for this project. Their ancestors have always been enthusiastic library users, and we felt it only proper that the present generation be included in this noble proposition. Among the three of us, we've already raised a substantial amount of money that will serve us well as we proceed with our plans. Shall we pause for a moment and give everyone involved a hand?"

The crowd responded enthusiastically, and Maura Beth had to struggle to keep her jaw from dropping, while noting similar astonishment on Nora's face.

"Furthermore, while this new library campaign is ongoing, your City Hall will undertake the repairs to the current facility on Shadow Alley and will do everything possible to keep it open until the new building construction has been completed. There will be some substantial improvements in the interim as well, including additional staff, computer terminals to access the Internet, and an increased materials budget for our hardworking librarian of six years standing, Miz Maura Beth Mayhew. Folks, let's all give her a hand, shall we?"

Maura Beth felt giddy as the applause washed over her. It was as if some gigantic, surreal spotlight had been focused upon her in broad daylight. Instinctively, she accepted the attention with a gracious nod and broad smile, but she was beginning to feel a bit like a trained monkey from the municipal zoo of Councilman Sparks. Here he was, stealing her thunder and taking full credit for everything, even if she and Nora were the only ones who knew the truth behind the ploy. That, she realized for not the first time, was the genius of the man, and she had to give him credit for being superbly skilled at covering his soft underbelly and rear end when cornered.

"I would also like to announce proudly that the name of this new library building will be The Charles Durden Sparks, Crumpton, and Duddney Public Library to honor its three main benefactors. I know it sounds a bit unwieldy or even like a law firm, but we'll all know better, won't we?"

Councilman Sparks now had the crowd in the vest pocket of his three-piece suit, and they responded with warm laughter. "I'd also like to point out that for those of you who wish to join this campaign and contribute whatever you can, there will be opportunities to sponsor certain elements of the new library. For instance, your name could be added to the genealogy room, or the reference collection, or the new high-tech computer room. If you need more information about any of these charitable opportunities, I direct you to Miz Mayhew, who will be running both the old and the new facility for as long as she chooses to. Isn't that right, Miz Mayhew?"

Once again, Maura Beth plastered a big smile across her face and did his bidding. "It most certainly is, and I look forward to being of continued service to all my fellow Chericoans."

There was scattered applause; then Councilman Sparks continued. "I will now take any questions from you good people."

Lester Bateman was the first to raise his arm and speak up. "Councilman Sparks, we'll be running your entire speech throughout the day on the news so the rest of the public knows about it. That ought to help get things started for you. Meanwhile, what is the time frame of this campaign? When do you hope to have raised all the money you need?"

It was clear that Councilman Sparks could not stop playing to the crowd, particularly with a microphone pointed in his general direction. Even his worst political stump speeches, however, avoided the stilted clichés pouring out of him at the moment. "First, I'd like to thank WHYY, The Vibrant Voice of Greater Cherico, for being here today. We both strive to maintain that public service spirit, always eager to tune in to the pulse of our citizens. Woe be unto him who ignores and refuses to march to the drumbeat of the voter who has elected him to office. And to answer your question, we'll be giving the campaign a solid year. We should have our blueprints in place by then. Of course, we'll expect our Miz Mayhew here to give the architect some guidance as to what a state-of-the-art library requires these days. I'm quite sure she'll be chock-full of helpful suggestions, won't you?"

Maura Beth continued to steel herself, feeling her jaw beginning to ache from such relentless smiling with so many eyes upon her. "I'll be literally overflowing, I'm sure," she said, giving him a Queen Elizabeth wave for good measure.

Lester Bateman continued his questioning. "Do you have a location yet for the new building?"

"We're still working on that. But you can trust your City Hall to find a location that is appropriate for this wonderful new facility. Nothing but the finest will do for all of you Chericoans out there."

Maura Beth began to think Councilman Sparks was going to go on pontificating forever, endlessly praising himself in thinly veiled prose, but he finally relented after fielding a few more questions from the crowd. It was obvious his announcement had gone over well, and there was prolonged applause right after his closing sentiment. "Thank you again, one and all, for coming out today. We here at City Hall look forward to making this journey together!"

Maura Beth breathed it all in deeply, closing her eyes while trying to make a mental picture of how her new library might look.

It was only after Maura Beth and Nora had sat down to their glasses of Chardonnay at The Twinkle that it truly registered. The endless smiling and standing in the sun atop the City Hall steps had taken its toll, pulling their focus somewhat. But now that they were sipping and relaxing in the midst of a very noisy lunch crowd, the reality of it all surged through their veins in the form of a very pleasant buzz.

Maura Beth was the first to put it in words as she gazed up at the gold and silver stars dangling above her head. "Can you even believe it? We actually got everything we wanted. I keep thinking I should just pinch myself and wake up. Maybe I have sunstroke."

"I know exactly what you mean. But the truth is, I haven't felt this good since . . . well, don't let me beat around the bush about it. I've never felt this good period," Nora said after another big swig of wine. "I was held back twice while I was in school because of my problem, so I wasn't able to stay in touch with any of the friends I'd made. I don't have to tell you the difference between grades is as wide as the Grand Canyon at that age. So most of the time, I felt like an ugly little bump on a log."

"But you were the one who brought this home for us," Maura Beth said, wagging her finger playfully. "Give yourself a pat on the back. It was you!"

The mutual admiration society continued. "Oh, no, Miz Maura Beth Mayhew. We couldn't have done it without *you*. Of course, it was a little galling to see Councilman Sparks all puffed up and claiming every bit of this was his idea, even if he was finally doing the right thing."

Maura Beth nodded emphatically. "Wrong reasons, right thing. I'll take that over the status quo any day."

Momentarily, Periwinkle emerged from the kitchen and spotted them. "How did you two characters sneak in here without checking in with me first?" she called out from across the room.

"You were busy," Maura Beth told her as she approached their table. "Lalie took our order. But we fully intended to catch up with you. In fact, do you have a second to spare right now?"

Periwinkle scanned the room quickly. "Yeah, I think I can spare just a second or two. What's up? I can tell something good's happened by those smug expressions on your faces."

Then Maura Beth telescoped the events in front of City Hall into a few sentences, and Periwinkle drew back in delight, throwing up her hands. "Well, my heartiest congratulations! I couldn't be happier for you. Matter a' fact, I was wondering what was going on down there. I got a peak looking out the window, and then a couple a' customers kept mentioning how something important must be in the works. Hey, but since there were no sirens or anything like that, I figured it was probably Councilman Sparks up to his usual blowhard tricks."

"Not this time," Maura Beth added, wrinkling up her nose and saucily wiggling around in her chair.

Periwinkle was clearly amused. "Now, that is just your first glass, isn't it, girl? Why do I get the feeling you're keeping something from me? Come on, now. Give Miz Periwinkle the lowdown."

Maura Beth took another sip and arched her eyebrows. "Everyone knows all they ever need to know. Let's just cut to the chase and say Councilman Sparks finally saw the light."

"With a little help I bet," Periwinkle added. Then she spotted the couple who had just entered for lunch, waiting to be seated. "Oops, gotta run now. Busy, busy traffic. I guess I can thank Councilman Sparks for that. Looks like he did all of us a big favor today."

Maura Beth watched her friend scurrying away like the ball of fire she usually was. She didn't seem to be particularly distraught, as Mr. Place had described recently. But then, this moment was just a snapshot of her daily routine, one that surely didn't give her much time to brood when the restaurant was as busy as it was now.

What did it matter, however? Periwinkle's surprise party was in the works behind the scenes, and that could only mean one thing: The heart of The Cherry Cola Book Club was on the way to save the day.

19

The Warbler Tour

Maura Beth could not remember a time in her life when she was this excited, and she was savoring every second of the feeling. Clearly, the early-afternoon phone call yesterday from Jeremy had set the tone.

"Get set, Maurie. I'm coming down there tomorrow, and I'm going to knock your socks off, sweetheart!"

Maura Beth had played along superbly. "I've been waiting a long time for something like that to happen to me. So you just come right on down here to Cherico and rock my world."

In truth, she did have some idea of what might be in store for her. Ratcheting up their relationship another notch was what she was hoping for, of course. It ended up costing her a good night's sleep with all the tossing and turning she had done in anticipation, but she wasn't going to complain about that. If any important part of page 25 of her college journal was about to come true, it would be well worth it.

Oddly, Jeremy seemed remarkably restrained after they hugged and kissed at the door of her apartment. "I don't know if you're ready for this or not, Maurie."

"Try me."

"Okay, but a person can only handle so much adrenaline in one day, and I intend to be a one-man tour de force."

Maura Beth showed him in and played along, as she had over the phone the previous day. "I get it. This is part of the big buildup. Well, I've done my part. Please direct your attention to my feet, if you haven't already."

He glanced down quickly and smirked. "Those are bobby socks you're wearing, right?"

"Went out and bought them especially for the occasion. You said you wanted to knock them off."

They laughed together and indulged another round of their playful hugging and kissing. "All right, then, if you'll just follow me outside where the grand tour will begin, sweetheart."

He took her by the hand, and she dutifully followed him all the way to the parking lot. "Here she is once again, but this time, all spruced up!" he announced, pointing proudly to the bright yellow, classic ride he had purchased soon after getting out of the hospital. He had made quite a to-do of introducing her to Maura Beth on his first trip down. "My genuine 1971 Triumph Spitfire with the four-cylinder, reworked engine now has a CD player so you and I can listen to beautiful music wherever we go. I had lots of the insurance money left over to bring her into the millennium, and now I'm going to take her out for another test drive down here."

Maura Beth didn't even have to think about her response. "Well, she looks as spiffy as ever, and I'm more than ready. Let's do this."

"And now that my pretty wheels can sing, so to speak," he explained, opening the door for her, "I've decided to tweak her name. Now, she officially goes from The Canary to The Warbler. You like?"

Maura Beth giggled as she slid into the front seat. "I do,

and I can't wait to hear what she's going to sing for us for her debut. Are we going anyplace special?"

"Well, the deal is I've been doing my homework. Got a map of Cherico and studied all the streets and roads carefully. I mean, every single intersection and every twist and turn, and I predict you'll see parts of this little town you've never seen before."

"Then full speed ahead!"

After he'd settled in behind the steering wheel, he slipped a CD into the newly installed slot, and they both waited for The Warbler to do her thing.

"What is that?" Maura Beth said, cocking her head as the jangling chords kicked in. "Wait . . . don't tell me. I should definitely know this." She took a while longer but finally broke through, touching a finger to her temple. "Stravinsky. *The Firebird Suite.* I took Music Appreciation my senior year at LSU. Even got an A."

"Very good. You're a girl after my own heart." He pulled out of his parking space and smiled at her approvingly. "I thought we needed some energetic music for our tour today."

Once they were well under way, Maura Beth began conjuring up her high-school fantasies involving dangerous boys with sporty cars. Now, more than a decade later, she was actually living it in a nearly danger-proof way, even if Jeremy had taken her command literally and was driving a little faster than he should. If he was showing off slightly, well then, that was just fine and dandy with her. She intended to go wherever he led her. That was part of the thrill come true.

"Of course, I'm not through sprucing her up just yet," he was saying as they sped along a deserted back road flanked by thick pine forests that were hemmed in by a continuous barbed-wire fence. The only sign of life was a hawk circling high overhead in the distance against the backdrop of the cloudless blue sky. "For starters, I was thinking about giving her a new paint job to brighten her up even more. You can only do so much with water and wax."

"Well, I know for a fact that she'll appreciate it very much. We girls like to look our best when we go out in public and strut our stuff. And for your further listening pleasure, Mr. Jeremy McShay, don't forget you can check out audio books at your friendly neighborhood library," she put in while the scenery flew by. "I'm sure you'll agree that there's nothing like riding around listening to great literature as well as classical music."

He gave her a quick glance and winked. "Spoken like the dedicated librarian you are."

The Warbler had now come to a fork in the road. Both choices looked a little foreboding, even derelict, but Jeremy did not hesitate. "We head off to the right. You'll find the scenery changes a bit and not for the better. But don't worry your sweet little head. I know exactly where I'm going."

Indeed, they entered a lengthy stretch of land that had been extensively cut over for timber. There was a desolate quality to it as weeds and saplings struggled for dominance among the multitude of forlorn stumps. The edgy, frenetic strains of Stravinsky even seemed to be deploring the damage that had been done.

"I trust you implicitly, of course," Maura Beth said. "But I could swear we were lost." Underneath it all, however, she was not the least bit concerned. There was a swagger about Jeremy behind the wheel that was thoroughly consistent with his promise to "knock her socks off," and she was loving it.

"Just a little farther ahead, Maurie. You'll see," he answered, his jaw firmly set.

Finally, Jeremy's circuitous tour of the outskirts of town ended up in the midst of a virgin stretch overlooking Lake Cherico. He shut off the engine and said, "And here we are."

Farther down and to the right were the high-end homes

and boathouses that Justin Brachle had developed; and beyond that, The Marina Bar and Grill. For once, there was nothing going on out on the lake—no fishing, no skiing, no recreation of any kind. There was only the placid brown water as far as the eye could see.

"Oh, I know where we are now," Maura Beth said, looking off in the distance. "You definitely took a roundabout way to get here, and I'd have absolutely no idea how to get back."

"Don't worry about that. I just want you to relax and listen to what I have to say." Then he leaned over and gave her another lingering kiss before continuing.

"You have my undivided attention," she said, catching her breath as her heart raced pleasantly.

"Good," he began, holding on to her hand. "First, I wanted to say that I never thought I'd be uprooting myself this way from the predictable life I had going up in Nashville. I think my students at New Gallatin Academy really liked me, even if cranky old Yelverton drove me crazy with his double standard for the football team. But I was still doing what I wanted to do—teaching classic literature and trying my best to convince the current impressionable generation that reading it was a worthwhile and a noble pursuit. Plus, my parents were nearby in Brentwood, so a home-cooked meal now and then was never very far away for a bachelor like myself. Of course, I dallied with this woman and that one, but none of my relationships ever seemed to amount to much. I was in a sort of safe, comfortable routine, and nothing seemed to be able to get me off dead center." He paused to gaze deeply into her eyes.

"Then two very unexpected and unforgettable things happened to me. First, I met you at my uncle's lodge one wonderful evening with my hands full of shrimp. Then, a few months later, I had a near-death experience that shook me to my roots. Both events had the effect of making me sit up straight and take notice of my life and just how precious it was; and after the dust had settled, I realized I was very much in love with you—and that was all that really mattered. Above all, I didn't want to waste any more time not doing something about it."

It was then that Jeremy dug down into his pocket and produced a small black jewelry box that he offered to Maura Beth. "Go ahead, sweetheart. Open it."

Maura Beth took it gingerly, opening it slowly and then softly sucking in air. "My God, Jeremy, this is so beautiful!"

Indeed, it was no conventional engagement ring. Instead of the traditional solitary diamond, he had ordered up a circle of diamonds in the shape of small stars and set in a narrow band of gold. "You are the star of my heart, Maurie. I love you so much," he told her, lifting it out gently and working it down her finger. "Will you marry me?"

Her response was immediate and breathless. "Oh, of course I will." They fell together in an effortless embrace and kissed once again. It was a kiss for the ages, not so much a matter of duration as it was undeniable passion.

When it was over, Maura Beth held up the ring to catch the light, flipping her hand back and forth to view it from every possible angle. "I just love you for creating these little stars for me. How did you think of this?"

He pulled back slightly, looking both proud and smug. "The truth is, I got the idea from all my visits to The Twinkle. All those gold and silver stars dangling from the ceiling got me started. And then I thought, 'I need to come up with something very special for my very special sweetheart.' So I bounced my idea off Mom. She runs Beads and Crafty Needs at the Cool Springs Galleria, you know, and she has all these connections down there, including one of the most creative jewelers in town. It all came together from there."

"It's every bit as original as you are," she told him, unable to take her eyes off her newfound treasure.

He chuckled softly. "Well, we both are, I think. That's why we're going to be such a good match."

Maura Beth finally put her hand down and caught his gaze. "I love you, Jeremy McShay, but this is just the beginning, you know. We have so much to decide. When and where the wedding will take place—how big, how small. Even when to announce it. But I just had a thought. Periwinkle's surprise birthday party is just a couple of days away, and all our close friends from the book club will be there. Why don't we announce our engagement to everyone then?"

"Sounds like a winner to me," he said. "Especially since The Twinkle was the inspiration for your ring. It would be the perfect place to show it off, and that's exactly what I want you to do."

"Jeremy McShay, you have just knocked my socks off as promised—metaphorically speaking, of course!"

He craned his neck to catch a glimpse of her feet. "Yeah, well, as an English teacher, I'm high on metaphors. Similes, too, for that matter."

They both laughed; then she grew serious. "I think here is where I should tell you when I first knew we were going to make it as a couple. You probably wouldn't guess that it was my first visit to the hospital after your horrible wreck. I was just a bundle of nerves, full of all sorts of conflicting emotions, despite a pep talk I'd just received from your aunt Connie. But I finally relaxed when you said, 'We can't go on meeting like this.' I mean, your sense of humor was nothing short of fantastic considering what you'd just been through, but it also made me realize that you were seriously thinking of how we were going to make our relationship work with you up in Nashville and me down here in Cherico. At that point I knew you really wanted this, and that made me care about you even more. Any doubts I'd had about our future together were erased."

He rewarded her words with a quick kiss and said, "Well, shall I steer The Warbler back to your apartment, and we'll see what develops?"

She took a deep breath while gazing out at the lake. "I think that would put the perfect exclamation point on our little tour today."

20

Changes Among Friends

Mr. Parker Place was trying his best to keep a lid on Periwinkle's appetite without giving the game away. After the lunch crowd and its dishes had been cleared, she had fixed herself a chicken salad sandwich with all the trimmings and sat down to that with one of her famous tomato aspics and a tall tumbler of sweet tea. Then came the challenge.

"You know, I'm feeling a little sweet-toothy this afternoon, Parker. I think I'll have a great big slice of your yummy grasshopper pie. Will you be an angel and cut me one, please?"

Mr. Place glanced at his watch. A little after three. He really shouldn't let her have such a rich, filling dessert and still expect her to appreciate all the potluck dishes everyone would be bringing just after nine. "I'm about to take a batch of my white chocolate macadamia nut cookies out of the oven. Why don't you have one of those instead?"

"Well, I have an even better idea. How about I have a slice of pie and a cookie, too?"

Now he was panicking. "Why don't you pace yourself, Periwinkle? Let's both have a warm cookie together and save the pie for tonight."

"Okay," she said. "You talked me into it. I can't resist anything fresh from the oven."

A minute or so later, they were nibbling at his cookies, sitting across from each other smiling. "I know what you're up to," she said, catching his gaze.

He could only hope the surprise surging throughout his body wasn't showing up on his face. "What do you mean?"

"Don't think I haven't noticed," she continued, breaking off another piece of her cookie. "It's very sweet of you to be holding my hand, so to speak. I mean, after I told you about my breakup with Harlan. You're a very sensitive man, Parker, and I do appreciate you trying to make things easier for me. But, you know, I think I may be pulling out of my little funk, slowly but surely."

"That's good to hear," he told her, feeling relief from head to toe. "Especially on your birthday. Yep, I remembered, and I have a little something to give you." He dug down into his apron pocket and handed over an envelope. "This is just a little poem I put together for you."

She smiled, put the rest of her cookie on her plate, opened the envelope, and began unfolding the paper. "That's really very sweet of you to think of me this way, Parker." Then she started reading out loud:

> *I'm here to keep the sweet tooth happy,*
> *And I think I do it well,*
> *At poems I think I'm less than snappy,*
> *Perhaps as thin as a pastry shell,*
> *But there is something I can utter,*
> *For I know it's very true,*
> *It goes together like sugar and butter,*
> *Happy Birthday just to you!*

She looked up and laughed her Periwinkle laugh of old.

"That bad, huh?" he said in a playful tone.

"As far as I'm concerned, you're the poet laureate of Cherico. Come right on over here and give me a big hug!"

He knew she probably wasn't feeling all he was feeling when she stood up and wrapped her arms around him, patting him on the back several times. He knew it was a gesture of friendship on her part more than anything else. But for now, it would do nicely.

Maura Beth and Jeremy were halfway out the door of her apartment headed toward The Twinkle when the phone rang. "Oh, I better get it. It might be Mr. Place with some last-minute thing about the surprise party," she said, turning around and heading back toward the kitchenette counter.

It turned out to be Miss Voncille at the other end, however, and she lost no time in getting to the purpose of her call. "We've been keeping this a secret until we could get in touch with Locke's children and get everything straightened out with them. At first we thought they were going to be a problem, but Locke laid down the law and brought them around. He told them, 'This is my life, and your mother would want me to be happy, so that settles it,' " she was explaining. "But tonight at the party, we were thinking about announcing to everyone that Locke and I are definitely getting married. We've set the date for August in his church."

Maura Beth was gazing fondly at Jeremy as she answered. "Well, congratulations to both of you, Miss Voncille. We've all been wondering when it would happen, not if. And I think your timing is perfect. You may not believe the coincidence, but Jeremy and I were planning on announcing our engagement, too. We just decided to make it official the other day. We were thinking of an August wedding as well—just before

Jeremy starts his new position down here at Cherico High." Then she paused to gather her thoughts. "Do you think we ought to coordinate who goes first tonight at The Twinkle, Miss Voncille?"

"Let me think." Then there was a sharp intake of air. "I know. We'll have some fun with this, do a New Year's countdown, and then the four of us will announce we're all getting married?"

Maura Beth couldn't help but giggle. "You're not worried everyone will think we're a foursome?"

"Oh, I see what you mean. What could I have been thinking?" There was further silence. "Well, we could do a twist. Locke and I could announce that you and Jeremy are getting married, and you could do the same for us."

Jeremy was brandishing his wrist and pointing emphatically to his watch, and Maura Beth nodded. "Or, we could just play it straight when we get there. Sometimes the simplest solution is the best. Now, we don't want to be late for the big occasion, so see you and Locke in just a few minutes. Bye now." She hung up and motioned Jeremy toward the door. "I'll tell you all about it in The Warbler on the way there. But in a nutshell—there are going to be lots of changes among friends."

Douglas was gazing out one of his great room windows at the lake, marveling once again at the feeling of redemption it always produced somewhere deep inside him. Whether at early dawn, sunset, or anywhere in between, it spoke to him in ways he could not put into words. Fishing was just the excuse he used to be near the lessons it was trying to teach him.

Connie soon joined him and began peering out into the night herself. "What is it we're looking for?" she said. "The Lake Cherico Monster? We could always get a myth started and make The Guinness Book of World Records."

He turned and put his arm around her, smiling. "I was just thinking that we haven't done enough yet. To help Cherico, I mean. I'm still not satisfied."

She pulled away just enough to catch the intensity in his dark eyes. "You want to do something more than help pay for the library repairs?"

He nodded slowly and then faced the lake and its shimmering moonlit surface again. "We have so much acreage out here. This was the biggest parcel Justin Brachle had for sale back then, and we got it for a song. I was halfway thinking at the time that we might build a guest house on it someday. It would give Lindy and Melissa a place of their own whenever they came to visit. But not so much anymore. My idea now is that we donate a couple of acres to Cherico as a site for the new library. Maura Beth says they haven't come up with the land yet. Well, there's plenty of room between our property line and the Milners. They've planted us out with all those willows and pines, so they wouldn't see it anyway. But imagine it—a library with a view. Maybe they could design a deck overlooking the water like The Marina Bar and Grill. A library like that couldn't help but have outstanding circulation."

Connie lifted her chin and narrowed her eyes, clearly trying to picture it. "I think it sounds lovely. But what about the location? Do you think people would want to drive out here to check out books and get on the Internet?"

"It's a five-minute drive," Douglas pointed out. "In fact, you know as well as I do that you can get anywhere you want in Cherico in five minutes. The inside joke here is that there really is no *greater* in Greater Cherico. It's a wonderfully funny expression, though."

"When you put it like that, I have to agree."

He pulled her in again, and their heads touched gently. "I was thinking we could announce our intentions tonight at The Twinkle."

"I know Maura Beth would be thrilled."

He took a moment and then pointed to the water. "When I was out there today, I didn't even cast my line. I just wanted to listen."

"To what?"

"To the lake. It laps at the shore very gently, and I just listen. And after I'd gotten my usual fill of the sun and started in to the pier, it came to me just what I ought to do with all this extra land we have. But you're my wife, and this is your land, too. So, tell me, would you like to do this together? I won't make a decision this big without you being on board."

Connie looked into his eyes again and kissed him gently on the lips. "You know I've been looking forward to sharing our retirement here, and I can't think of a better way to do it. We'll tell Maura Beth and the others tonight. Speaking of which, I'll round up the baked chicken, and we better get going or we'll be late."

About a quarter past nine Periwinkle was back in the kitchen getting ready to pour herself a steaming bowl of chicken gumbo and then have that postponed slice of sinful grasshopper pie when she heard the relentless knocking at the front door. "Will you go see what that's about, Parker? Can't people read the sign and see we're closed? You'd think they'd know our hours by now anyway. I don't know what gets into people."

Mr. Place could barely contain his excitement as he headed out. "Will do. Can't imagine what's going on, either." But once he'd let the Brachles, McShays, Miss Voncille, Locke Linwood, Nora Duddney, Maura Beth, and Jeremy inside, he shouted back. "Oh, Periwinkle, there are some people out here to see you, and they just won't take no for an answer!"

"What on earth are you talking about!" she cried out, her

irritation beginning to bubble over. "Stand up to them, for heaven's sake!"

"They won't listen to me. They really insist on seeing you. You need to come out here and take care of this!"

The ploy worked, and a few seconds later, Periwinkle was greeted with the loudest orchestrated "Happy Surprise Birthday!" of her life. It was clear from her expression and the way she clasped her hands together that she was genuinely caught off guard. But she quickly recovered.

"Well, dang-it-all, it looks like a girl just can't keep her age a secret these days, can she?"

Many hugs and kisses on the cheek followed, and it took a while for everyone to get settled in, particularly with the covered dishes they had brought along with them. "I'll take all of those back to the kitchen," Mr. Place offered. "I'll be officially in charge of the warming and serving, too. This is your special night, Periwinkle, so you just sit back and relax and let us do all the work."

Periwinkle scanned the faces of her friends and asked, "Whose idea was this? Was it yours, Maura Beth?"

"Afraid not," she answered, pointing to Mr. Place. "You can thank your right-hand man there for this little scheme."

Periwinkle turned and gave him a sweet smile. "So that's what you've been up to all day. Really, Parker, I thought you might have joined Weight Watchers or something the way you were paying so much attention to my diet today."

Mr. Place shrugged with a display of his hands. "What can I say? I guess I'm not a very good actor."

"But you're a very good friend, Parker, and I thank you for thinking of me from the bottom of my heart. Come on over here, and let's hug it out again."

Everyone looked on, smiling and making noises of approval at the spontaneous display of affection, and then it was time to get the celebration under way.

"We all decided that the best gifts to bring you would be lots of potluck choices so you wouldn't have to serve your own food at your own birthday party," Maura Beth said. "Let's see, if I remember correctly, I made some stuffed mushrooms, Nora whipped up a layered salad, Becca brought clam canapés and hot fruit, Connie brought some baked chicken, and, oh, yes, Miss Voncille brought her wonderful biscuits and green pepper jelly. I think that about covers it."

"Except for the chocolate caramel sheet cake I made that's been hiding at the back of the fridge all this time," Mr. Place put in.

"Aha!" Periwinkle exclaimed, pouncing upon his words. "You mean the one you kept on describing as an experimental dessert, and I'd better not peek under the aluminum foil in case it didn't turn out well? I thought you were probably up to something, but I gave you the benefit of the doubt. Experimental, my foot! Meanwhile, I don't know about the rest of you, but I'm starving. So let's heat up all this good food and chow down on my birthday feast!"

In the end, Maura Beth and Miss Voncille had decided to draw straws in the ladies' room to see who went first with the straightforward engagement announcements. Well, not straws exactly. Lacking a broom, they had each offered up their lipsticks, and Maura Beth had concealed them behind her back, one in each hand.

"You pick," Maura Beth had told her. "If it's yours, you go first."

"Right hand," Miss Voncille had said, touching a spot in midair with her finger.

She had chosen her own but had been gracious about it. "Age before beauty, I suppose."

"Now, none of that, Miss Voncille," Maura Beth had returned with equal aplomb. "The fact is, you are both ageless and a beauty."

Miss Voncille nodded in her general direction. "Why, thank you, my dear. You are a true Southern lady. I've thought so from the day you took over from Annie Scott, who was always out of sorts and let you know about it, too."

When it was time for the actual announcements after everyone had eaten their fill of all the delicious offerings, Miss Voncille chimed her glass of white wine several times. Both she and Locke then stood up while everyone seated around the well-lubricated table halted their chatter and gave them their quizzical attention. After all, Periwinkle had been toasted several times over. Was there anything more left to say?

"My friends," she began, making eye contact with everyone in turn, "Locke and I have an important announcement to make tonight on this joyous occasion of Periwinkle's birthday. No doubt some of you think it has been long in coming, but here it is at last. We intend to get married in August at St. Peter's Episcopal Church, and, of course, we will want all of you to attend. It just wouldn't be the same without you. As for my engagement ring, Locke has taken my breath away with this little gem." She briefly displayed the elegant diamond on her finger. "Now, Locke, do you have anything to add?"

He looked at once sly and subversive, yet still maintained his gentlemanly demeanor. "I just want to thank Voncille for making me see that getting married was my idea from the very beginning." He paused just long enough to collect a few titters and giggles. "But in all seriousness, she has a certain way about her, and fortunately for me, I fell head over heels as a result. So don't let anyone ever tell you that you can't fall in love twice in a lifetime." There was an outburst of applause, "Awws!" and congratulatory phrases as the couple hugged and kissed. Then Periwinkle rose and hoisted her glass. "A toast to the soon-to-be bride and groom. We couldn't be happier for you both!"

"To Locke and Voncille!" everyone shouted before tossing back generous swallows of their drinks.

"Thank you, one and all. As a wise retired schoolteacher once said, it's never too late to change your life for the better," said Miss Voncille. Then she gestured toward Maura Beth and Jeremy. "And now, ladies and gentlemen, get ready for an encore presentation!"

There was general buzzing throughout the room, along with a lineup of genuinely surprised faces.

"Yes, my friends," Maura Beth began, rising from her seat with her fiancé. "It's true. Jeremy and I are also going to be married in August, and all of you are the first to hear the good news." Jeremy inched a bit closer, put his arm around her shoulder, and gave her a peck on the cheek. "As you already know, he's going to be moving down here to Cherico to teach English to our bright young minds. How's that for the makings of a devoted husband? All told, I think we're off to an amazing start." Then she brandished her ring finger. "And you ladies can all take turns checking out this gorgeous circle of stars Jeremy gave me."

The already-boisterous group exploded further, and the flurry of hugs, kisses, and congratulations—not to mention the *oohs* and *aahs* over the ring—lasted several minutes.

"Well, I think I may need to have birthdays more often," Periwinkle told Maura Beth, taking her aside at one point. "Good things are happening right and left."

Maura Beth nodded enthusiastically. "Good things deserve to happen to us. We're The Cherry Cola Book Club."

"You bet we are!" Periwinkle exclaimed, feeling the warm, fuzzy effects of the several glasses of wine she had enjoyed. Then she turned to address the others, raising her voice further. "Folks, if you'll indulge me, I'd like to make a little speech of my own right now!" Everyone eventually settled down and waited for her to begin. "Tonight, I fully intend to show all of you what a liberated woman I truly am. I will no longer keep secrets from my fellow Chericoans. It so happens I have in the past, but no more. The truth is, I officially turned forty-one today. Yes, you heard me right, and I know you all thought I was celebrating The Big Four-Oh. But I was one of those women who tried to hold off forty as long as I could. I kept shaving a year or two off my age thinking it mattered. But I'm here to tell you tonight that it doesn't amount to a hill of baked beans—which, by the way, is not on the menu of The Twinkle and never will be. I like to think I'm a lot more creative than that."

Everyone laughed, and Stout Fella even started up a chant: "No baked beans! No baked beans! No baked beans . . . !"

"So here's to no baked beans and definitely no fear of birthdays. Never, ever!" Periwinkle cried out once the chanting had died off. Eventually, she took up a different train of thought.

"I know I've said this before, my friends, but you'll never know how much this surprise birthday party means to me. It's really nice to know that you like me and my restaurant this much. I guess you could say it's my passion, and maybe it was in the stars for me all along." She pointed dramatically to one of the mobiles dangling above them, which immediately produced some *oohs* and *aahs*. "Well, I think I've finally run out of things to say. You take it, Maura Beth."

"Gladly. I'd have to say everything has been in the stars for all of us lately. We've shared so much with each other tonight—good food and drink to start with—and then these life-changing announcements such as August weddings one after another."

"And guess what?" Douglas said, putting his arm around Connie and giving her a gentle squeeze. "We're not through with the announcements yet. Tonight, Douglas and Connie

McShay proudly announce to all of you, but particularly to Maura Beth, that we will be donating two acres of our lake-front property for the construction of Cherico's new library. We know the site hasn't been picked out yet, but we thought a state-of-the-art library with a view of the lake would put Cherico on the map."

Maura Beth was nearly as speechless as she had been during Councilman Sparks's press conference in which he had waved the white flag and claimed victory at the same time. But finally she gathered herself. "Douglas . . . Connie . . . this is unbeliev-ably generous of you. It's more than anyone had a right to ex-pect." She clasped her hands together and pointed them in their direction. "I just want to make sure. Do you really want to do this? Keep in mind that a year from now you'll have a busy pub-lic library next door. You'll be giving up some of your privacy, and I can't promise you there won't be a little traffic from time to time."

"We understand that, but we've given it a great deal of thought, and this is our time to do something significant for Cherico," Douglas answered, sounding not the least bit fazed. "I think we'd both be proud to wake up every morning, look out the window and see our handiwork rising right there on the lakeshore. Plus, we'd have no excuse for not returning our books and CDs on time."

Maura Beth and the others laughed brightly, and she said, "You two are the best, and I think I could find it in my heart to forgive any fines you might have."

"I do have a serious question, though," Connie added. "You think Councilman Sparks will be okay with our pro-posal? For instance, would there be a zoning problem?"

"Oh, believe me," Maura Beth began, rolling her eyes, "if it won't cost City Hall a cent, he'll be just fine with it. You won't hear a peep out of him, and that will be music to my ears. I'm ready for a little peace and quiet after all the flak he's given me and the library all this time. Zoning, schmoning. And even if there is a problem, Councilman Sparks will find a way around it. Just trust me on this one."

Then Maura Beth and Jeremy made their way over to the McShays for an exchange of hugs. "Looks like everyone is full of surprises tonight," Maura Beth said in the midst of all the excitement.

"Wow!" Jeremy exclaimed. "Uncle Doug . . . Aunt Connie—I'm so proud of you both. I'm sure I'll be sending my students out there to do research after hours. You're my heroes!"

"Hey, nephew," Douglas said, patting his shoulder, "we think you're a great teacher, too!"

"Well, as long as we're celebrating all this good news with each other, don't forget that Justin and I have a little one on the way," Becca put in. "We've been waiting a long time to get pregnant, and now it's finally happened. And just so you know, I've been thinking about an episode of my show that gives pregnant mothers with morning sickness something to swear by. You know, what to eat when you don't feel like eating, or can't keep it down. I'll be able to say without a doubt that I've done the research myself."

"Oh, we've all been so excited for you since you told us a few days ago. Not about the morning sickness, of course. But I think maybe some of us are hoping we're in the running for godmother and godfather when the time comes," Maura Beth said.

Becca and Justin exchanged smiles, and she said, "I can't think of a better group of friends to choose from, can you, Stout Fella?"

"No, ma'am, I can't. Any one of 'em would do us proud. But maybe I should just say that if we don't choose you this time, we might next time. We plan on having a nice, big family before we're through, and when you get that new children's librarian, we'll keep her plenty busy, Maura Beth."

"I can't wait for them to grow up under her nose—and mine, too," she answered.

Then Periwinkle stepped in. "Since we're all about announcements tonight, Parker and I have one of our own we'd like to make right now. We've just been waiting for the right moment." She gestured in his direction. "Will you do the honors, please?"

Mr. Place straightened up in his chair and cleared his throat. "Last year, Periwinkle and I started considering the possibility of a takeout and delivery service for The Twinkle. Someone had suggested it before, and just this past month we worked out all the details. Next month we will officially unveil our new 'Twinkle in a Twinkle' takeout menu. You can call in your order and pick it up, or we'll deliver it to you anywhere within a five-mile radius of Greater Cherico. Now, your choices will be more limited than if you ate with us on Commerce Street, but just about all your favorites will be available. Hey, we know which side our bread is buttered on."

There was muted laughter and a smattering of applause.

"I for one will be your first customer, I'm sure," Connie said. "You know how much Douglas and I crave your tomato aspics."

"Hey, Parker and I have it documented. You're our best customer. At any rate, what really got us off dead center with this whole concept was our waitress, Lalie Bevins," Periwinkle continued. "She wanted to know if we had anything for her teenaged son to do this summer, as he had nearly driven her crazy last year asking for an allowance for doing nothing. She couldn't even get him to cut the grass every other week. But since he got his driver's license, he loves to run around town the way teenaged boys like to do. So young Mr. Barry Bevins will be our very first driver, and we just bought a new van with our logo on it and everything to do it up right. It's parked around in back if any of you care to take a look sometime. We're so proud we're about to pop."

"And I'm sure I'll be taking advantage of your service, too," Maura Beth said. "There are lots of times when I'm just too tired at the end of the day and don't feel like eating out. But I don't want to go home and cook, either. Your food will be the solution every time. I can't stay away from it too long."

"That's what we're counting on to make a go of our 'Twinkle in a Twinkle,'" Periwinkle said, exuding confidence. "My personal opinion is that it'll become the rage of Greater Cherico."

Perhaps he was imagining things, but after everyone had finally cleared out and he and Periwinkle were left alone to put The Twinkle to bed, Mr. Place thought he was the recipient of a very special smile. To be sure, it was just a moment in time, but it was magnified by the fact that he was constantly on the lookout for a sea change in his workplace relationship with the woman who had caught his fancy. And there were words of praise for him following that smile to encourage him further.

"I think you did a wonderful job of unveiling our new service to the gang, Parker," Periwinkle told him as they were busily wiping down surfaces and putting things away. "I could tell everyone was really excited about it. But that was the easy part, of course. The hard part comes in a few weeks when we have to keep our promise and deliver. And I mean that literally."

"Well, you and I know we can flat turn out the food," he replied, chuckling at her remark. "And Miz Bevins seems to think her son is trustworthy. I've been meaning to tell you that I had a long talk with him when he came in the other day to get the lay of the land. Oh sure, he's a typical teenager with all his loud music and his cool phrases, but he reminded me of myself at that age. I went along with some of the fads back in the day, too. The bottom line here is that I believe he's basically responsible and will get the job done for us."

"I'll trust your judgment on that one, then."

Mr. Place put the last of the leftovers in the fridge and continued. "As a matter of fact, I was even thinking that maybe I ought to ride along with him for the first few deliveries. That way if anything goes wrong, I'll be there to help out."

"You think of everything, you know?"

"Well, I was the best at what I did up in Memphis, and I'm gonna be the best down here, too."

When they were just about ready to lock up a few minutes later, there was another special moment, and Mr. Place felt the subtle change that had taken place. "I just wanted to tell you how much your poem meant to me, Parker. It was even more unexpected than my surprise party. I don't think I've ever enjoyed working with anyone as much as I do with you. I've come to count on you for so many things, and you do them without asking."

He lost no time in following her lead. "Well, I take pride in my work and in this restaurant, and I think we make a great team."

She reached out and gently grasped his hand. "I know you realize all too well what I've just been through with Harlan. You saw it unfold before your very eyes, and I'm sure it was hard on you being the innocent bystander. But I wanted to let you know that I value your friendship above all. It's also nice to know that not all men are like he is. It—well, it just gives me hope." Then she gave him a hug, lingering longer than was necessary.

They finally pulled away from each other, and somehow he found the perfect words as he gazed at her fondly. "Happy birthday again, Periwinkle. And here's to hope!"

21

A Wedding with a View

Maura Beth and Jeremy were standing in tall, swaying grass, shading their eyes from the late-morning sun as they gazed at the surface of Lake Cherico a scant few feet away. A fisherman in his bass boat out in the middle was casting his line leisurely into the brown water, and they watched the ritual for a while, finally growing bored when it produced no results.

"Your uncle Doug said that muddy little strip just ahead might be about where the library deck could be built overlooking the lake," Maura Beth was saying. "That is, if such a deck got included in the plans. But even if it didn't, this will still be an incredibly spectacular view for all the patrons. I can see myself spending a lot of time just looking out the windows and not getting much work done. But, of course, that will be my little secret."

Jeremy was scanning the shore from right to left. "This plot of land really is a beautiful ground zero, isn't it?"

"To say the least. There won't be too many libraries in the world with this kind of setting."

They began heading back to the lodge, but they were in no hurry. "Out here you can breathe the fresh air off the lake and feel like you're actually a part of the world going on around you," Maura Beth continued. "I've tried my best to keep that claustrophobic old warehouse of a library from getting to me these past six years, but it's been very hard on me. More times than you'll ever know, I was sorely tempted to hand in my resignation and call it quits. Councilman Sparks did his part in always making that an option for me, as you know. But something inside kept me fighting on. Of course, I'll still have another year or so of construction to endure while I go to work every morning to that dark, depressing office of mine; but just knowing that this kind of vista is waiting for me at the end should see me through. For all practical purposes, it will seem like a pot of gold at the end of a rainbow."

Jeremy stopped and turned his head back toward the lake for a moment. "Believe me, I don't want to play devil's advocate, but you're sure that Councilman Sparks will follow through on all he promised?"

"Oh, I'm pretty sure," she told him without hesitation. "There are some things I know that nobody else ever needs to know. I say this to you believing with all my heart that I'm on the side of the angels in this one."

They resumed their walking. "I guess this little town of Greater Cherico, as they insist on calling it around here, is where we're going to be living and working for a while," he said. "But we should definitely both be flexible about the future, don't you think?"

"You're not missing Nashville already, are you? You haven't even moved down here yet."

Impulsively, he took her in his arms and kissed her with great feeling. "That should tell you how much I miss Nashville. I shouldn't have even said that about our future. What just happened between us is all that really counts. I've had a tendency to get ahead of myself too often in life. I've just got to learn to be patient and let things work out the way they're supposed to."

"I've been guilty of that, too," Maura Beth said, still enjoying the buzz from his kiss. "I look back on it all and see that I practically galloped out of library school, got this job without even half-trying, and thought nothing could possibly happen to stop me from setting the world on fire. Oh, I was a pistol, a real firecracker ready to explode. Then the reality of small-town politics kicked in at just about the same time it kicked me in the teeth."

Jeremy's laugh was carefree and aimed up at the cloudless blue sky. "And the jackass who did it was one Councilman Sparks!"

She joined him in laughter, but then eventually grew quiet. "Have you thought any more about your Uncle Doug and Aunt Connie's invitation to host our wedding out here at the lodge? The more I've thought about it, the more I like the idea. I mean, here the town of Cherico will be building a fantastic new library with a view. Why not have a wedding with a view out here, too? If nothing else, it would be different and certainly memorable."

He stopped again and looked into her eyes. "It's entirely up to you, Maurie. The bride and her family usually decide such things, and if it's going to cause you problems with your parents down in Covington, maybe you should just go along with having the ceremony down there in Louisiana and keep the peace. After all, you are their only daughter, and this will be their only chance to go all out for you. I definitely don't want them thinking this was my idea and get off on the wrong foot with the in-laws. You need to think this over carefully."

Maura Beth looked decidedly distressed. "My mother in particular could be a problem. Both my parents have lobbied me insistently all these years to move back home and stop beating my head against the wall up here. But I was determined to make it on my own here in Cherico, and now I have, big time. At the moment, I'm leaning toward taking Connie and Doug up on their generous offer. I may be in for it, but I'm the sort of woman who intends to get married only once, and I think I'm entitled to have it the way I want."

"You're very brave," he said. "But that's probably the main reason I fell in love with you."

"And what won me over to your side was that I saw clearly that you wanted the world to be so much better and so much smarter than it is. I like the fact that you're always aiming high," she answered.

"So, do you think maybe marriage really is a good idea for us, after all?"

"I do. See, I just recited my part of the vows."

He was pointing to the imposing lodge ahead of them where they had first met. "Then let's go in right now and tell Uncle Doug and Aunt Connie what we've decided about our wedding with a view."

They held hands and walked ahead with the unshakeable confidence of two people in love. For them, August could not come soon enough.

Treats and Tongue Pleasers from The Twinkle Café

Since reaction to our recipe section in the debut novel in this series—*The Cherry Cola Book Club*—was so enthusiastic, we've decided to return to Greater Cherico for more of the same. This time, we were able to obtain the cooperation of Ms. Periwinkle Lattimore and Mr. Parker Place, owner and pastry chef, respectively, at The Twinkle. Following are some of their favorite recipes—both on the café menu and for their personal enjoyment at home. We predict you'll find something to your liking for snacking, entertaining, and formal dining—in short, for every occasion year-round.

Mr. Parker Place's
Egg Custard Pie

Ingredients you will need

4 eggs
1 cup sugar
1½ cups half-and-half
1 tablespoon vanilla extract
½ tablespoon almond extract
1 whole nutmeg grated
1 deep-dish pie shell
1 tablespoon butter

Beat eggs well. Slowly add sugar while beating with mixer. Add half-and-half, vanilla and almond extracts, and grated nutmeg. Beat on medium speed for 1½ minutes; pour into pie shell (may be raw or slightly baked). Slice butter and lay super-thin slivers all over top of pie; place on cookie sheet with a deep lip. Add water under pie and bake in 350-degree Fahrenheit oven for 1 hour or till brown crust has formed over pie. Allow to cool and refrigerate. Best if made a day ahead.

—Courtesy Abigail Jenkins Healy, Natchez, Mississippi

Periwinkle Lattimore's
Easy Banana / Cranberry Bread

Ingredients you will need

2 very ripe bananas
1 cup Stevia sweetener
1 box Chiquita Banana Bread mix
⅓ cup water
1 egg
1 cup dried cranberries

Mash bananas well. Add Stevia, banana bread mix, water, egg, and cranberries. Spray loaf pan with cooking spray; then pour batter into pan. Bake at 350 degrees for 50 minutes, allow to cool, then turn out onto paper towel. May be stored in refrigerator or breadbox. Good cold or toasted with jelly.

—Courtesy Abigail Jenkins Healy, Natchez, Mississippi

Mr. Parker Place's
Clam Canapés

Ingredients you will need

1 package (8 ounces) cream cheese
1 small can minced clams, drained
3 teaspoons Worcestershire sauce
1 teaspoon minced green onions
Salt to taste
Dash of red pepper
Paprika (optional)
Parsley (optional)

Whip the cream cheese with a fork. Add clams and mix well; add other ingredients and whip well. Place in refrigerator in covered dish until ready to bake. Spread on plain Saltines and bake at 300 degrees for 20 minutes. Sprinkle with paprika or parsley and serve.

—Courtesy Helen Byrnes Jenkins, Natchez, Mississippi

Periwinkle Lattimore's
Cashew Cheese Log

Ingredients you will need

1 pound yellow cheese
2–3 ounces of cream cheese
1 cup cashew nuts, salted or unsalted
2 cloves minced garlic
Paprika

Put yellow cheese through meat grinder or in blender. Whip softened cream cheese. Put cashew nuts through grinder or in blender. Mix all ingredients except paprika; shape into log about 1½ inches in diameter; then roll in lots of paprika. Wrap in waxed paper and refrigerate. To serve, slice very thin and place on round crackers; log may be frozen for later use.

—Courtesy Helen Byrnes Jenkins, Natchez, Mississippi

Mr. Parker Place's
Chicken Gumbo

Ingredients you will need

1 whole chicken, boiled, deboned, and chopped
2 large bags of frozen baby okra
1 cup of any cooking oil
3 onions, chopped
1 celery stalk, chopped
1 large green bell pepper, chopped
2 large cans of chopped tomatoes
2 cups flour
3 large bay leaves
Salt and pepper to taste
Hot sauce to taste

Boil, debone, and chop chicken meat; refrigerate meat and strained cooking stock. Grind the frozen okra. Cook ground okra in oil slowly until okra is bright green; add all vegetables and cook slowly for about 2 hours. Add in silted flour a little at a time and mix; add more oil if needed; cook about 40 minutes or until everything is well-mixed and smooth. Add the stock from the chicken a small amount at a time; add chopped chicken (or seafood such as shrimp, oysters, or crawfish, if you prefer). Add salt, pepper, and hot sauce to taste. Serve as is or over rice.

—Courtesy Mrs. Rose Williams Turner, Natchez, Mississippi

Periwinkle Lattimore's
Hot Fruit

Ingredients you will need

1 orange
1 lemon
2–3 tablespoons light brown sugar
8-ounce can of apricots
8-ounce can of pineapple pieces
8-ounce can of sliced peaches
8-ounce can of pitted Bing cherries
Nutmeg to taste
1 container of sour cream

Grate the orange and lemon rind; add the zest into the brown sugar. Cut the orange and lemon pulp into thin slices, removing seeds and as much of the white membrane as possible; mix these slices in with the rest of the fruit pieces and make a bottom layer of it in a baking dish; sprinkle in zest and sugar mixture and a dash of nutmeg. Repeat layers until all has been used up. Heat in a 300-degree oven for 30 minutes. Top with cold sour cream before serving.

—Courtesy Helen Byrnes Jenkins, Natchez, Mississippi

Bon appétit!

THE READING CIRCLE

Ashton Lee

ABOUT THIS GUIDE

The suggested questions are included to enhance
your group's reading of Ashton Lee's
The Reading Circle!

DISCUSSION QUESTIONS

1. Revisit the book club argument between Maura Beth and Jeremy early in the novel. Pick a side and tell why you support it.

2. Have you changed your opinion positively or negatively about a character or characters after reading this second novel in the series?

3. What was the biggest surprise for you in this plot?

4. What is your favorite sequence?

5. Would you like to live in Cherico? If so, why? If not, why not?

6. Do you think Maura Beth is making/can make a difference in Cherico?

7. Of all the couples in the series, who do you think has the most realistic, well-adjusted relationship?

8. Which character touches you the most?

9. Which character annoys you the most?

10. How do you view Maura Beth's notion that the book club is an "alternative family" of sorts?